MW00763853

Also by the author:

Elizabeth's Knights
Elizabeth's Quest
Elizabeth's Trials

In Your Dreams

Writing as Mela Barrows Bennett:

Murder Makes The Rounds
Double Helix: DNA Never Lies
Murder in Exam Room Three

A Lawyer For Soda Flats

BARBARA WILHELM

ISBN: 978-1-4834-7814-2 (sc)
ISBN: 978-1-4834-7813-5 (e)

Library of Congress Control Number: 2017918918

Lulu Publishing Services rev. date: 12/27/2017

Acknowledgement

To my sister, Jeanne, for her help and encouragement with proofreading and promoting.

Introduction

Much of this story takes place in the fictional town
of Soda Flats, Colorado, located approximately
fifty miles northeast of Colorado Springs

Historical Note:

Pittsburgh, PA had an "h" when it was founded in 1794. However, it was spelled "Pittsburg" between 1890 and 1911 when the National Board on Geographic Names tried to standardize spellings across the nation. Bowing to public and political pressure, the board reversed its decision in 1911 and the city won back its beloved H.

Chapter One

May 1896
Pittsburg, PA

Charlie Fletcher was headed west. He checked his appearance in the mirror over the dresser before leaving his lodgings. His clear brown eyes reflected honesty and hope. His brown hair was a bit long, but he had tied it back, and a stylish hat helped make him appear more business-like. The dark blue suit he wore was new. He smiled at the sight of seeing himself so well-dressed. Straightening his tie, he decided this neat, conservative look would help him appear older than his twenty-seven years, as well as command more respect.

By habit, he rented a room at a boarding house, to conserve his funds. Here, he could pay for a week at the price of a night in an average hotel. Because there was never money for extras when he was growing up, it was hard for him to spend more than necessary, even now that he had the means. The place served its purpose, giving him time and privacy to prepare for his trip. Besides, the room was clean and in a decent area of town. What else did he need?

He adjusted the brim of his hat to be sure that he didn't make himself appear any more of a dandy than he already did, given his fine features. He laughed. The ability to assume an effeminate visage was an advantage when he and his twin sister Charlotte fooled people by switching places growing up. But he was no longer a kid, and he and Char didn't even share the same last name anymore. No, he was going out West, and it was important to look as masculine as possible. His lanky build might not look like much, but he had developed his strength working in his uncle's furniture store. Lifting furniture and bolts of materials for years after school and during the summers had served him well. Charlie picked up his suitcase, and took a deep breath. His steamer trunks had been sent on ahead to the station. Time to go.

Waiting for his train in the lobby of the spacious Pennsylvania Railroad station, he bought a copy of the *Pittsburg Post.* He found a vacant seat on one of the polished wooden benches and placed the paper on his lap. He had some time to kill before his train arrived. He opened the paper and thought about what section he would look at first. Maybe there would be some interesting news to read on the train. For several days, he had been following a story concerning a missing Philadelphia woman. If there were nothing new on that, perhaps he might find a report about what was going on in Chicago or Denver. He could use some leads on finding a good position in the West. Before he could page through to look further, his eyes were drawn to an article on the front section, just below the fold. It was about the missing woman. Had she been found?

He skimmed through the review of the case: The police had been looking throughout the state for this particular young woman. She was wanted for questioning in a theft from a prominent family in Philadelphia. There was a reward for information leading to her arrest. According to the reporter in today's paper, the wanted woman was no longer missing. She had been identified as the person who had fallen or jumped from the Sixth Street Bridge right here in Pittsburg three days ago.

Until yesterday, the police were not able to connect the two incidents. Charlie recalled a mention of the bridge death in the paper, but had not paid much attention at the time. There was so much tragedy in the world. He did not want to dwell on any more of it than necessary. However, today's development compelled him to look in the paper for anything else connected to this story. He noted a quote from an eyewitness. Charlie read on, his curiosity increasing with each line. The paper had included an interview with a local worker, Henry Duralczyk. He had been heading home from his night warehouse job and was crossing the Allegheny River on the walkway along the side of the bridge. The reporter quoted the man's observations.

"It was about seven-thirty in the mornin'. The air was still pretty thick and the light was not so good. I saw this woman standin' on the bridge. I thought it was odd, her being alone and all, but I figured she was out lookin' at the water or waitin' for someone. She had somethin' in her hand and put it down. It could have been a rock. Then she climbed up on the railing. She stood there, just starin' at the water. I was afraid she might jump, but before I could get any closer, she vanished. Maybe she slipped. Maybe she did jump. I don't know."

The police detective stated that Duralczyk's description of the woman fit the information they had for the missing suspected thief. There was more to the detective's statement. "We found a suicide note under a rock on the pedestrian sidewalk at the spot he had seen the mysterious woman. We also found her scarf. It was caught on a bridge support nearby, just blowing in the breeze. The note indicated that her suffering was too much for her to bear. When she knew we were closing in, she decided to end it all. There's something about those three sister bridges." (Editor's note: The detective refers to the Sixth, Seventh and Ninth street bridges that are nearly identical and unique to Pittsburg.) "We have a few jumpers every year. Water was running fast that night. Could be a long time before she turns up downstream. Maybe never. One thing for sure, she's a goner. We've only fished one out alive ever, and that was blind luck. Boat happened to be right under the fellow, and the water was warm. Guy nearly fell right onto the deck."

The article went on to report that there was an active search for the body, but at the time of publication, no other clothing had turned up, nor had the body been recovered. There was a statement from the coroner as well. "It's not so unusual for the remains of jumpers to never be found. Sometimes, they do wash up on shore. Their bodies have been discovered as far away as fifty miles downstream in the Ohio River. Regardless of where a body is recovered, the longer it remains in the water, the less likely that the remains will be in an identifiable condition. Between the bloating from the water and scavenging by marine life, it's not something for a person with a weak stomach to see, let alone a family member." A review of the more notorious cases of recovered remains from the past followed. Charlie had no interest in the history of this nasty business. He scanned the remainder of the front page for other news, then turned the page.

What he found on page four was the contents of the suicide message. It was even more pathetic than the detective had indicated. The unfortunate woman had poured her heart out on paper: "I have run out of options and have nowhere else to go. I have been falsely accused of stealing from the family I was promised to join. I would never do such a terrible thing, though I have just cause. My fiancé broke our engagement, broke my heart and finally, broke my spirit. Now, he believes that I have sought retribution through theft. I have been hounded by his privileged family for my perceived sins, the worst of which was having been born poor. Rather than face a life of continual persecution, I choose the freedom of the world beyond."

In the next column was an exclusive interview with the ex-fiancé. Charlie skipped through the introductory paragraphs. They merely repeated the charges of theft and deception, in more detail than in the suicide note. The article chronicled the family's wealth, which was considerable, their indignation at being robbed by someone they knew, and the man's search for the stolen valuables. He claimed that several pieces of family jewelry, a large sum of cash and "other items of value" were missing. Finally, Charlie came to the heart of the interview. "The police asked me to examine the suicide note. The handwriting in the message found on the bridge is most definitely hers. Of course, her death is a shock and terribly sad, but I feel vindicated. While she proclaimed her innocence in her pathetic letter, the fact that she went to such desperate lengths only proves her guilt. All that remains is to recover the stolen property."

Charlie paused in his reading. How could someone be so cold? He believed that any man who had been engaged to marry a woman who died tragically should be more upset about the loss of her life than the loss of his property. Even if this fellow was no longer in love with this poor woman, should he not have expressed some measure of sadness upon learning of her death? He sounded like one of the haughty rich men who owned great businesses and cared nothing for the people who made the money for them.

With the identification of the handwriting in the suicide note, the reporter opined that the police would likely close the case, body recovery or no. As there was no other suspect, the matter of the theft was also now closed, despite none of the allegedly stolen items having been recovered. The police had searched the woman's last known whereabouts and turned up no leads. Charlie nodded. His train was pulling in, and he tucked the paper under his arm.

As he moved toward the platform, a gentleman in a black suit and bowler hat pointed at the headline and said, "Some story, eh? Those reporters are going to have a field day. Love, larceny, betrayal, old money, tragic death." He smiled wistfully. "Doesn't get much better than that."

Charlie shook his head and shrugged.

The man pressed on. "Friend of mine is the associate editor. A story like that sells a lot of papers."

Charlie then nodded in agreement. It did have everything.

"The body will wash up somewhere eventually." The man gestured out towards the river. "You have to be patient and watch for it. And when that happens, that'll *really* give them something to write about. Most people won't admit it, but they can't get enough of the nasty details. And this will be *very* nasty. The public is like a bunch of vultures."

Though Charlie wouldn't be reading the Post again any time soon, he simply nodded again and let the man go on his way. He doubted there would be many further articles about this case. For Charlie knew something that the police did not: They would never find the woman they sought by watching the water.

Chapter Two

Giving the post of her bed a vicious kick, Charlotte Baker cursed inwardly. She had no choice but to accept a drastic change in her plans. She had wanted to stay in Philadelphia until her brother Charlie sent for her. After everything that had happened in the past week, this was no longer possible. She was not welcome in this town, and she did not feel safe. Since she went to attend The University of Pennsylvania School of Law (or "U Penn"), life had seemed to get better. The last few years were one step upwards after another. She was about to reach the top of her dreams. Everything was working out better than she dared hope for. For a gal born of modest means, it was like finding the pot of gold at the end of a rainbow.

Charlotte wagged her head sadly. Now, her world was falling apart. She had to leave without delay, before all of her hard work was for nothing. She pulled out her trunks. They were already packed for a different sort of move, a happier move, one that would never happen. She laid two small valises on the bed and opened them. As she pulled hose, undergarments and camisoles from her dresser and placed them neatly into her bags, she reflected on her life. Nothing she experienced had gone according to plan, but where did she go so far off track that she was being virtually run out of town?

Her life had started off well enough. Born in 1869 in Boston, the War Between the States was not long past. The wounds were still deep and fresh. Families remained staunchly divided in their allegiances. Her father was a lawyer, son of Irish immigrants, an idealist who cared more for principles than fees. He did well enough with his practice in Boston to enable him to pursue his sense of social justice. Her practical mother was an exotic beauty, daughter of a wealthy mercantile owner. Charlotte barely knew her grandfather. Even in his later years, the man was an unconventional sort. He had traveled the country to find exceptional wares for wealthy Easterners, and on one of his more memorable trips, he returned with a wife, her grandmother.

Charlotte closed up the first valise and started to pack her personal items into the second. There was a set of a brush, comb and mirror that had been a gift from her grandmother. Placing it carefully between more of her clothing, she thought about Grandmother Baker. So pretty, with dark eyes, sun-kissed skin and hair that was nearly black... She'd asked her mother about where Grandmother was from. To Charlotte, she looked like pictures she'd seen in books of Indians. Her mother had only laughed and told her that her imagination was much too overactive. Still, no one knew, or at least *said*, much about Grandmother Baker's life before she had appeared with her grandfather. Charlotte found this all fodder for her vivid imagination.

During her childhood, she had envisioned all manner of possibilities. Was her grandmother the descendent of an Indian princess? Or perhaps, a Far Eastern beauty that her grandfather met in the wilds of California? People usually went West to seek their fortune. They either found something and stayed or deemed it too rustic and returned East. She had not heard of anyone who was *from* the West coming to the East. Indeed, was *anyone* really from there? The West was a destination, a place that promised a fresh start and freedom from many of the constraints of so-called civilization. It inspired tales of discovery and adventure.

Both of her parents were staunchly antislavery, and her father went to the South a number of times to help settle the lingering land and property disputes that arose in the years after the war. She had only the vaguest notion of how dangerous this could be, but had overheard her mother express her apprehensions on several occasions. One exchange in particular was burned into her memory. Charlotte was ten years old at the time.

"Shawn, why must you go now?" her mother pleaded. "Shouldn't you wait until that lawyer in Mississippi writes you? You're an outsider to them. Being invited is better than storming in."

"You worry too much, Lillian. The terrible war has been over for years, now. We're all one country again." Her father always saw the best in everything.

"I admire your spirit, sweetheart, and I wish that were true. The law may call us all one, but feelings run deeper." Her mother paused and extended her hands in a pleading gesture. "People aren't about to start treating former slaves like people instead of property merely because a piece of paper says they should."

"Believe me, my dear, I know that. But they need people like me to help set things right. I try to show them that getting along is best for everyone." He stopped speaking, and for a moment, Charlotte had thought that was the end of it. "All I'm being asked to do is clarify property issues. It's not like I'm going into the army, and I'm not going to preach. The case is no more than glorified clerical work."

"If you say so." Her mother's reply seemed matter-of-fact at the time, to a child. Regardless, it was the end of the discussion. Her mother had called her to supper.

Remembering this exchange many times over the years, she came to understand the tone of her mother's voice. It said to Charlotte that she was resigned to her husband's decision, not reassured. All Charlotte understood at the time was that her father had a deep love of the law. She had no concept that the same sense of justice and fairness that she admired and that won him great respect at home, made him unpopular with many of the old plantation owners. During his trips south, Shawn Baker won a string of contentious cases, obtaining portions of land for former slaves and indentured servants.

Charlotte had hoped that her father would not be gone very long on that trip. Most of his other missions had not lasted more than a month. In truth, he was gone only a week. One of the members of the old guard decided that it was time to put a stop to what they perceived as a "great foolishness." Their method was direct: a shotgun. Her father came home in a pine box.

Charlotte and her mother dressed in black as they stood in the cemetery. The pastor said that her father was in a "better place." For the young girl, the only place she wanted her father to be was beside them.

She wanted to be just like him. He was supposed to be there to lead the way. She could not understand why some people were so hateful. Now, she had seen it up close and knew that some just were. For them, it was as natural as breathing.

Her mother sobbed quietly at the gravesite, but when the preacher asked if anyone wished to speak, she stepped forward. "Why couldn't those people understand that Shawn only wanted to do what was right within the law? He never railed. He was the calmest, most rational person I have ever known." Lillian Baker stopped and wiped her eyes on a handkerchief. "It's like everything I've ever believed in is a lie. How could God allow this to happen?" Her voice lowered, but Charlotte could hear her. "It makes me wonder if there *is* a God.'

Clearly, Charlotte's aunt had also heard. "Now, Lillian! Don't go saying things like that!" She put an arm around her sister. "We're all in shock. You can't blame the Lord for this."

"No? Prove to me that God protects the righteous."

Charlotte never heard the remainder of their conversation. Her aunt had hustled her mother away from the gravesite, and mumbled apologies to the pastor. The small group dispersed.

After the burial, her mother was never the same. Her eyes no longer sparkled. She spoke in low, flat tones. Charlotte thought that all the joy had been drained from her mother's spirit. She went through the motions of caring for Charlotte, preparing meals that she herself barely partook of. Her face became pale and thin. It seemed nothing that Charlotte or anyone else did would bring a smile to her mother's lips. Charlotte missed her father, but like her aunt and Charlie, she had reached a place inside where she accepted his absence. However, the fear for her mother was harder to bear.

Lillian Baker spent her time and money on psychics and séances, hoping to contact her dead husband. She even had one of these sessions in her own home, with Charlotte present. It was quite a show, with the lilting voice of the medium calling forth the spirits. Charlotte recalled feeling the table move and hearing the "voice" of her father speaking through the medium. Even at that age, Charlotte didn't buy into any of it. Her hope was that this sideshow would bring her mother peace, regardless of how outrageous it was. But no matter how many psychics, fortune-tellers and mediums her mother consulted, none of it led to any improvement in her mood. It only drained her finances and her strength.

When Charlotte's mother died of grief barely a year after her husband, Charlotte's world suddenly became very small. At eleven years old, Charlotte had only Charlie- no other sibs, first cousins, or living grandparents. They promised that each would always look out for the other, no matter what came along. Who else could they rely on? Her father's generosity and her mother's search for answers to his murder meant that there was limited cash remaining. Fortunately, there was money left in trust for the children's education.

Charlotte and Charlie went to live with her mother's sister and her husband, Seth and Bertha Fletcher, in Worcester. Seth Fletcher ran the local upholstery store. Charlotte concentrated on her schoolwork, striving to make grades that would get her into college in Boston. She made few close friends at school, merely acquaintances. There was no time for school activities or socializing. She read as much as she could, feeling that to be a good lawyer one day, she needed to know more than what was in the law books.

Charlie preferred working with his hands. Uncle Seth needed help at the shop and encouraged Charlie to learn the trade. Charlie did not object. He felt grateful to his relatives for taking them in. After school and during the summers, Charlie spent his time working hard in the store, hauling chairs and settees. He learned how to help the customers choose fabric, and how to apply it. He cut and padded and tacked, learning how to re-web old frames and stitch matching bolsters and cushions. He loved the satisfaction of making things, of getting his hands dirty and the challenge of a difficult task well done. Once he entered high school, he took to using the surname Fletcher, as many of the customers assumed he was the owner's son. Between the number of hours he spent there and the family resemblance, the assumption was natural.

Charlotte was the scholar of the family, like her father. Tall and lanky, her figure was hardly the Victorian ideal. She looked more like her brother than a debutant. This was of no real concern to her. She had no time for frivolous social events or suitors, had there been any. She worked hard, made top grades and got accepted to Boston University. She knew that given the rate of tuition and fees, there was only enough in the trust for one to go. It was not an issue. Charlie preferred the life of a tradesman.

University was the next step on her journey and she would make the most of it. Women had to be twice as qualified to get into professional schools and she made it her mission to be among the top students in her class. They would not be able to deny her. When she was accepted into the University of Pennsylvania School of Law, it meant moving to Philadelphia and leaving Charlie behind. She had only enough money left for the first semester, but had hopes of securing a scholarship. She had to try. With luck, something would work out. Eventually, her circumstances *did* improve. She got her scholarship. However, it came at a high price. Now, she had to leave, or the last of her dreams would die.

Chapter Three

Fall 1896
Soda Flats, Colorado

Charlie Fletcher wiped his brow with the sleeve of his flannel shirt. He stood back to admire the cabin that he had built with the help of his new friends. The cabin still needed a lot inside, but after two weeks of working every minute of daylight, it was habitable. It had a root cellar ready to stock for the winter, and the adjacent woodshed and modest sized barn were nearly complete. He smiled. He'd accomplished a lot since arriving in Soda Flats less than two months ago. It had taken weeks to get everything arranged for the move. He'd needed time to ship his possessions to Denver, get his finances in order and coordinate it all with Charlotte.

His image since coming to Colorado had changed significantly. He no longer looked like a fellow from the city. His brown hair, now past his shoulders, was tied back with a piece of leather and topped with a beat-up wide-brimmed hat. His face was perpetually smudged with dirt from the nature of the work. A blue bandana was tied loosely around his neck. He wore faded denim overalls and a patched flannel shirt.

Back East, he would have felt embarrassed to appear in public looking so scruffy, so wild, but here... Well, it just seemed the way it should be. His one prized piece of new clothing was the pair of fringed leather gloves he wore to do his work. They were not only the sturdiest and most comfortable gloves he had ever worn, they were adorned on the backs with intricate beadwork depicting red birds. They were a fitting symbol of his new life. Charlie found them at an Indian trading post on his way to Colorado. He bought a different pair for Charlotte, thinking she would like to display them, but she was a practical gal. She would wear and use them well.

When he arrived in town, he booked a room in the hotel next to the saloon. Within a week, he located a suitable piece of land to buy, and started to assemble plans and materials for a dwelling. He looked at his friends, standing with him in front of the cabin. Ward Parker was a carpenter. Charlie had met him at the mercantile, when he went into town to purchase his building supplies. Ward was average height, shorter than Charlie, broad and fit. He had a wide, winning smile framed by a moustache and a close-cropped beard. Ward's dark hair was graying at the temples. Charlie estimated him to be in his mid-fifties. This was based more on the time the man had been in Colorado and what he had done in his life than by his appearance. If Charlie didn't know all this about him, he'd have placed Ward at about forty.

Ward was the first guy in Soda Flats to reach out to anyone in need. He had befriended the greenhorn easterner and offered his help with the cabin. Charlie knew how to handle tools, having worked in the furniture store, but Ward was teaching him the basics of carpentry. He also taught him to ride. This was an essential skill in Colorado. Ward had also let Charlie stay in his old cabin these last weeks, so he could leave the hotel and be closer to the homestead.

"It isn't much, Charlie. There's no furniture, but we could probably find you a few things."

"I'll be fine, thanks," Charlie declared. He had made a fairly comfortable "bed" from fresh straw covered by a blanket and had put a board across some stones for a makeshift table. For him, it was still better than the hotel. He no longer had to waste time going in and out of town and could spend his money on building supplies. Even though his own cabin was not much more than a shell, he looked forward to putting a bedroll on the straw and no longer imposing on Ward. He truly cherished his privacy. He'd have that at his homestead. Soon, there would even be a few amenities, like a real bed.

The other man with them today was Niels Sorensen. Niels was an immigrant from Norway, a stonemason. He was a few years older than Charlie, and much more introverted than Ward. He was a good man—quiet and focused on his work. He made an interesting contrast to Ward. Niels was tall, lean, blond and blue-eyed. He sported an untrimmed beard and had let his hair grow nearly as long as Charlie's. Like the others, he was a bit dirty from the work on the cabin.

Ward nudged Charlie in the arm. "Well? Going to stand there daydreaming forever? Looks darned good, if I say so myself. Your sister's going to be impressed, even though she *is* a city gal."

Charlie smiled. He was a man of few words, but he felt compelled to defend Charlotte, even with his weak voice. He was all too aware how cracked and scratchy it sounded. When he met Ward, he explained why that was. A freak accident with a furniture delivery two years back had made it painful for him to speak much above a whisper. "I wouldn't call sis 'citified'. She's not so different from me, though she speaks a lot better." He shook his head, and thought about Charlotte. "She says I had a real nice baritone voice once," he croaked. "I've gotten used to this one."

"So, when do you expect her?" Niels asked.

"Not until spring. Hard to travel in the winter, especially as she's coming out by herself. Besides, I've got a lot of work yet to do to get this place ready," Charlie responded.

Ward nodded. "What does she plan to do out here? She a teacher? I think they're looking for one the next town over."

"No." Charlie paused. He knew they would ask more eventually and hoped the news would be well received. "She's a lawyer."

Ward scratched at his beard. He did not say anything for a bit. "Is she the one who answered the town's advertisement? Is C. Baker your sister Charlotte?"

Charlie owned that was true. "She wanted to get the position based on her qualifications."

Ward grinned. "We do need one here. I can't wait to tell Harriet. She'll be glad to have another educated lady in town."

Charlie was more or less counting on that. Ward's wife, Harriet, was the town's doctor, and had been for nearly twenty years. When she came here, had she met with a lot of opposition? Would it be too nosy to ask? He'd soon have the chance.

Ward added, "You and Niels are invited to Sunday supper. Now that the heavy work is done, we should celebrate."

"Sorry, Ward." Niels knelt to pack up his tools. "I have a job in Colorado Springs. I leave tomorrow. Perhaps another time." He stood and put his hand out to Charlie. "I look forward to meeting your sister."

The Parker home was only a mile from where Charlie lived. It was an easy ride. He was getting used to the different ways of getting around in the West. He hitched his horse in front of the house and walked up to the front entrance. The Parkers lived in one of the nicer homes that Charlie had seen since he had come to Soda Flats. It had touches that reminded him of the fine homes of Boston, such as the leaded glass window set in the front wall. Ward opened the door and motioned him in.

"Thanks for inviting me. Your home is impressive."

An outgoing woman in her fifties, with graying hair and a bright smile, approached. "I'm so glad you could come. I'm Harriet, as you probably guessed." She was pleasant-looking and by the way she looked at Ward, theirs was a strong partnership. "Ward did most of the work himself."

Ward grinned. He slipped an arm around his wife's waist. "It wasn't always like this. We've added to it and replaced a lot," Ward explained. "Got that fancy glass for the front window just a few years ago. Came all the way from New York City."

"I always wanted a little touch of luxury out here," Harriet explained.

"Well, you've got that now," Charlie said, "I think—" Charlie coughed and then spoke in a squeak. "Sorry," he pointed to his throat. "Old injury. I do my best. I'd rather hear about you and Ward." As they moved into the house, Charlie saw two children setting the table.

Ward spoke as he motioned toward the children. "Victoria, Jonas, meet Charlie Fletcher. He's the one putting up the house on the next property." He turned to Charlie. "Their older sister, Rachel, is back East at college." Victoria looked to be about twelve and favored her father. Jonas was tall and gangly, perhaps fifteen or sixteen. They smiled, murmured "hello's" and continued to set the table.

Over supper, Ward mentioned that Charlie was building the house for his sister and that she planned to set up a law practice in Soda Flats. Charlie ventured a question. "What kind of reception can she expect? Is there office space available in town?"

"Well, she's going to get a mixed reaction, for sure, but life gets more complicated every day," Harriet said. We need someone in town who can deal with legal issues. Going to Denver for help all the time, even with the train from Cedar Springs, is simply not practical. People have to work. They have children, farms and animals to care for. They can't be running off to Denver every time they have a dispute or have to get papers signed."

"You can talk to Buck Larson about space," Ward added.

"Buck? Who is he? Is that really his name?" Charlie wondered aloud.

"His name is George, but don't call him that unless you want to start a fight," Jonas advised. This generated much laughter at the table.

Ward put up his hand and the group grew quiet. "Back to why you want to talk to Buck. He owns several buildings in town, including the saloon."

"The saloon?" Charlie responded.

"Yeah, where those ladies with all the face paint are," Victoria offered.

"That's enough about that, young lady," her father admonished. "Charlie can talk to Buck and see for himself. He's just interested in renting space in one of his buildings."

"Well, lawyers have a lot of books, right?" she countered.

"True, Victoria," Harriet granted. "But what does that have to do with the saloon?"

"The old boarding house across the street. Mr. Larson owns it. The barbershop only took over part of the building. The rest is still empty. It has lots of room for bookshelves."

Ward rubbed his chin. "Actually, you may be on to something there, Victoria. You really should have a talk with Buck, Charlie."

"When is your sister coming?" Jonas asked.

Charlie smiled. "Depends on the weather. And when I get the inside of the house done."

"Holler if you need any help, Charlie," Ward offered.

"Thanks, but if I get all my supplies in before winter, I can hole up indoors and have the place done by spring. Make some furniture, too." Charlie coughed, then smiled. "I'm not one for long conversations."

"Fair enough," Harriet said. "Just be sure to bring your sister by when she gets to town."

Charlie nodded. Charlotte was sure to like the warm-hearted town doc. This would be a good place for her to set up her practice.

After the fine supper and listening to Ward and Harriet's stories of their early days in Soda Flats, Charlie rode back to his cabin. His first project, he decided, was to build a proper bed. Camping inside was not so bad, and with the solid chimney and fireplace Niels built, he needn't fear the winter's blast. He had time to fill the woodshed and could work on other furniture later.

He'd venture into town in the morning and see about buying a wagon. Now that the barn was up, he had a place to keep it. This would be a big help when his crates came in from Denver, and when Charlotte shipped her things later on. He'd put up some fencing and get a few cows and chickens. Once he planted a garden in the spring, he could be nearly self-sufficient.

What did he want to put in the house? Better question: What would Charlotte need? He planned to build another cabin or move on after she arrived. This cabin had two rooms. There was one large area that would be for eating, cooking and living space, and a smaller one for a bedroom. He'd need at least a bed and chest for that room, and maybe a chair. Charlotte would like a mirror. Charlie would ask in town about ordering one. The main room required at least a table and a few chairs. A small sideboard would be nice. Charlotte had the china from Grandmother Baker. She'd want to show it off, or at least have a place to put it.

I really love this place. The town is just big enough, it's not far from the railroad, and there's such a sense of freedom. Okay, so there are also bank robbers and cattle rustlers, but I haven't met any of those yet. I was such a tenderfoot when I got here! He remembered how little he knew about living off the land. For a strong, able person, he had been next to worthless with many of the routine skills of the West. He couldn't ride, didn't know the first thing about raising chickens, or milking cows. But he did know about gardening. His aunt and uncle had grown their own vegetables. Looking back on the last weeks, it was hard to believe he had done and learned so much in so short a time. He would need it all—no doubt about it.

Charlie knew that he had been purposely selective about what he told anyone about himself or why he was here. What would they think if they knew the whole truth?

Chapter Four

Charlie went into town two days later for supplies and to buy a wagon. It was as good a time as any to make the acquaintance of Buck Larson. Charlie hitched his horse in front of the saloon, and walked in. There were a number of men scattered about the saloon. One table of five was playing cards. Three of them wore large-brimmed hats, one fellow had a bandana and the fifth man was dealing the cards. He was missing a finger on his right hand. Three men stood at the bar drinking, one with a gun belt slung low across his hips. Charlie noticed several saloon girls, all with fancy dresses and some kind of feather plumes in their hair. One was serving drinks to two men at a corner table and two were standing close to the man dealing at the card table. The brunette had a hand on his shoulder.

Charlie walked up to the bar. The bartender was a middle aged, squatty fellow with a receding hairline and pockmarked skin. He was wiping shot glasses and setting them on the back wall of the bar area. Charlie caught his eye and asked, "Is Buck here?"

"What did you say?" The bartender took a step closer. "You have to speak up in here." He pointed to his right ear. "Don't hear so well anymore. Took a few bottles over the head."

"Sorry." Charlie spoke up as best he could. "Is Buck Larson here? Ward Parker said I should come and talk with him."

The bartender jerked his thumb in the direction of a tall, lanky, long-haired fellow at the far end of the bar. "Not sure what you want, but be my guest." He wiped the bar surface. "Don't try to get in on the card game unless you got a big roll of bills."

Charlie nodded. He walked down to the end of the bar. Buck Larson turned to look at him. Buck was a couple of inches taller than

Charlie, had medium brown hair and hazel eyes. He was not a bad-looking fellow, though Charlie noted a long vertical scar on the man's left cheek.

"You lookin' for me? Now why would a young fella like you want to talk to me? Are you sure you wouldn't rather spend some time with one of my girls?" Buck smiled and took a sip from his whiskey glass. "Hey, Pearl, come on over and talk to my new friend." The woman standing with the card players turned and smiled. She was pretty, with jet-black hair and a curvaceous figure. She walked over toward them. Charlie noticed that she was older than the servers- maybe in her late thirties. It was hard to tell. She was very attractive and had an air of refinement about her, despite the liberal amount of face paint. Her eyes were bright and hinted of a keen mind, no matter the costume.

Buck nudged Charlie. "What's your name, fella?"

"Charlie. Charlie Fletcher."

"Well, Charlie, this here's Pearl." He nodded towards her. "How about you let her get you a drink?"

"Another time." Charlie coughed into his fist. Buck motioned to Pearl to rejoin the card game. "Pardon. Old injury." He pointed to his throat. "Caught a chair leg. I can't speak very loud."

Buck pointed to his scar. "Bar fight. Got hit with a bottle. Was cut up real bad. Doc Harriet had her hands full. A drunk was beatin' on one of my girls. Don't nobody beat up on my girls." He gave Charlie a direct look. "That includes you."

Charlie put his palms up in surrender. "Hey, wouldn't think of it." He put his hand out to Buck. The man had a strong grip. "Good to meet you, Buck. Ward Parker says that you know everything there is to know about this town."

This drew a laugh from Buck. "I 'spose that's true, but what is it that *you* want to know?"

Charlie drew himself up. Time to get to the point. He spoke softly, as best he could. "Ward says that you own the building across the street. The one that used to be the boarding house."

"So?"

"So, I wondered if you want to rent the place out? For an office." Charlie coughed again. Trying to speak up was hard.

"Office? What kind of business you in?" Buck gave him the once-over. "We already got ourselves a banker, a barber and the lady sawbones."

"It's for my sister."

"I haven't seen any sister of yours around town."

"She'll be coming out in the spring."

Buck pursed his lips in thought. "So...what does *she* do? I'm guessin' she's not lookin' for any work here." He gave a significant look to the gals at the card game. "'Course, if she's a looker..." Buck chuckled to himself. Charlie could see that the man's easy-going charm was a major asset to his business.

Charlie waved him off but smiled as he did so. He found the idea amusing. "She's my identical twin. Well, not *quite* identical." This drew another chuckle from Buck. "She's a lawyer. Said she saw an ad the town put in one of the eastern law journals."

"Yeah, that was the town council's idea. Since the railroad came through, life's gotten a lot more complicated out here. Could use a little legal advice myself from time to time." He rubbed his chin and looked at Charlie. "Your twin, eh?"

This was Charlie's turn to laugh. "When we were little, we liked to fool people as to which was which. Gets harder when you're older."

"Still...if things don't work out, she could come talk to me. Always need new girls." Buck raised a brow and grinned.

As crazy as this conversation was, Charlie was having fun talking with Buck. What a character this guy was! But it was clear that his easy charm was why he knew everything about everybody. Charlie returned the smile. "She's really not the type you hire. No, not just for that reason." He relaxed and found he could speak more easily. "She's as tall as I am, more on the lean side and damned strong. We had a hard life growing up. She had to work while she was in school."

"As tall as you, eh?" Buck stroked his chin again. "Yeah, I'll have to meet her." He finished his drink. "Want to see the building?"

"So, you would consider renting to her?"

"Hey, business is business and if she's got the cash, why shouldn't I be the guy to collect the rent? Come on."

Well, Charlie thought, Buck was nothing if not pragmatic. Who was he to judge what he did for a living? "Sure. Lead the way."

Charlie followed Buck across the street and into the empty former boarding house. The building had two floors, with large common areas on the first floor and rooms for the boarders on the second. As Charlie walked through the building with Buck, he tried to imagine it converted into offices.

"How much space would you say your sister is looking for, Charlie?"

That was a good question. "Half of this building. I mean- two floors, but only half the length of it."

Buck nodded. "The way the rooms are laid out, that could work." He walked around the large first-floor room that had been used as a parlor, studying the space. "Yeah, I like that. It would be easier to rent out that way- as two businesses. I might even have an idea on someone who'd take the other side."

As the two men concluded their tour, Charlie shook hands with Buck. "I'll be back soon to talk terms and sign the papers."

"Anytime. Ain't going' nowhere. You can always find me at the saloon."

Heading back out of the town, Charlie decided that the space in the former rooming house was more suitable than he could have hoped for. The larger first floor room would be the office, the smaller a receiving area. The upstairs would need some modification, primarily to add shelves for law books and cabinets for files. He would get to that in the spring. The house had to come first. His plan was to gather his supplies and finish the inside work during the cold months. In the meantime, he'd work up an agreement with Buck, secure the building and make some drawings of the interior, so that he could plan out the changes and estimate the amount of lumber and other supplies he would need. If Ward was available, he'd hire his new friend to take the lead on the cabinetry. The work would go much faster with two, and Ward was a master.

That week, Charlie took delivery on his wagon and a second horse. He would need both for hauling supplies and purchases to the cabin and new office space. The first load he took out to the house included the stove he had ordered. It came in on the train and he picked it up at the railway station in the next town. Charlotte had made sure he learned some basic cooking. Next, he laid in stores of flour and some canned goods. With chickens and a cow in the barn now, he was ready for whatever the winter would bring.

As Charlie went about town to lay in the last of his supplies, he encountered Ward and Niels leaving the general store.

"Charlie!" Ward greeted him. "How's it going? Harriet tells me you've found an office for your sister."

Niels added, "I hear she's your twin."

He'd been warned that news traveled fast in a small town. If he didn't believe it before, he did now. He hadn't seen Ward since talking to Buck and hadn't mentioned the transaction to anyone. Charlie simply nodded. "Thanks for sending me over to Buck's, Ward." He liked talking to Ward and Niels. They were used to his soft croaking voice and Charlie no longer felt so self-conscious about how he sounded to them.

"Glad to do it," Ward replied. "Even life in Soda Flats is getting more complicated."

"Why would she want to come all the way out here?" Niels asked. "Aren't there jobs for lawyers back East?"

"Yes, but mostly for men," Ward noted. "I know we've been out here a few years, but Harriet couldn't find a practice willing to take her when she graduated. I'd hoped things might have changed by now."

"Not so much," Charlie said. "Charlotte saw the notice the town sent to the Eastern papers and figured that a place advertising so far away would look beyond her gender. Besides, regardless of what you might be told, everything back East isn't wonderful. There are some terrible things in the cities: slums, overcrowding, the smells of the factories."

Ward indicated agreement.

"Charlotte is coming out West for breathing room like you both did," Charlie added.

"This open country. It is so beautiful- almost as beautiful as where I came from in Norway," Niels offered. "What is your sister like?"

Charlie shrugged. "Hey, if you get along with *me*, you'll like her."

"You're that identical?" Ward raised a brow. "We'll see."

"We've done a lot of the same work since we were kids**,"** Charlie added.

Niels shifted his weight. "As to work, when should I come out to lay the stones for the hearth? We should have enough in the pile beside the house."

Charlie thought about it. He, Ward and Niels had stacked a wagonload of stones near the house specifically for that part of the construction. The weather was getting colder at night. "Can you do it this week, Niels? Anytime. I'll be at the house doing finish work." Niels agreed.

"I'd better get my supplies home," Ward said. "Join us for supper tomorrow, Charlie?"

"Wouldn't miss it."

Three days later, Niels came out to Charlie's house to lay the hearth stones and make a final check on the chimney work. Charlie was unpacking some of the household goods from Denver that his sister had sent on ahead.

"Help me with these stones, Charlie?" Niels asked. "We'll get a few at a time so I can see how they fit."

Charlie set aside the crate of dishes and went outside with Niels. They brought in a modest sized pile of stones and Niels got to work laying out the hearth.

After a while, Niels stood back and surveyed the work so far. "Think she'll like the cabin? Not the same as those fine houses in the East."

Charlie smiled. "She's not one of those spoiled, delicate types," he replied quietly. "Really, we're not so different in what we like. This is a comfortable, solid house. I'm sure it will feel like home to her."

At the end of the day, with the hearth laid in, Charlie thought about what Charlotte and Niels might think of each other. His sister needed to meet someone better than the man who had courted her before. Why not Niels? He would make the introductions and see what happened.

Chapter Five

Charlotte continued her packing, folding the remainder of her clothes carefully to fit into her wardrobe trunk. She was not about to leave anything behind. Who knew when she would be able to replace any of these items if she left them? It had taken her years to acquire a decent wardrobe, as well as to collect her books and personal effects. Placing a folded nightdress into the trunk, she sighed. It was impossible not to go over the details of her life as she prepared to move into another stage of it. Maybe, just maybe, she could see where it had all gone off the rails. She had to set her path in a direction that would avoid future disaster.

She resumed her mental cataloging of her life. She had worked hard in school, even from the early grades. She loved reading and learning about a variety of subjects. Her father's work fascinated her and she tried to find out as much about it as she could. She liked the logical approach it embraced and hoped that all disputes could be settled reasonably. Her father's death had only made her more determined to see that happen.

At the furniture store, she put her knowledge of figures to good use keeping the books. Charlie had helped with repairing and upholstering. She continued working at the store, even as she entered college. Her aunt and uncle paid her a small salary that helped to stretch her remaining funds. College had meant a time of great fulfillment with new learning, but she had no time for socializing or courting. In many ways, Charlotte was not so different from other young ladies her age. She had always wanted to marry and raise a family, no matter her other ambitions. Having lost so much, she yearned to be part of a real family again. The only way that was going to happen was to have her own.

Would she ever have that family now, considering all that had happened? She shoved these thoughts aside. They were not helpful. She turned her thoughts to college. Colleges were nearly all single sex, so of course, her college was all women. She supposed that society feared that too much proximity of the sexes could lead to all sorts of deviltry and debauchery. Her opinion was that this was nonsense. Deviltry could happen anywhere. If she ever doubted this before, she no longer did.

College was a busy time, but happy. Making friends, participating in college activities... She had such fun whirling about the maypole on the May Day celebrations, dressing in her best on Sundays to go to chapel services, and taking part in student plays and tableaux. Oh, how she loved those days! The whole world seemed to be open to her. She had been determined to fulfill her dreams. The tremendous sense of achievement at graduation also meant an end to her carefree life.

Charlotte worked and studied and prepared for a career in the law, even though she had no idea where the money would come from. The trust had held enough to get her started. She was thrilled to be accepted to the law program at the University of Pennsylvania, and refused to let any pessimism spoil her joy. She packed her few belongings and moved to Philadelphia. There was so much less to pack then! One valise and a small handbag. When she arrived, she found herself a room at the cheapest boarding house she could find. She enrolled at the university, using the last of her funds to pay the tuition for her first semester and two month's rent. This was her dream, despite her uncle's warnings that women were not well accepted in the legal profession. Charlie was often her only supporter.

Law school was a very different place from college. There were only two other women in the entire class, and she had not succeeded in making friends with either of them. They, along with the majority of her male classmates, were from wealthy and prominent families. She had little in common with people who never had concerns about money, lived in homes tended by servants and spent their lives in private schools, attending a continual whirl of social events. They were expected to marry well, which meant within their elite social class. She was clearly not one of *them.*

The men in her class had many reasons not to show interest in her. Choosing a career in a "man's" field was a black mark against her from the outset. She was not of their social standing, which made her doubly unacceptable. She could not dress as well as they, or afford to attend the same events. Many of her classmates already knew each other from their college or prep school days, so the social circles were already closed. A number of them also knew the professors, as they had a father, uncle, brother or grandfather in the law.

Wherever she could, she tried to minimize her expenses. She scrounged for food, mended her clothes, used the books in the library, saved bits of paper and stubs of pencils for her notes. She kept telling herself that somehow, someway, she could stretch her money to last long enough. Despite her frugality, she could see by the end of the first month that it would not be enough. She would have to find another source of funds. First, she made the rounds of the Philadelphia banks. She needn't have wasted her time. The same scene played out in each financial institution.

Charlotte would approach the nearest teller and start again. "May I please speak to a loan officer?"

"I'll see who's available." The teller spoke to another employee, and soon Charlotte was shown to an office. The last loan officer she spoke with was typical: a balding, middle-aged man who was not terribly interested in her.

"And what business do you wish to discuss, young lady? Is your father or perhaps your husband, one of our customers?" The man crossed his hands across his ample middle and waited.

"Sir, I am here on my own behalf." The loan officer appeared puzzled. "I am a student at the University of Pennsylvania School of Law. I wish to take out a loan to cover my expenses."

"Harrumph. That's highly irregular. Can your father or husband sign for you?"

"Sir, my father is dead and I am not married." The loan officer scowled. "I assure you, that when I complete my studies, I shall be more than able to repay the loan."

"Miss, what about your family? Surely they could help you."

She shook her head. "The family's resources are...limited. Is not the degree I shall earn worth the loan?"

He sighed deeply. "Were you a man, undoubtedly. However, this bank is not in the habit of lending money to foolish young women with delusions of competing with men." He waved his hand dismissively. "Good day."

Yes, this scene had played out with few changes at every bank she approached. Though she grew more determined with each one she entered, determination alone was not going to keep her in school. Her next thought was to consider employment, but where could she work that would pay enough? Even if such a dream job existed, how could she still attend class at the same time, or find time to sleep? No, she would have to see what resources were available at the school.

She gathered her courage and went to the Bursar's office, hoping to either extend her time to pay for the following semester or to hope that some new scholarship funds existed. When she had inquired about financial help prior to her enrollment, she was told that all available scholarships had been awarded. She suspected that these were meant only for the men, but she had to try.

"Miss Baker," the secretary said. "Here to pay your bill, I trust?"

"I wish to speak with the Bursar, please."

"Let me see if he has a moment." The secretary rose from her chair and went into the inner office. After a few minutes she returned. "His last appointment cancelled. He can spare you a few minutes. I'd advise you to make the most of them."

Charlotte took a deep breath. Entering the Bursar's office she smoothed out her skirt and offered greetings.

He pointed her to a chair. "What is your concern, Miss Baker? I understand that you are not here to settle your account. Time grows short. The semester is nearly over."

"I know, sir. I am here to ask for your forbearance and hope you will grant me additional time to meet my obligations."

"That would be highly irregular."

"But certainly not against any rule."

"I cannot show favoritism. Have you approached your family?"

"I have no living family of any means. Might there be any additional scholarship funding available now? I was told to ask again each semester."

The Bursar returned the same expression that the bankers had: some pity but mostly disinterest. "No, there is no additional funding. You can either pay on time or pack your books. We have no place for charity cases."

"Sir, I have completed all the work that my professors have assigned and done well on my exams. Surely, that should prove that I belong here."

"Miss Baker, that is all very fine, but do not return to this office unless you are prepared to pay your bill. You may go."

Charlotte left, having no idea what to do next. Outside the office she nearly collided with one of her classmates. He had been one of the few who had, of late, been civil to her. Conrad James Walker III (she had an immediate distrust for anyone who was a "third" but he *had* been nice to her) smiled and excused himself.

"Miss Baker? You look distressed." Walker was tall, dark haired and had hypnotic dark eyes. He seemed genuinely interested.

Should she say anything? She felt drawn in by those eyes. Had she ever seen anyone as handsome? "I...I was just making an inquiry...to see if they had any scholarships available."

"And did they?"

"Well, no."

"I certainly hope that isn't going to mean that you might have to leave the university."

"That would not be my wish, no."

"Might it be your wish to join me for supper? I hate to see such a lovely, and clearly intelligent, young woman so upset." His smile was dazzling.

Charlotte was under his spell from that moment on. Their dinner was wonderful and she hadn't had such good food in months. Over the next three weeks, she spent a great deal of time with Conrad Walker. They studied together in the library and he took her to supper nearly every evening. He was not the best student, but he was eager to learn and accepted Charlotte's help without judgment, even praising her for her logic and insight. He was a perfect gentleman—never a hair or a cuff out of place, manners circumspect and always respectful of her in public or private. Day-to-day life was good and she started to forget about her looming deadline with the Bursar.

When Charlotte was summoned to the Bursar's office the day after final exams began for the semester, she was rudely brought down to earth. This was it, she assumed. This was when she would be dismissed, sent away to no longer pursue her dream. Her heart was heavy, but she would face her fate with dignity.

"Miss Baker," the bursar said as he rose to greet her. "How good of you to come so promptly."

She wondered why he was being so pleasant. She supposed that he wanted to preserve an air of professionalism. Even such nasty business as booting a student could be handled with decency. "Yes, sir. Your message sounded important."

"Yes, indeed. You shall be having a change in status here soon and I wished to explain this to you myself, in private." He shifted in his seat.

"I anticipated as much. I shall pack up my things as soon as the exams are completed. It was kind of you to handle this discreetly."

"Yes, quite. Now as to your packing. It shall only be to move to more suitable quarters."

"Oh?"

"Yes. You recall you had inquired about scholarships. I am pleased to inform you that a full scholarship has been endowed for you, along with funds to provide for your room and board."

Charlotte blinked. "How? When?"

The bursar waved his hand. "The details are unimportant. Between us, I am pleased that you shall stay. I have seen your exams. It would be a shame to lose such a fine student, though your life will be a challenge even as you leave here. I fear the world is not ready for a woman as determined as you."

Could this be true? All she could say was, "Thank you, sir," as she left his office in a fog. What had happened? She had a charming beau and her place at the school was secure. Life was perfect. Or so she thought.

Chapter Six

Charlie read the latest letter from Charlotte. He received a letter about every other week and looked forward to them, while he anticipated her arrival. This one mentioned that she had made it through a very rough year and would explain more when she came out West.

"Thank you for helping me get my house and office set up before I arrive. This will make the move so much easier for me. I may even have clients waiting for me, as I know you will be singing my praises. I certainly will not discourage you from doing so. However, please do not say overly much about my personal situation. I would rather not have to answer too many questions. If you are pressed, as you may well be, simply say that I am a widow. It is a respectable condition for an unattached woman."

This gave Charlie pause. In her letters, Charlotte had shared many of the painful details of her last days in law school and what she had been doing since her graduation. Clearly, she did not mean for him to disclose these to anyone else. He never had any intention of doing so, but apparently Charlotte was more concerned about this than he thought. He read more.

"I am looking forward to moving to Soda Flats in the spring. This chance for a new challenge in the state of Colorado, both in the practice of law and in my life is like a new birth." Charlie smiled. All of his hard work would be worth it.

In early October, with the cabin at least habitable, Charlie decided it was time he explored Soda Flats more closely. With the pressure of finding a homestead, getting a cabin and barn put up and finding office space for Charlotte, there had been little opportunity for a full tour of the town. In addition to the general store, the saloon and the now-empty former boarding house, Soda Flats boasted quite a number of other shops. It also had wooden-planked walkways in front of all of the buildings on Main Street. Not as durable as the brick and stone of the East, but far better than simple dirt paths, as in many of the small hamlets Charlie had seen on his way here.

He walked down the main street, stopping in front of the barbershop. As his long hair was acceptable here, especially when tied back neatly, and given the fact that he had never been able to grow a beard, this was not a place he had patronized. The shop had a traditional barber pole in front and a sign listing the hours of business. Charlie could see through the window. The barber had a customer in the chair and another waiting. He moved on, not wishing to appear too curious, and explored the alley next to the barbershop. At the end of the alley was the livery where he had bought his wagon. He discovered that there was a smithy behind the livery. Why had he not noticed this before? Perhaps he had been more focused on getting things done than he thought. He returned to the walkway.

The next building was the hotel, which was next to the saloon. He knew that some of the hotel rooms were actually above the saloon, since the room he had occupied for a week was one of them. The hotel was clean and basic, and the lobby was done up well. It was not at the same level of opulence as any of the large city hotels in Boston, but it was surprisingly well-appointed for being in what Charlie considered the middle of nowhere. The saloon was the unofficial town meeting place and de-facto men's club. Even if one didn't drink much, important business was conducted there and avoiding the saloon meant missing much of the necessary news.

On the far side of the saloon was the town café. Charlie had taken his meals there during his first days in Soda Flats. It served good, hot, simple food, reasonably priced. The house specialty was a roast beef dinner. He crossed a small alleyway to the next section of sidewalk, and took a detour down the alley behind the café. There, he found a different path to the lumberyard and farm supply. Again, why had he not made the connection? He should have seen it from the livery, shouldn't he? They were both set well back of the buildings on Main Street. Maybe he was being too hard on himself. He had only been there a few times. Ward and Niels had brought out most of the supplies for the cabin.

Returning to the walkway, he was soon at the mercantile, at the end of the street, across from the sheriff's office and jail. Was this location planned? Had the original owner wished to protect his business by putting it there? The mercantile sold an impressive variety of items, from canned goods to clothing and patent medicines. One could also order from a catalog and have merchandise shipped out by train to Cedar Springs.

Charlie crossed the street and worked his way back on the opposite walkway. After a dirt alley next to the sheriff's office, there was a small building with a sign indicating it was a library. A plaque on the door explained that the books had been donated by several of the town business folk, including Doc Harriet. Adjacent was Doc Harriet's office and clinic, a fairly large two-story building, with another dirt alley on the far side. Charlie saw nothing but rain barrels and storage behind the clinic.

The next building was familiar to Charlie. It was the old boarding house. Charlotte would have her office in one section. Rumor was that Buck had been speaking with a tobacconist from Denver about putting a shop in Soda Flats. Buck wanted the additional rent and the saloon crowd would certainly be pleased by the choice. By the end of the vacant building was another unpaved alley. It held nothing of interest. In a few steps, Charlie was in front of the Soda Flats Savings and Loan. The town must be doing well, Charlie thought. The bank had the fanciest front in town, with gold lettering on the window and brass fittings on the door.

At the end of the street was the office of the Soda Flats Gazette. On the door of the newspaper office, Charlie saw a posting for a town meeting later that week. He had never attended one and was curious to see how this mode of government worked. The meeting would be held at six in the evening at the town church, as it had a social hall adjacent. It was the only place in the town that could accommodate a crowd indoors.

He could see the church steeple a few hundred feet away. The church was at the end of the town limits, its steeple making its presence known from any point in the town. Across the meadow was a school building. Charlie had no idea how many children were in the town, but had seen a number on their way to or from the schoolhouse. Regardless, Charlie had spent enough time exploring. It was time to go back to his cabin and get to work.

On Wednesday evening, Charlie rode over to the church to attend the town meeting. As he glanced around and entered the social hall, he counted at least a hundred people. Clearly, there was great interest in the topics for discussion. Before he could get a seat, he heard a voice call out to him.

"Charlie! Hey, over here! Saved you a seat." It was Ward Parker, there with Doc Harriet, two rows up from where he was standing.

Charlie made his way over and went to sit down. "Seems like the place to be." He coughed lightly. "Guess most everyone in town must be here."

"Not everyone," Harriet said. "Niels had to work out of town this week."

At the front of the hall, an average-looking man in a fine three-piece suit and bowler hat pounded a gavel. He looked to be in his mid-forties and his demeanor was of a man used to being in charge. "Ladies and gentlemen. I call this meeting to order."

Charlie leaned over and whispered to Ward, "Who's he?"

"That's Edward Lowell, the mayor. He's worked hard to make this town a better place."

Nodding, Charlie sat back to listen to the mayor.

"Now," Lowell continued, "We have several proposals to consider. First, is the call to reinforce the jail. Sheriff, would you like to come up and explain this?"

A tall man with sandy hair got up from the second row. He was dressed in a simple brown suit, had a string tie and wore a broad-brimmed hat. Charlie estimated him to be in his late forties. He turned to Ward with a questioning look.

"Grant Turner. He's been sheriff for the past ten years. Does a good job and I don't think anyone else wants to do it." When the sheriff turned to address the crowd, he revealed a face with lines and a cleft chin. Charlie wondered about the life that had led to these features.

"As you all know," Turner began, "our town has grown and the rails have come within a few miles of us. This has allowed us to expand commerce with the rest of the country. It also means that we have become accessible to outside criminals. When they cause trouble in our town, we need to be able to keep them away from our good citizens until the circuit judge arrives. I wish we didn't have to, but after the jailbreak last year, we need to build a stone building with bars. There's no way a couple of friends with horses and a rope would be able to pull out the window from that!" There was a general murmuring of agreement through the crowd.

"Thank you, Sheriff Turner," the mayor said. "Are there any questions before we vote on the proposal?"

Charlie listened as several of the other citizens asked about the cost and the time involved to build the jail. The budget was modest, and after some discussion, was approved. He also learned that the town raised most of its funds from taxing property: land, livestock, buildings and so forth. He then realized that Charlotte would be taxed for her homestead, but not for her office, as long as she rented the space.

The next topic was a proposal to build a firehouse. There seemed to be general agreement that this was a good idea, as fire could take down a frame building in minutes during a hot summer. However, there was a lengthy debate about how much money to spend on what type of equipment. Ultimately, the decision was that a brick and stone building would be constructed, and the equipment would be discussed at a later meeting. A committee was appointed to determine the costs of the various options available.

After a long week of work on the interior of his cabin, Charlie went into town to see what was going on at the saloon. Ward had told him that there were frequent card games, mostly penny-ante. He assured Charlie that tales of shoot-outs at Western card games were highly overblown by Eastern journalists. In the saloon that evening, he spotted many of the men he had seen at the town meeting, including the mayor. Ed Lowell was seated at a corner table playing cards with three other fellows in fancy suits.

Charlie asked at the bar about a low-stakes game and the barkeep motioned him toward a table towards the back. Charlie sat and introduced himself. "What's the minimum bet? Might be too rich for my blood."

The men at the table laughed. One who said his name was George, pointed at the center of the table. "For now, we're playing for toothpicks."

Charlie played a few hands, then folded when another player joined them and the group moved on to play for money. He got up and stretched. He saw Buck at the bar and went over. "Business is good, Buck."

"True enough. Card games always help sell drinks...and entertainment." He chuckled and finished his drink.

A man came into the saloon and walked over to Buck. He was at least sixty, had a remarkably innocent-looking face for his age and wore a clerical collar. "Buck!" He clapped the saloon owner on the back. "When am I going to see you in church? I told you that the ladies are welcome, as long as they dress modestly."

Buck smiled. "Sure, Rev. I'll remember. You might have better luck with Charlie here." He motioned. "Charlie Fletcher, meet Reverend Bob Miller. He's been in Soda Flats since before I was born."

"Pleasure to meet you, Reverend," Charlie managed.

Buck motioned Rev. Miller over to a table and sat down with him. Charlie turned and saw Pearl. He spoke in a loud whisper. "Pearl? Care to join me for a drink?"

Pearl raised an eyebrow. "Last we met, I had the impression that I wasn't your type."

Charlie felt slightly embarrassed. "Well, maybe not for... but I'd like to sit and talk. I'd pay you for your time, of course."

This elicited an expression of skepticism. "It's your money." She motioned to the barkeep. "Two drinks over at the far table, Fred." She waved Charlie over to a table.

The two sat and one of the other girls brought drinks. They each took a sip. Charlie didn't know where to start. Pearl spoke first. "Did I hear you tell Buck you have a throat problem? Not that it matters." He nodded. "So, Mr. Charlie Fletcher, what is so fascinating about me that you want to pay me to talk? Or is it because you have trouble with that yourself?"

He smiled. "That's only part of it. I don't have many friends here and something tells me this," he gestured, "is not why you came West. I'd ask your full name, if that's not too personal."

Pearl lifted her glass. "Here's to either the smartest man I have ever met, or a psychic." When Charlie did not reply, she continued. "My name is Pearl Hudson. I grew up in Philadelphia, youngest of four daughters. We were not exactly rich, but we were well-off. Father sent us all to finishing school, but by the time my sisters got married, there wasn't anything left for a dowry. Truthfully, I couldn't stand the fellows of the social standing my parents found appropriate. I wanted to see more of the world. So, I headed West."

"With your education, why not teach school rather than..."

"Be a saloon girl?" She laughed. "I did consider it, but there are so many rules and it doesn't pay so well. I put in my time and Buck has been fair with me. Actually, my job now is mostly serving drinks to customers during the card games and helping him find new girls."

"Have you ever considered, well, retirement?"

"To what? Marry some old coot or be a rancher's wife? I'm not really cut out for that. I'm used to doing as I please."

"Maybe you heard. My sister, Charlotte, is coming here in the spring."

"The lady lawyer? Who hasn't?"

"She's going to need office help. Interested?"

"Are you serious?"

Charlie nodded. "No promises, but I'll talk to her about it."

"Okay, then you can let me know what she says."

Charlie smiled. "Wonderful." He saw Buck motion to Pearl. "Guess my time's up." He stood and tipped his hat. "Nice speaking with you, Pearl."

"Likewise. Does this mean you're not going to be in to talk to me again?"

"No, Pearl. Just the opposite. I'd very much like another drink with you, or dinner at the café. I want to be able to tell Charlotte all about you."

Was Charlie imagining it or did Pearl, the saloon girl, actually blush?

CHAPTER SEVEN

During the remainder of October and November, Charlie spent all of his time working on his house and laying in supplies. The inside work would wait until the winter, but there were many other tasks remaining. He took a break to have a drink or share dinner with Pearl nearly every week. The first time he took her to the café, she laughed. "Okay, are you ever going to explain to me why all you want to do with me is talk? Not that I mind being paid to sit and tell you my life story, but you're not the usual kind of man I meet."

Charlie conceded this was probably true. "Well, I told you that my sister will be here in the spring. She trusted me to get things set up for her. That means building a cabin, finding a place for her office and interviewing for an assistant."

"And you figured that a saloon was a good place to look for one?"

That made Charlie grin. "Well, she wants a woman for the job and what better place to find one?"

"You are one strange fellow." Pearl leaned in to speak softly. "What will your friends think about your spending time with one of Buck's girls outside the saloon?"

He shrugged. "Jealousy?" This brought a laugh from Pearl. "I hardly think they concern themselves with such things. Tell me more about your life back East."

Charlie knew that Charlotte would like this bright, spirited woman. He enjoyed learning more of the details of Pearl's life before Soda Flats and was more than happy to let her do most of the talking during their times out. She had been dismissive of her finishing school education at first, but when pressed, admitted the details.

"I was a much better student than my sisters. They were more interested in the social calendar and snaring a proper husband than anything in a book. By proper, I mean someone of the right social standing, and, of course, with serious money."

"Did you have a favorite subject?" Charlie asked.

"Figures...the number kind," she laughed. "I help Buck at the saloon and make sure he doesn't get swindled by any of his suppliers." Charlie smiled. "I can't wait to meet your sister. It's such a hoot that you two are twins."

Charlie shrugged. "Sometimes it seems strange to us, too. Another person so like you and yet so different."

After their first meeting at the cafe, Pearl would meet him on her off time, as she conceded that she now considered him a friend and not a customer. Charlie also looked forward to seeing her. He was more certain with each meeting that Pearl and Charlotte would do well together in their new business. In the meantime, Charlie was pleased to increase his small circle of friends.

The center of this circle was the Parker family, who treated him as an extension of their own. Ward came by Charlie's cabin frequently, mostly to offer advice and occasionally lend a hand when a job required two to accomplish. When Charlie joined the Wards for supper, he always tried to bring a contribution to the meal. His days were full even with the delay on the inside work. He had to gauge his progress by the week and month, and assure himself that he would finish.

By December, Charlie was ready to hunker down for the winter in his log house. With help and advice from carpenter Ward, he had completed the posts and slats for a bed, started on a table and had plans drawn up for the chairs. He still had some finish work left on the barn and sheds. He had made good progress on laying in a supply of wood and had filled the woodbin closest to the cabin. He hadn't bothered to cut his hair in months, but by doubling over his tied-back tail, it didn't look any different. It was simpler than going into town for a cut.

Ward had advised him to attach metal loops to the sides of his outbuildings, that he might thread guide ropes. In the event of a severe snowstorm, he would be able to find his way out to the barn or wood shed and back without getting lost in a whiteout. Charlie had never even considered this.

"We've lost a couple of folks over the years and had some close calls. Anyone who's been through a bad one has learned to be prepared," Ward told him. "Mother Nature is not to be taken for granted."

Besides the cows and chickens (which provided his milk and eggs), he laid in a supply of canned goods, salted meats, flour, salt, sugar, and potatoes. He was glad that Charlotte had insisted that he learn some basic cooking skills. "Remember what our aunt told us. You should be sure you eat proper meals when you're out on your own," his sister had said. Well, he would. Come spring, he would even put in a garden and have fresh vegetables. Maybe he or Charlotte would learn to can as well.

Meanwhile, he busied himself finishing the inside of the house. Some of Charlotte's crates had arrived, as well as an upholstered chair from back home and he wanted to get things put away properly before she came in the spring. His list of projects included shelving for books, a cabinet in the dining area and making simple wooden chairs to put around the table. The cabin should have at least four or five. He might not be much for company, but Charlotte was. Ward promised to help him acquire or fashion parts for the chairs and then Charlie would have to smooth, sand, assemble and finish them, to make the piles of parts into useful furniture.

Charlie wasn't going to spend the entire winter in the house, but he *was* going to keep close to home. He doubted that he would need to take a trip to town for weeks. Fortunately, should he have to, he had learned to ride, thanks again to Ward, with some coaching from Niels. Though he had acquired the necessary skills, the first lessons had been painful. He fell several times before mastering them, and was glad the lessons started in the meadow. Truthfully, Niels' "coaching" consisted mostly of helping him up from the ground when he fell. The grass there was thick and provided some cushion, at least enough to avoid broken bones.

The barn required a small amount of additional work. Charlie had to finish the stalls for his cows and two horses. He and Ward had completed the chicken coop earlier, so he had a good supply of eggs.

By spending some time every day splitting and stacking wood, he was well on his way to having enough in the sheds for the entire winter. He'd keep at it until the weather stopped him.

Charlie had supper once or twice a week with the Parkers, weather permitting. Their oldest child, Rachel, away at college in Pittsburg, sent sporadic letters. "She's doing very well," Harriet told him. "Loves everything, so she changes her mind about what she wants to do about every month or so." Victoria and Jonas were seeing to their assigned chores around the house. Victoria had her mother's dark eyes and her father's smile. Jonas was tall and lean, with his father's hazel eyes.

Charlie's contributions to these gatherings varied depending on his day—a string of fish, fancy tinned items from the mercantile, or fresh eggs, to name a few. One night he brought a pan of freshly baked biscuits, much to the amusement of Jonas and Victoria.

"Sis told me I'd better learn to cook before I struck out on my own. Afraid I might starve. But I'd rather know more about you two."

"Jonas has a real talent for building things. He thinks up designs I've never even imagined." Ward beamed proudly and roughed up his son's hair. "He's also good with his hands, so I don't know if he's going to be a carpenter or an architect."

"And I want to be a doctor, just like mother," Victoria declared.

Once they sat down for their meal, Charlie asked Ward and Harriet how they came to be in Soda Flats. He spoke quietly, as always, and was pleased that his voice only gave out a few times that evening.

"We've been here for, what, twenty-two years, Ward?" Harriet answered. "I was born in a small town in Pennsylvania. We came out here from Philadelphia after I graduated. I wanted to go where I could be of the most use. There were plenty of doctors in the East, but so few west of the Mississippi."

Ward picked up the story. "I was born and raised in Philadelphia. Learned carpentry from my father and uncle." He smiled. "I met Harriet when I was installing cabinets at the hospital where she worked during her training. She didn't have to sell me on the idea of moving West. The thought of open spaces and being able to create things from the ground up? That was a dream I could share in a heartbeat." He grinned. "We left on the train about a week after we got married. Never looked back."

Two days later, Charlie rode over to the Parkers, taking along a fresh pan of cornbread. Harriet invited him to have supper with them the following evening, as Niels would be joining them. "We should all enjoy this break from winter. We'll see how long it lasts."

"It'll give you a chance to ask Niels about other work you need on the cabin, as well," Ward added.

Charlie agreed. As much as he enjoyed his privacy and time away from the bustle of the town, he did find the occasional company of friends most enjoyable.

When Charlie returned to the Parkers, he greeted Ward and Harriet, then spotted Niels. He put out his hand.

"Charlie! How do you like our winter?" Niels asked.

"Winter? Is that what this is?" He coughed. "Until you go through winter back East, you haven't lived," he joked.

Niels shook his head. "You cannot fool me, Charlie. I came over from Norway when I was sixteen. Spent a number of seasons East. Winters can be hard in all of these places."

"I'm ready for it." Charlie decided to venture a question. When he came to Soda Flats, he had been hesitant to ask too many questions about anyone, lest they ask probing questions about him in return. He now felt more comfortable with both ideas. "Did you learn the stonework trade there?"

"Yes, my uncle lives in New York City," Niels said. "He is a stone mason and taught me."

"That's how Ward learned carpentry," Harriet added. "His father taught him. What of your sister, Charlie? How did she come to study law?"

Charlie thought. What could he say and still honor his sister's wishes to not say too much? Her education was a safe enough subject. "Our father was a lawyer and worked hard to restore order in the South after the War." He paused. "Charlotte always wanted to follow in his footsteps. She studied law at the University of Pennsylvania in Philadelphia."

"Were there many women in her school?" Harriet asked. "I remember how it was for me."

"No, but that only made her more determined," Charlie replied.

"Ah, another strong woman," Ward said. "Just what Soda Flats needs." He nudged Niels, who shrugged.

Charlie was relieved that there were no further questions about Charlotte. He needed time to consider everything he said and to let the bits of her story that she wished to share be revealed a little at a time. He changed the subject. "What can I do to add a woman's touch to the cabin?"

"Ah, good question," Ward responded. "Harriet, tell Charlie about what you found for his house."

Ward's wife smiled. "One of my patients made me a quilt and I already have many. I was thinking it would make the perfect housewarming gift."

Charlie breathed a sigh of relief. She was right. A fine quilt would be just the thing.

Back at his cabin that night, Charlie pulled out the upholstered chair. He fondly remembered seeing other members of his family sitting in it over the years. Settled in front of the fire, he reread some of Charlotte's letters. So many plans. So much to look forward to come spring. He smiled. Charlotte should write a book about her life, he thought. Would anyone believe it? Did she really mean to tell everyone in Soda Flats the version in her letters? Some of it was true. But where was that story leading?

Chapter Eight

On that early May morning as she prepared to leave Philadelphia, Charlotte found herself lost in memories. Her packing was temporarily forgotten. It was so easy to drift back in time. The scholarship had saved her dream and made it possible for her to complete her studies. While she remained curious as to its circumstances, with each passing month this became less important to her. She was focused on her studies, and had a handsome suitor. He was more than enough distraction. She allowed herself the luxury of bathing in pleasant memories.

Ah yes, Conrad Walker. How very happy she was to be romanced by the handsome and wealthy Conrad James Walker III! He had thick, dark, wavy hair and the most compelling eyes. Those eyes were like deep, dark pools that made you want to dive into them. Charlotte knew he would never have trouble winning cases if women were allowed on the jury. One long look and they would believe anything he said. She sighed. He was so wonderful, so well-bred and charming. His manners were perfection. He treated her like a lady and never pressed his suit. Their future was going to be secure. He told her over and over how they would both join his father's law firm after graduation and being accepted to the bar. This was an incredible opportunity. His father headed one of the most prestigious firms in the city. Most of her classmates would have killed for it.

As Conrad's interest in her became obvious to her classmates, she endured some of their bad temper and foul comments. Conrad made no secret of the fact that he felt she would make a great law partner. Several of the men would snicker when he said this. "I'll bet I know how she earned *that* position," was one of the more polite remarks. Others who thought she couldn't hear said worse. The implication in each case was that she was whoring for a job. Conrad never failed to come to her defense. She didn't catch all of what they said, but did see Conrad's reaction when he told one fellow to "take it outside."

While her classmates may have thought that Conrad "had it made" and that his future had been secure from birth, Charlotte did not entirely agree. Yes, Conrad had a tremendously successful and powerful father. And yes, his family's wealth went back three generations. And no, neither Conrad nor his father had ever wanted for anything. However, Conrad had also told her repeatedly that if he did not meet his father's high expectations, he would be out on his own. His father had a spot for him, *if* he deemed Conrad worthy. That was a tremendous burden, in Charlotte's opinion. She was pushing herself hard, but somehow, that seemed easier. Her destiny would be determined solely by her ability, not by some artificial measure with an automatic reward at the end.

The first time she saw Conrad's father was at one of the many Walker family parties. Conrad invited her, along with a half-dozen of his male classmates, to a spring celebration at their estate. Her initial impression of Conrad Walker II was that he had a very detached relationship with his son, and perhaps his entire family. The man was formal and polite, but paid little attention to his son or the friends he had invited. Conrad herded the group from the school over to meet him.

"Father, I'd like to introduce some of my fellow law students." Conrad smiled in his engaging way and waited for his father's response.

The senior Walker was tall and imposing, broader than his son and had a commanding personality. He did not seem to be a man one would challenge lightly. "Oh? Well, then."

Conrad started to introduce the group by name. "Yes, father, as I was saying, this is Charles Pike, son of the banker, and Fred Sommers, whose father owns the department store, and.." Conrad continued the introductions, but his father seemed only minimally interested.

"Yes, yes, son. It's good to form contacts with your colleagues early. It will serve you well." He swept his eyes across the group. "And the young lady came as your guest as well?"

"Yes, father, if you will permit me to continue-"

"Where did you meet her?" His father was clearly not interested in what Conrad had to say. "Is she...related to one of your other friends? Or, perhaps she is one of the secretaries?"

"No, father. She is one of the law students."

"A law student? What is a woman doing in the law school? I heard that the Trustees were considering admitting a few, but it is misguided. They don't have the right temperament, you know." Walker senior shook his head. "Far too emotional."

Before his father could offer another comment, Conrad put up his hand. "She is quite capable. I'll hear no further slights. Her name is Charlotte, Charlotte Baker."

Charlotte blinked. Someone was defending her to the host? And Conrad no less. Well, this certainly increased her good impression of him. "Pleased to meet you, sir," she offered, along with her most pleasant expression. With that, Conrad steered the group away from his father and back to the banquet table.

The remainder of the evening was pleasant but uneventful. Conrad's mother was the perfect hostess, but clearly saw her place as support for her husband. She smiled and circulated through the crowd, but kept her comments to polite small talk.

After the party, Conrad escorted her home to her boarding house. "Please accept my apologies for my father's rude remarks. I would not wish you to think that I share his opinions. You are living proof that his ideas belong in the past."

"Why, Conrad! I had no idea that you felt so strongly!"

"What do you mean? Haven't I said a dozen times that you are sharper than half the professors? Little do they know what power is in that mind of yours." Conrad's expression radiated sincerity.

Basking in the glow of Conrad's praise, Charlotte beamed. Then she was taken by surprise when Conrad leaned in and gave her a light kiss on the cheek. "Good night. I shall see you in class."

Ah, such sweet memories. She hated to leave them. So, she wouldn't. There were more. As Charlotte floated through a series of pleasant scenes, she also thought about Charlie. She admitted that she envied

Charlie at times. Charlotte never shied away from heavy work, but "ladies" weren't supposed to like getting dirty or sweaty.

While Charlotte studied in high school and college, Charlie worked at the store. When she went to law school, she visited him and her aunt and uncle on holidays. Conrad was not entirely pleased. "Why do you mind my visiting with family, Conrad? You certainly spend much time with yours."

"It's purely selfish. I simply wish that you could spend the holiday with me." He flashed her the smile that always won her over. "Enjoy the time with them."

She had wondered what Charlie's plans would be after she finished her studying and passed the bar. They had been there for each other through so much. Would they be ready to go their separate ways? But their destinies were so divergent, it was hard to imagine otherwise. Charlie loved working with wood and upholstery and turning old pieces into new treasures. Charlotte appreciated that. She had spent time in the shop with Charlie and understood the satisfaction of making something with your own hands and being able to use it. Her profession was not measurable in the same concrete way. Researching points of law, preparing arguments, trying to persuade a judge that your point of view was more just than the other side's...these goals were all so nebulous. They were not something you could measure or hold in your hand. She envied the fact that the result of Charlie's labor was so visible.

So, though she did not create or repair chairs and settees, she did her work diligently and received high marks. She knew that some of her professors would rather have given her lower grades, but by working twice as hard and presenting work that she humbly felt was also twice as good, they had no choice but to recognize her scholarship.

Gradually, as the months progressed into the remaining semesters of school, Charlotte did more and more of Conrad's work for him, including writing his briefs. She was so in love, she didn't see a problem with helping Conrad. After all, they were a team, were they not? She was the superior scholar, but Conrad had the personality to win over clients and juries, as well as valued social contacts. Both of them had to complete school and pass the bar for them to join his father's firm.

At a summer party at the Walker estate, months after the occasion when she first encountered Conrad's father, Charlotte met Conrad's uncle. It would be the beginning of an enlightening relationship.

Soon after they arrived at the party, Conrad escorted her over to the buffet table. An elderly man, leaning on a cane near the buffet, waved them over. Charlotte assumed this must be a family member. She turned to Conrad.

"That's my uncle, Benjamin Walker," Conrad whispered.

Benjamin Walker was in his late seventies and did not appear to be in the best of health, but his smile and mental energy were robust. He had grey hair and his blue eyes were clear behind his spectacles. "Conrad! Is this the young law student you brought with you before?"

"Yes, uncle, this is Charlotte Baker."

"Well, then." He put out his hand to Charlotte. "So nice to meet you. Conrad, your father wants to see you about who knows what, so if Miss Baker doesn't mind, I'll keep her company. Is that agreeable to you, Miss Baker?" Benjamin Walker smiled. She could see where Conrad got his charm.

"I'd be pleased to, sir." Charlotte was intrigued by this interesting man.

"Well," Conrad looked at Charlotte and then at his uncle. "If that suits you. This might take some time."

"Then we shall make ourselves comfortable." Benjamin Walker motioned toward a group of chairs nearby. "Run along, Conrad. We shall be fine." Conrad cast a skeptical look at Charlotte but went off to meet his father. Charlotte followed his uncle to a group of chairs. She couldn't help notice that the older gentleman had a pronounced limp.

"I hope you don't mind sitting," Walker said. "Working my way up in the business, I learned a great deal. Unfortunately, a textile mill can also be a dangerous place."

"Textiles?" She thought for a minute. "You're *the* Walker, as in Walker Textiles?"

He nodded. "Founder and owner. Though these days, I don't do much of the leg work anymore." He tapped his foot with his cane and chuckled.

She tipped her head to him. *Impressive.*

"Building a company from the ground up is quite an accomplishment." This family was even more wealthy than she had imagined. Walker Textiles was one of the biggest of its kind in the country. Conrad's father was a banker, so she had never considered a connection.

"Enough about me. I'd like to know how a lovely young woman got into the law. You're clearly bright, but it can be such a nasty business."

Charlotte smiled. The more she spoke with him the more she liked this older man. Would Conrad emulate his uncle when he was older? "My father was a lawyer. He inspired me." She continued to tell Conrad's uncle about herself and her family until Conrad returned, nearly an hour later.

"Sorry to be so long. Father wanted to go over the plans for the office. He'll be adding consulting rooms." He turned to Charlotte. "There are some people I should introduce you to." He put out his arm.

Charlotte got up. "It was a pleasure to speak with you, Mr. Walker."

"Likewise, Miss Baker. I wish you all the best." She joined Conrad and made the rounds of the room. Later, Conrad apologized to her. "I feel bad for sticking you with the old guy. He tends to go on about bygone days and how he built his company. He's a bit of a bore, but he *is* my uncle."

A bore? Hardly, she thought, though she supposed that the same stories heard over and over might wear on a person. "I found him to be quite charming, Conrad. Actually he reminded me of you."

"Oh? Really?" Conrad seemed momentarily annoyed.

Charlotte thought his reply was odd but did not wish to start an argument. At the end of the evening, Conrad escorted her home and offered his usual chaste kiss goodnight. By this time, Charlotte was confused. His kisses were nice but she couldn't help wondering if there should be more, if she should *feel* more. Was this all there was? Maybe it was a silly romantic notion. She had heard rumors about Conrad being with other women. Did he save more for someone else? Should she ask him?

Chapter Nine

On their next evening out, Charlotte decided she would ask Conrad about the rumors she had heard. Of late, she was more concerned about these stories than ever. One of her classmates had seen Conrad out with a young woman. It was on an evening when he had planned a dinner with Charlotte, but had abruptly cancelled. His excuse was that he had a business meeting with his father. She thought nothing of this until she learned about where he actually was. She was confused, but felt confident that Conrad could explain.

Over their dessert, Charlotte spoke up. "Conrad, do you remember last week when you were unable to keep our dinner date?"

Conrad put down his forkful of cake. "Of course, sweetheart. It couldn't be helped. You know how my father is. When he wants to meet with me, I have to go."

"But Conrad, you weren't with him, were you?"

"What are you talking about? Of course I was with my father. What ever gave you the idea that I wasn't?" He stabbed the bite of cake and stuffed it in his mouth.

"Someone saw you at the opera. You were in a box seat with a very attractive young lady." Charlotte took a sip from her water glass and waited for a reply. For a moment, she thought Conrad seemed flustered, but his smile came so quickly, she decided that she had only imagined this.

"Charlotte! Don't look at me like that! The reason my father wanted to see me was to talk me into escorting his client at the last minute." He waved his fork dismissively. "It meant nothing. I didn't think it was important enough to even mention. You know I clerk for my father. Part of my job is to be supportive of clients who are victims of divorce and property disputes." He put down his fork, then reached across the table to touch her face. "You know how hectic it's been for us, with only a semester left before graduation. I didn't give it a thought. Forgive me?" He turned on that smile that made her melt like ice on a hot summer day.

Charlotte felt embarrassed. At the time, she decided she should never have doubted his word. She felt fortunate that her doubts had not soured their relationship, whatever it was. While Conrad had spoken of their being in his father's law practice together, he had been much less specific about other aspects of their relationship. They spent time together in the library and he took her to dinner or the theatre nearly every week. His behavior was generally circumspect. He would give her a polite kiss goodnight, but never pressured her for more. Charlotte assumed that this was a sign that he was a gentleman. After all, she had nothing to compare to.

This memory of her questioning Conrad's motives stressed her a bit. Her happy, breezy feeling was starting to fade. Had this incident with Conrad been a harbinger of things to come? She dismissed it at the time. Now, she returned to drifting through more pleasant thoughts.

When Conrad invited her to dinner just two weeks after that awkward conversation, he told her they were going to a new restaurant on the other side of town. She attached no particular importance to it. It was exciting to go somewhere new, even though it required a train trip to travel there and back. At the restaurant, Conrad further surprised her by having the waiter take them to a private booth.

Once they settled in and ordered, Conrad asked the waiter to bring them a bottle of wine. "What's the occasion, Conrad?" she asked. "Has your father decided to let you have your own consulting room at the office?"

Conrad chuckled. "No, but I still think he will eventually. No, this is something more important." The waiter returned with the wine and poured a glass for each of them. Conrad nodded to him. "That will be all."

Charlotte took a sip of the wine. It was exceptional and probably very expensive. What was up? She looked at Conrad and waited. He rose from the table and came over to her. He reached into his pocket and got down on one knee.

"Charlotte Baker, will you marry me?" He opened a small box to reveal a dazzling ring.

She blinked. Did he really say that? Her answer was never in doubt. She had been head over heels for him since their first dinner together. How had she missed the signs that he returned her feelings?

"Charlotte?"

"Oh! Yes, Conrad. I will. It's just such a surprise." He slid into the booth next to her and gave her a hug, then moved back to his seat. He passed her the ring box. With shaky hands, she put the ring on her finger. Had she ever been happier in her life?

The next few weeks were a busy blur of work and wedding planning. Classes and exams ended and between sessions in the library to study for the bar exam, Conrad and Charlotte moved ahead with their personal plans. The first order of business was to make the announcement to his family. Conrad's father was not enthusiastic, but Charlotte was satisfied that he gave Conrad his approval. She knew she was not what his family expected. Whatever she had to do, she would prove them wrong.

His parents hosted a small, but lavish engagement party at their estate. Charlotte hardly knew anyone there, but recognized some of the same faces from the family holiday parties.

Conrad took her to the jewelry store where he had purchased her ring. "Our family has shopped here for decades. It's tradition. I thought you could select our wedding bands."

"Will you wear a ring, Conrad?" Not every man did. He nodded. Charlotte was pleased that he would willingly wear such a symbol. It helped to allay her concerns about attractive clients trying to steal away her husband.

Charlotte looked over the offerings at the store. So many beautiful rings! She was favoring a simple design until Conrad pointed to a gorgeous set with small diamonds flush-mounted into the top of the rings. "Conrad! They're perfect, but aren't they expensive? Plain gold would be fine."

"Fine maybe, but not good enough for the wife of Conrad Walker III. It must be the best."

Charlotte smiled and felt warm all over when Conrad put his arm around her shoulders. It was a good day to be alive.

When the jeweler put the rings in a box for them, Conrad handed them to her, "Keep these in a safe place until the big day. They could get lost at the estate, given its size." Awash in her happy fog, this was fine with Charlotte. "Now, let's go to Henri's and have some lunch. We need to pick a date for this wedding."

"Is there any rush?" Charlotte was truly overwhelmed. "I though we were going to be engaged for a while."

"We are, sweetheart. In my family, a wedding is a major event. We have to pick a date at least a year ahead."

Over their elegant lunch, they decided on August 28th of the following year. "I'll have Ernest book the date with the church." Ernest was the family's longtime butler. Conrad's family were members of the enormous Episcopalian church downtown. Charlotte had heard that the congregation dated from the Revolutionary War. "Mother will want to have a catered party in the ballroom at the estate, of course."

Oh my! This wedding was going to be a major social event, she realized. "Conrad, I don't know how to say this, but what can I possibly wear for such an elegant ceremony? Your church is a landmark."

"Don't give it a thought. Mother will *insist* that you have something spectacular." He put up his hand. "Don't think about the cost. It's taken care of. You will be representing our family. We have a reputation to protect."

That is how Charlotte ended up at the priciest dressmaker's shop in Philadelphia. Never in her wildest dreams had she thought she would ever be a client at such a place. She felt entirely out of her element, but was soon swept up into the moment.

"Oh! Miss Baker!" The sturdy middle-aged dressmaker was a sweet lady, but no-nonsense when it came to fitting her clients. She introduced herself as Mrs. Bertha James and immediately took charge of the appointment. "Mr. Walker said to be sure that you have a dress that everyone will talk about, a creation that will be the envy of every other bride in the East, so let me show you some of my ideas." She beckoned Charlotte to sit and pulled out a sheaf of papers. "Now, I thought that this one would be nice, but now that we have met, it might be too fussy for your taste." The seamstress showed Charlotte a sketch of an elaborate gown with a long train and endless amounts of lace.

"Indeed. I would feel very overdressed in such a gown," Charlotte replied. "What else have to show me?"

She shuffled through her sketches. "Ah! Now, here's one I favor for you. My last client thought it too simple." She passed the sketch to Charlotte. "I would make it with silk and the best French lace."

The sketch showed a lovely, flowing gown with lace detailing on the bodice and sleeves. The sleeves reminded Charlotte of trumpets, as they were open at the wrist and tapering to the shoulder. "Oh my! That is exquisite! But a gown such as that would be very expensive."

Mrs. James waved her hand. "Tut, tut. Do not worry about that. Mr. Walker has assured me that the cost is of no concern. So, shall we get some measurements?"

The dress that Mrs. James made for her was even more amazing than the sketch and after a few trips back to the shop for fittings, it was completed. She had been so happy when it was delivered to her, just days ago. So happy, and so recently. She let her mind drift on.

Soon after her first trip to the dress shop, she and Conrad attended the expected party at his family estate. She was happy to show her ring to Conrad's uncle, Benjamin Walker. He was the one member of Conrad's family that she genuinely liked.

"Mr. Walker! I'm so glad to see you again."

"Miss Baker, a pleasure. I do hope my nephew is treating you well." He took her hand in both of his and nodded his approval at her ring.

She smiled. "Very well, thank you. I couldn't be happier. This ring is beautiful and Conrad has arranged for the services of a dressmaker." Though she was intimidated about marrying into this family, and most of those family members she met had been rather cold to her, she felt a closeness to Conrad's bachelor uncle.

"I'm pleased to hear that, Miss Baker. Conrad can be, well..."

He never got to finish. Conrad came up and greeted the pair.

"Uncle Benjamin! Sorry, but she's spoken for." He offered Charlotte a dazzling smile and steered her away. Charlotte turned and waved at his uncle.

Charlotte's thoughts started to turn more analytic. She had spent a lot of time with Conrad helping him study for his exams and in preparing him for being admitted to the bar. Conrad pleaded that he needed more help. His father would disown him if he did not get accepted to the bar. She was exhausted, between her own preparations and papers and doing his, but soon it would all pay off. They only had to get through this exam.

Ultimately, they both were accepted to the bar, though Conrad passed only by the slimmest of margins. Charlotte wondered if it had been her talk with one of the lawyers after her exam. She had mentioned how very important it was for Conrad to pass and that his father, who was a very prominent local attorney, would cause a major incident if he did not. Regardless of how they had reached this point, she was relieved. She looked forward to having a partnership in work and at home.

Only last week, at the end of April, they celebrated with his family and then Conrad took her back to her flat. He had far too much to drink and came on strong to Charlotte. She found this more annoying than passionate, but attributed it to the drink. He persisted, and said all the right words. Charlotte was won over by his pleas and let him make love to her. After all, he reminded her, they were getting married soon. With all his sweet talk and maneuvering, when it came time, Conrad had drunk so much that he was barely able to complete the act. Afterwards, he fell asleep. In the morning, she got up to make them breakfast.

"Don't bother making anything for me," Conrad told her.

"Oh?"

Conrad's expression was unreadable. "I have to go over to my father's office to ask about my appointment to the firm."

Chapter Ten

Charlotte coughed. "Conrad, I believe you mean *our* appointments."

Conrad laughed. "No, my dear gullible girl. I *do* mean *my* appointment."

"But you said that we would *both* be joining your father's firm, so long as we passed the bar. How many days and nights did I spend helping you prepare?" Charlotte felt her head start to pound. This could not be what she was hearing.

"I do thank you for that." Conrad's face twisted into a satisfied smirk. "Oh, and while I think of it, I must say that last night was a pleasant bonus, but certainly not good enough to change my plans."

"*Your* plans? For the past...nearly two years all you have talked about is *our* plans." Indeed, Conrad had talked ad nauseam about what *they* needed to study, what *they* would be doing, where *they* would live, what *they* would make of their lives together.

The smirk dissolved into a look of pure innocence. "And what plans might those be? I do not recall signing any papers."

"Conrad! What is this madness? How many times have you told me that we would *both* be part of your father's firm?" Cold fear began to grip her heart.

Conrad simply shrugged. "You know what the most successful lawyers say. If you don't have it in writing, it doesn't exist."

This couldn't be happening, Charlotte thought. "What about what you told your father?"

"Father?" Conrad laughed again. "All Father cares about is having me in his firm. Carrying on the family legacy and all. He bought my way into law school and then expected me to measure up to his standards. It was a gamble, but he desperately wants me in the firm."

Charlotte kept quiet. She was still in shock and now to find that Conrad's father had *bought* him his admission? How many more shocks were coming?

"Imagine my good fortune to have met you." Conrad flashed that winning smile.

She brightened. Maybe this wasn't *all* bad news. "So, you do not regret our time together?"

"Of course not. You were a godsend." Just as Charlotte was breathing a sigh of relief, Conrad continued. "I knew from that first day in class that despite being a woman, you were brilliant." He put his hand on his chest and sighed. "When I met you outside the bursar's office, it was like Fate had shown me the way."

"Conrad, I don't know what you are talking about. Shown you the way to what?" Charlotte had a bad feeling about this, but had no idea where he was going. "You aren't making any sense."

Conrad shook his head. "Let me make this clear then." He took a step away from her and started to pace. Charlotte had seen him do this when he practiced speaking before a jury. What was he trying to tell her? "Look, Father could buy me a place in the class, but I still had to successfully complete the courses and pass the bar. I knew I was in trouble the very first month. My only hope was to latch on to someone who could help me. Father got me in, but he couldn't get me through."

"Why didn't he simply hire a tutor for you?" she asked quietly.

Conrad stopped in his tracks. "Are you serious? I would have had to admit to him that I couldn't do it on my own. Father would *never* have stood for such a thing. I had to find a person who would willingly help me and also be acceptable in his eyes." He paused. "He knew we studied together, but he will *never* know that you did most of my work."

"What if I told him?"

"Ha!" Conrad's grin grew wider, if that were even possible. "I have already told him that you are not to be trusted. He sees you as a scheming woman who wants to latch on to the family fortune and weasel her way into the firm."

"Where would he ever get that idea?" Charlotte struggled for composure.

Conrad shrugged. The angelic look returned.

"Why, you... What about the proposal? The rings? Did you mean any of it?"

"Have I not made myself clear? A *Walker* could never be serious about a nobody like you." Conrad laughed. "I needed you so I could graduate and pass the bar. Now Father will see to it that I get everything I want. What do I need you for now?"

"What about last night? What about everything you said?" Charlotte felt a cold chill over her heart. "What we...did?"

Conrad yawned. "A pleasant diversion, but I know plenty of other women who are better bed partners. I was so bored I could barely stay awake through it."

Charlotte was stunned. "So drunk, you mean," she muttered. She could not believe he said any of this, but Conrad wasn't done.

"My dear girl, you really should be grateful to me and my family."

"Grateful?" Charlotte felt her pain being replaced by anger. The nerve!

"You wouldn't be anything without me. Where do you think that so-called 'scholarship' came from? That was a stroke of genius on my part, I must say." Conrad could not have looked more pleased with himself. It made Charlotte ill.

"What could *you* have to do with my scholarship?"

"You seriously think that such a large award fell out of the sky with your name on it?" He laughed. "Well, I guess in a way it did. I had been scouting the class for the brightest student that I could buy. You being female made it all the easier. I convinced my family that it was a noble thing to put up money for a deserving student and I saw to it that it went to you. Your tuition and stipend were cheaper than a full-time tutor and I never had to admit the truth to Father." His expression was triumphant.

Charlotte could barely focus. "What am I to do, now? Join another firm? Set out on my own?"

"I really don't care." Before Charlotte could counter, Conrad added, "But don't plan on opening an office here in Philadelphia. Father will ruin what's left of you. Women don't belong in the law anyway."

As she stammered in protest, he sighed condescendingly, and for the first time, she saw his true character in his next words. "Now then, enough of this. I'm not a complete cad. You have some time to make arrangements to leave. But, by the end of the month, I'd best not hear about you being here." He offered a self-satisfied half-smile and left.

Charlotte stood, staring at the door after Conrad shut it behind him. She wanted to believe this had been a nightmare, that Conrad had not said any of those awful things. How had she been so completely taken in? Was she so pathetic that she had fallen for Conrad's promises because she needed so desperately to believe in love?

I did everything for him. How many extra hours had she spent in the law library working on Conrad's assignments? How many nights of sleep had she given up to help him study when he was having trouble getting all the details right for his courses?

Conrad thought that *he* was the master of clever persuasion, that *he* was the best at turning others to his way of thinking. *Ha!* Sadly, she might never get to display her courtroom skills. Not if Conrad and his family had their way. And that last insane push to get them *both* to pass the bar exam? She had been so exhausted that afterwards, she had slept for the better part of two days.

As she packed the last of her belongings, stuffing them into her trunks in anger through the tears, she realized he did not ask for the rings back. *He's not getting anything more from me.* She'd keep the dress, too, since it had just been delivered to her and was still carefully packed. If all else failed, she could sell them. For now, they would go with her, wherever she was headed.

She did have a few saleable items in her small apartment. It was unlikely that she would be able to take *everything* with her. Certainly she would take two or three trunks of clothes, her law books and some personal items. She would not attempt to move any furniture or other large items. These she would sell to finance her move. She would buy a train ticket to Pittsburg, and arrange to send her trunks and the crate of books ahead. This would keep her in the state, but hopefully, far enough away from Conrad and his family.

With luck, she would have enough money left to pay for a room while she looked for work. Pittsburg was the second largest city in the state, and there were a number of good law firms that she could approach for a job. Even if all she found was the lowest clerk position, she could surely be hired for that. Any reasonable offer that kept her in the law and paid her enough to scrape by would give her time to plan her next step.

Over the next four days as the calendar turned over into May, she completed her packing and felt more resolute about the changes in her life. It did not take long to tell her landlady that she would be leaving and make arrangements to ship her things. In a pleasant surprise, her landlady bought her few pieces of furniture, saying she could now rent the flat as fully furnished and charge more. With all of the misery Charlotte had faced in the week prior, she welcomed anything positive. She had some cash, her ticket, and her trunks were on their way.

Returning from the station after buying her train ticket, Charlotte's landlady approached her. "I know you'll be leavin' soon, but a feller stopped by and left this note for you."

"Thank you." Her landlady left and Charlotte wondered who in the world would be sending her a message. Certainly not Conrad. He had made it more than clear that he wanted nothing else to do with her... ever. She took the envelope and opened it. She quickly scanned to the bottom. The letter was from Conrad's uncle. This was strange. Though she had a warm spot in her heart for the old man and had always felt that he held her in high regard, she had never before received a letter from him.

Was this related to Conrad's ultimatum about leaving town? Was his uncle going to back up his demand in some way? No use speculating. She took a deep breath, sat down and read the note.

"Dear Miss Baker,

"Please be so kind as to come to my house tonight. It is very important that I speak with you as soon as possible, before you leave Philadelphia. I shall send a coach for you at 7 this evening. I have something for you, but you must come to my home.

"I implore you, this is a matter of utmost importance. I look forward to seeing you again,

Signed,

Benjamin Walker."

Charlotte put the letter down and thought about her next move. She would get ready and go when the coach arrived. It was only one stop to make before she could leave. She was concerned for the man's health, and hoped it was not bad news. Besides, she was grateful to have the opportunity to say goodbye to this delightful and fascinating man. Surely, if he was going to the bother of sending transportation for her, he was not planning to give her a dressing-down.

An hour later, there was a knock at her door. It was her landlady. "Miss Baker, there is a coach outside and the driver tells me you are expecting him." She put her hand to her chest. "It's the fanciest coach I've ever seen."

"Thank you." Charlotte picked up her handbag and cloak and went outside.

At Benjamin Walker's house, the coachman assisted her out and escorted her to the door. The butler admitted her and showed her to the drawing room. He motioned for her to sit. She did so and after a few moments of waiting, saw Benjamin Walker enter the room. His expression was grave.

Chapter Eleven

Charlotte was immediately concerned. She had never seen Conrad's uncle look so serious. Was he ill? Had he not heard about the broken engagement? "Mr. Walker? What is the matter? Are you ailing?" She rose from her chair and walked toward him, her anxiety building with each step.

"Please, Miss Baker, sit here. The problem is not with me." He pointed to the settee and after she sat, he took the other end and settled in. "I heard only yesterday of my nephew's rash decision to break your engagement." He sighed. He muttered. She thought she heard him say, "That boy is a fool." How could she respond to that? She didn't. "I had no idea that he would do that. Not even after what I heard."

Before the older man could comment further, a servant appeared. "Mr. Walker? Would you and your guest care for some tea and light refreshment?"

"An excellent idea, Miles, though under the circumstances, something stronger might be more appropriate."

"Sir?"

Walker waved his hand. "Never mind. Tea will do." He coughed and pulled out a kerchief.

Charlotte felt anxious. *Something stronger?* What kind of awful news was Benjamin Walker about to share? "Are you certain you are well?"

"Well enough." He cleared his throat. "We are not here to discuss me." He relaxed into a sly smile for a moment. "Though, were I much younger, I would welcome the chance to impress you with tales of my life and travels. Contrary to what Conrad may think, I have had a most interesting life."

This was a side of Benjamin Walker she had not considered. He was likely quite the lady's man in his youth. The lighthearted moment passed quickly, though.

His face clouded. "A few weeks ago, I happened to overhear Conrad discussing his plans with one of his friends. There was something in his tone, as well as the fact that he never mentioned you, that struck me as odd. Then he said something more perplexing."

"Oh?" *What in the world?*

"He said that his father would never know how he really got through school." Walker paused. "I know he has never been a great student. Figured he must have cheated to get through college." He coughed. "I assumed what he meant was that he had some extra tutoring. My nephew may be many things, but he does not have the kind of sharp legal mind that his father has. Personally, I was surprised that my brother, dear Conrad the second, pushed him to go to law school. I was even more surprised when I heard that he wanted him to join his firm."

"Oh." Charlotte didn't know about all that. Of course, her only source of information had been son Conrad. "I thought he did very well in college."

"Only because of who he is and because he had a tremendous amount of help." Walker frowned. "He is a very charming lad, and can be most persuasive, but he is not a towering example of superior intellect."

Miles returned with a large silver tray and set it down on the table before them. Charlotte noted a matching teapot, delicate china teacups set on saucers and a crystal plate full of fancy small biscuits and cookies. Miles poured tea and offered the treats.

Despite her anxiety, Charlotte realized her stomach was growling. She was glad to accept a cup of tea and selected a cookie and two biscuits. A few sips of the tea seemed to steady her. "Mr. Walker, I am well aware that Conrad was not...the best student in the class, but I sense that you had more reason to invite me over than to discuss his study habits."

Benjamin Walker nodded. "I see why my nephew took up with you. You don't miss anything." He sighed, took a sip of his tea and put the cup down on the table. "What I could not fathom, not at first, was why he would ever break your engagement."

"Perhaps you'd best ask him."

"I prefer to keep my dealings with my nephew to a minimum. He's a sniveling leech who is throwing away the only good thing in his life." Walker coughed and reached for the tea.

Of all the things she thought Benjamin Walker might say, this was not something she had been prepared to hear. "And what evidence brought you to this conclusion?"

"After I overheard that bit of conversation from the lad, I kept my eyes and ears open. Did a little investigating on my own. Funny how no one pays much attention to an old man, especially one with a cane." He laughed and took a sip of his tea.

Charlotte nibbled on a biscuit and waited for Walker to continue.

"A fellow like my nephew can't help but brag to someone when he thinks he's pulled off a fast one." He stopped to cough and take a sip of tea. "I invited him and five of his friends over to celebrate his passing the bar. I had a nice spread laid out for them and stayed close enough to hear their conversation." He paused again. "Conrad boasted that he sailed through school by keeping company with one of the best students. The next week was the engagement party at the family estate. You recall that we spoke at some length that night, as your fiancé was too busy rubbing elbows with my brother's associates to do more than bring you and take you home. I thought about that afterwards and it all fell into place." He sipped more tea, then put down the cup and clasped her arm. His grip was stronger that she had expected. "You wrote all of Conrad's briefs for him, didn't you?" He released her and patted her arm.

What could Charlotte say? Benjamin Walker had cut through his own nephew's deceptions and knew the ugly truth. She could barely find her voice. All that came out was a whisper. "Yes."

He nodded. "I suspect that you did a great deal more. Tutored him through every class?" She nodded. "Helped him prepare for the bar exam?" Again, she nodded. "Did you perhaps have anything to do with his being named to the law review?"

"Well..."

"Now, Miss Baker, this is not the time to be modest. Did you have a role in his selection?" She lowered her head and nodded. "I really want to hear about what you did."

Charlotte looked up at him and tried to read his intent. She prayed he was being sincere. But what could it hurt now to tell him? She was already being run out of town. "I called in all the favors I could in order to speak before the selection committee. Once I got there, I pointed out to them that it would be a major embarrassment if the son of one of their biggest contributors did not make the law review, but that his fiancé *did*."

"Were you not fearful that they would simply take that honor away from you?"

She paused for a deep breath. "They had already announced my name as being on the review, so it would have been very difficult for them to do so. I must admit, though, it did occur to me."

"And yet you still stood before the committee to make a plea for him?"

She shrugged. "I was in love. I felt I had to do whatever I could for him. And the committee bought it. After some consideration, they thought it was *their* bright idea, and acted as if there had never been a question that Conrad would be included. They likely assumed it would get them another fat check from Conrad's father. It did."

"And now?" Walker put his teacup down.

"I was a fool." She wagged her head. "Now I have to start over somewhere else." She sat quietly and finished her tea. "What about you? It is clear that you are not so fond of Conrad, but what does he say to you? Do you think he holds you in the high regard that he tells me he does? Is that another lie?"

Benjamin Walker did not answer immediately. Instead, he poured another cup of tea and took a long sip. "I suspect he is pleasant to my face only. His real feelings?" Walker put his cup down and rubbed his chin. "My guess is that he tolerates me in hopes that I will leave my money to him, as I have no children."

Her eyebrows flew up on their own accord. Was the man she thought to marry even more of a lowlife that she knew?

Walker smiled slightly. "He's in for a big surprise, and sooner than he thinks."

Charlotte felt a sense of alarm. "What do you mean sooner, sir? I thought you said you were well. Please do not tell me otherwise." She genuinely liked Conrad's uncle. He was the only one of his family she would miss.

"No, no, nothing like that. I have my problems, but no more than I have grown used to." He smiled. "I called you here tonight to give you something. I want you to have it, not any of my family."

"But why me? I am no longer engaged to Conrad. I'm not even going to be family by marriage."

"Because you are worth ten of him and I am not afraid to say so." He shifted his position on the settee and picked up a box on the end table next to him. She had been so focused on the conversation that she had not noticed it before. It was a beautiful wood box, the size of a large cigar box. Why in the world did he wish her to have this? Walker coughed and placed it on his lap. "This is for you."

"Mr. Walker, I can't possibly accept such a lovely gift."

"That is what makes you so different from Conrad. You don't even know what's in it and you already show more gratitude than I have even seen from him." He handed her the box. "Please. I can think of no one I wish to have this more than you."

"I suppose, if you insist. But why me and why now?"

"I like your spirit and you need it. Please, take it and go far away from my worthless nephew and the rest of my miserable family. My brother listens only to what his conniving son says and is inclined to run you out of town as a gold-digger. He would smear your reputation by twisting the story of your scholarship."

"You know?"

"Yes. The silly boy told his friends about that, too. I should have realized there was an ulterior motive for that donation to the scholarship fund. Look in the box, Miss Baker."

At his urging, she opened the lid and peeked inside. She saw cash and some jewels. "Oh my!" She shut the lid. "I can't...I mean I don't know what to say."

"You don't have to say anything. Accept it. The contents of that box should be enough to get you set up where they will appreciate you. You're a smart gal. I was suspicious of Conrad's motives from the first. He never brought around any young ladies with a brain. They were too much of a threat."

Charlotte knew the truth of that now. "That does not surprise me."

"I'm ashamed of him. He's nothing more than a good-looking twerp." He coughed. "Take that box and keep it with you all the time. Remember, no matter what my scheming nephew tries to do, you will have what you need to beat him."

Supremely grateful and stunned into near silence, she accepted the man's gift. She placed the box on the table and gave Benjamin Walker a heartfelt hug. "I've made plans to go to Pittsburg."

After muttering, "I hope that is far enough," Benjamin Walker gave her a long look. "Alright now, go on, or my reputation for being a hateful old miser will be ruined."

Walker rang a bell on the table. Miles appeared as if from thin air.

"Sir?" The butler bent at the waist for a moment. "How may I be of service?"

"The young lady and I have completed our business. Please tell the coachman to come around to take her home."

Charlotte blinked back tears and left in a fog. She could not even remember the return trip and as she sat in her small flat, the only thing that made her believe any of the evening was the box. It was very real. She went through the motions of finishing her packing.

The following morning, on her way to the train station, she stopped in a bookstore. Her idea was to find an interesting volume for the trip. She bought a copy of "Nurse and Spy in the Civil War." She had wanted to read it since she first heard of it, but did not feel she could spare the money for a non-textbook, nor would she have had time to read it. It certainly was not the kind of book that Conrad would buy her. She heard the call to board and tucked the book into her bag. It was time to leave.

Chapter Twelve

Charlotte checked her ticket to be sure everything was in order, then boarded the westbound train. With as much as she had been through to get this far, the last thing she wanted to do was be on the wrong train. She had booked a sleeper so she could be alone and looked forward to the privacy and some rest. As much as she could, she would avoid thinking about Conrad or her missed opportunities in Philadelphia. With the assistance of the conductor, she found her compartment and stowed her baggage. She pulled her book out of her carpetbag. Taking a seat next to the window, Charlotte settled in to read as the train pulled out of the station. She took a deep breath and opened her book.

As she read, she learned that the author, S. Emma Edmonds, was born in 1841 and had served in the second Michigan volunteer infantry as "Franklin Thompson." Charlotte wanted to know all the details and eagerly dove into the story. Soon, she learned that Emma was from Canada and had fled to the United States to avoid an arranged marriage. To hide her identity from anyone who might try to track her, she cut her hair, changed her name, put on men's clothing and assumed the persona of a traveling Bible salesman from Connecticut.

In 1861, Edmonds moved to Michigan. When the War Between the States broke out, she found herself unable to be content as a bystander. There was so much at stake. Emma felt grateful to the people of the "Northern States," her adopted country, and felt compelled to express this through service. As Franklin Thompson, she enlisted in the Union Army. She was mustered in as a three-year recruit with the Second Michigan. Her unit encamped in Washington DC in June of 1861. They saw their first battle in July. Later that month, the unit covered the Union retreat at Bull Run and Edmonds helped to nurse wounded soldiers at Centerville.

Edmonds witnessed the battle of the Monitor versus the Virginia (also known as the Merrimac) at Hampton Roads, Virginia in March, 1862. At the Battle of Yorktown, she was involved in procuring supplies for the hospitals. In the spring of 1862, she completed her first mission as a spy, disguising herself as a male "contraband" or slave. While working at Yorktown, she discovered a Confederate spy. During her second secret mission that summer, she posed as an Irish peddler. Later on, she had the first of many episodes of severe chills.

In mid-1862, Edmonds became regional postmaster, and her regiment participated in the Battle of Williamsburg. She also served as an orderly to a general, and witnessed Prof. Thaddeus Lowe's use of the *Intrepid,* a hot air balloon used to report Confederate troop movements. In her capacity as a regimental mail carrier, a rather dangerous assignment, she covered a distance of some one hundred miles round-trip and sometimes slept on the side of the road where she risked run-ins with robbers. Her regiment fought in the Peninsula campaign, going through Mechanicsville, Gaines Mill and Malvern Hill. During this time, Edmonds wrote that she witnessed a military execution. In the course of her service, she reported that she aided in the care of wounded soldiers on both sides.

Edmonds served at the battle of Antietam and described an incident when she tended a dying female soldier after the battle. This made Charlotte wonder how many other women had secretly enlisted, and in how many units. Would there ever be a way of accounting? Some, if fallen in battle, may have been discovered posthumously, she presumed. What of those who served and lived to return home? Had they simply faded into their old lives and told no one?

Charlotte stretched and returned to her reading. In the fall of 1862 as Edmonds carried out another spy mission, she narrowly avoided being shot by guerillas. Her horse was killed and she played "possum" to escape and avoid further injury. In December, she served as an orderly to a colonel at the Battle of Fredericksburg, and in the spring of 1863, she was sent on an intelligence mission in Kentucky. At some point during the spy mission Emma contracted malaria. She requested a furlough so that she might seek medical attention elsewhere, but was denied.

This illness led "Franklin Thompson" to abruptly leave her unit and become classified a deserter. She could not risk being sent to a military hospital. There would be no chance to avoid having her identity exposed in that setting. Thus, she simply left. A publisher's addendum noted that the author had succeeded in having the charge of desertion removed in 1884 and had been granted a military pension for her service. The addendum also mentioned that Edmonds married in 1867 and raised a family. Charlotte thought about this last bit of information. It gave her hope. An unconventional life did not necessarily mean giving up on more conventional dreams.

On the train ride, Charlotte slept fitfully, spending most of the time reading her book and thinking about what she knew of the war. When she did sleep, her head was filled with strange dreams. Events in the book, events in her life, things she had read in the papers, her hopes for her life in Pittsburg, were all mixed up like some kind of brain salad. The stress of the previous weeks, between the long hours of study, her bar exams and the frightful breakup with Conrad was extracting its due. She replayed the events over and over, with the worst of them dominating her mind's stage.

The book was fascinating and further fueled her imagination. That a woman, one Sarah Emma Edmonds, could pass as a soldier and work as a spy? How amazing that was. Edmonds had also tended to the wounded as a nurse, and took great pains to write to the families of those who died, sending them their last words or a special token that they wished to have returned to their family. Charlotte could not help but admire the other woman's stamina and courage.

The thought of such a life was exciting, in no small part because it was so dangerous. Charlotte hung on every detail of how Edmonds had achieved her transformation and how she eluded capture during her courier missions. However, not all of her convoluted thoughts about the soldier and spy were positive. As she thought about the military execution, she shuddered at the thought of a cold dispatching of a human being. Her life had not been easy, but she had never had to witness such a violent act. What would it be like to be present? To be one of the participants? With all she had been through of late, her mind could not hold all these distressing thoughts. In the next part of her dream, *she* was the one being executed and it was Conrad who held the rifle.

In the Pittsburg train station, Charlotte saw postings for lodgings, restaurants, and available jobs, as well as wanted posters for the most recent notorious criminals. Avoiding the wanted posters, she turned her attention to the ads for lodgings and made note of several promising listings. She had arrived on the fifth of May and immediately set about finding a place to live. With no job and no clear idea on how long it would take her to secure one, she settled on renting a small flat in a rooming house. It offered the option of payment by the week or month, and until her plans were set, this was a perfect arrangement. It was billed as "furnished" but she found the rooms met only the bare minimum for this description: a bed, a washstand, one small chest of drawers, a small table, and two wooden chairs. She decided to unpack only what she absolutely needed, and wait until she was more permanently situated before treating her rooms like home.

Each day for the first week, she read the *Pittsburg Post* to check the classifieds, and canvassed the local law firms asking about any openings for clerks. At the end of her rounds, she would retire to her flat to read and rest. She had not slept well since her fight with Conrad, but each day since she had arrived in Pittsburg was better. The increased distance helped. She was starting to feel relaxed and confident, which would surely help her to find gainful employment. Her plan was to get a job, almost *any* job, at one of the law firms and work her way up by showing what she could do. She had no doubts about her abilities, only in the capacity of others to recognize them.

Once Charlotte had her belongings in her flat and answered several of the advertisements for employment, she inventoried the box. On her journey from Philadelphia, she debated about what to do with her generous gift. She had not decided whether to place the money in a bank, or simply keep it secret. How would she ever explain having such a sum of cash, or the fine jewelry? Even settling in a new town, this would be hard to explain. Best she kept it to herself. She lived in a modest rooming house and relied on the wardrobe she had acquired when Conrad was paying the bill. The contents of this box was worthy of someone from the upper crust.

When she finally got the courage to count the money, she was astonished at the total amount of cash, but was determined to spend it as slowly as possible. This might have to provide for her living expenses for years. The jewelry was exquisite but she dared not wear it, or even think about selling it. The pieces were much too distinctive. The last thing she wished was to attract suspicious attention.

For now, she carried the box with her in her carpetbag whenever she left her flat. She was still fearful that she might have to pack up again and leave Pittsburg in a great hurry and wanted to keep her valuables nearby. The box from Mr. Walker was all that she had to fall back on, should trouble follow her. As she explored the city, she tried to decide whether to strike out on her own, or apply for a position in an established firm.

She had been in Pittsburg for just shy of two weeks when she finally felt more secure. She had interviewed for several positions, and was called back for a second look by two of them. One of these was for a clerkship in the largest firm in town. Such a position could be a path to her dream. She was more hopeful with each passing day. The idea of being able to have a career in the law was now something real to her, not an abstraction.

As she left her latest interview, she was full of energy. She felt ready to take on the world, as she was certain she would be offered the position. She stopped at a newsstand and bought a copy of the *Post*. She had not paid much attention to anything in the paper of late, other than the classifieds, but today she had some extra time to sit and read while she waited for a streetcar.

Charlotte unfolded the paper. Before she could start to read, a gentleman with a large briefcase and an umbrella came up to her.

"Mind if I sit here, young lady?" He tipped his hat to her.

"Oh! No, of course not. Please have a seat. We may have a bit of a wait. I got here as the last car pulled out." She moved to the end of the bench to give him more room.

The gentleman sat down on the bench and put his briefcase down next to her. He had a large sheaf of papers under his arm. She waited for him to settle in. Turning her attention back to the paper, she started to read. There was a story about a fire, an arrest in a recent bank robbery and a business merger. As she scanned the remaining headlines, her blood ran cold. There was a story below the fold about the death of a prominent Philadelphia businessman. She could not believe what she was reading.

Benjamin Walker was dead. He had suffered a stroke and the family was planning a private funeral. Her eyes welled with tears. He had shown her such kindness and now she would never be able to have him know that his help had truly made the difference in her life. She had wanted to write him later and tell him how she had done. She took a deep breath. How long would it be before the family discovered that there was missing cash and jewels? Did Conrad know of his uncle's gift? Would there be trouble over it if he did? Would Conrad try to trace the missing items and thereby find her? Was Pittsburg indeed far enough away to be safe? She would need Charlie's help to get beyond Conrad's reach.

Chapter Thirteen

By December, Charlie had made a list of the furniture he would need for Charlotte's cabin when she arrived. With help from Ward, he drew up plans for these pieces and ordered the needed supplies: wood of various sizes, finishing materials to smooth and preserve the individual pieces, tools (chisels, a planer, and a fine-toothed saw) and a small treadle lathe. Charlie already had a saw for large work, an axe, hammer and other basic tools for building. Ward showed him how to work the lathe and suggested some less ambitious projects to practice his skill with the machine. Charlie started with a simple bedside stand.

"You should have no trouble selling the lathe when you finish with these pieces, if you like," Ward advised.

"Oh?"

"Unless you plan a change to a career in carpentry."

Charlie laughed. "Not a chance. I can make a few things with a lot of help from you, but... Perhaps you would have better use of it."

Furniture construction was work that was best done indoors, which was opportune, as winter was approaching. Everyone Charlie had met in Soda Flats had warned him that the winters were unpredictable, and often severe. The older residents recalled winters with the snow piled so high that only the roofs of the houses showed above the snowline. Charlie thought they were exaggerating, but he had witnessed a few bad winters back East. Maybe they weren't. Best to be prepared and plan accordingly.

He had also been warned about the spells of severe cold and had been stockpiling wood for months. He and Ward had built a substantial woodshed, which was now nearly filled with cut and split wood. Charlotte had sent out a quilt and blankets and Charlie was collecting pelts to possibly be made into a coat later. He had put up curtains in the cabin not so much for decoration, but as to hold in the heat. If a hard freeze was coming, best to be ready beforehand. Charlie did not fear the cold of the winter, but preferred to be comfortable, if that be within his means.

Working on the furniture proved to be a pleasurable task after Charlie's initial struggles with learning all of the needed techniques. Having become passably skilled with the treadle lathe, and increasingly facile with the saw and other tools while building the cabin, he worked out the steps to build a set of chairs, a table and a basic bed. Working with the finer saw was tricky business, as either the small pieces of wood or the thin blade could snap if not handled properly.

Ward provided valuable instruction as he worked on the first chair. "You have to shape the spindles for the back just so, and gouge the holes in the seat at an angle. We'll make the first one together and you can repeat the steps. Precision is the key. If you are off-center by even a small amount, the pieces will never fit together."

After they finished the first chair, Charlie understood the importance of having paid attention to the details. He finally had a second one completed, after having to discard a few parts. As he had the first chair as a pattern for the rest, he was able to avoid more mistakes. Charlie found the various types of joinery fascinating. He had learned how to place spindles in the correct sized holes to make a type of mortise and tenon joint when he made his chair, and later applied this skill to making a small footstool.

When it came to working on larger pieces, there were more skills to master. Years ago, he had studied some of the construction styles when he worked in the furniture store and was familiar with how they looked and went together. Sometimes small dowels were used to reinforce joints that needed to withstand more stress. He was amazed by the process of fashioning dovetail joints and impressed with the strength of such simple construction. Without the use of nails, carpenters could make chairs, tables, shelving, dressers and anything else within their imagination.

Charlie repeated the process of cutting blocks of wood, using the lathe and chisels to fashion spindles, and sawing the larger pieces until he had enough parts to work with. These would become the seats and arms of more chairs, a tabletop, and a headboard and footboard. After smoothing the parts, he would proceed to assemble his projects and oil them to a fine finish. What seemed like a monumental task at first became a most rewarding way to pass the time during the long winter days. With each completed piece, his anticipation for how Charlotte would use and enjoy his handiwork grew.

Charlie had been intimidated at first with the task of constructing the table and bed, but as he worked with the wood, cutting, shaping, evening the surfaces with the planer, making the pieces fit together, he had a sense of pride. He had always liked working with his hands when he was in the upholstery shop. This was even better. He was making the furniture and if he wished, he knew how to upholster the chairs. He had made a nice cover for the footstool. Charlotte would like that. At the end of a busy day, she could put her feet up and think of the brother who had made it for her.

The bedding he ordered from Denver came days before the first big snow. He had already received a shipment of dishes and cooking pots and pans and tested a few of them on the cast iron stove that came in on the train from Chicago. Charlotte had supplied him with family recipes for cornbread, biscuits, stew and other simple dishes. He made arrangements for the shelving, desk and cabinets for her office space to be sent in the spring, a month before her expected arrival. Charlotte would send out her legal books when she was ready to leave.

He constructed a tall bookcase for the cabin. Charlie had a dozen or so books of his own, mostly adventure and history. Charlotte also liked to read books other than her legal references. He figured that when she was at her cabin, she would prefer to relax by the hearth with a novel.

For the office, Charlie had acquired shelving, a large desk with file drawers, and several upholstered chairs. He purchased these items second-hand and planned to repair the chair seats himself. Buck had given Charlie a lead on an auction house in Denver and this proved to be the key to furnishing Charlotte's office. When people came West and decided that they were not cut out for the change in lifestyle from the big cities of the East, they rarely took everything back with them. If you knew the right people, one could find many useful things at a surprisingly low cost.

At the auction, he had also purchased some framed pictures and a small sculpture for next to nothing. No one else seemed to want them. It was their loss. These pieces would grace the walls and a table in the waiting room. Maybe these would not produce an office as fancy as the plush anterooms of the top firms in Philadelphia, but it would definitely be a sight that would impress clients in rural Colorado. The signature piece was the short marble column topped with a bust of a man. Charlie had no idea who it was supposed to be, but it had a classic look. He would let others speculate on the subject's identity.

In January, a brief thaw allowed Charlie to go into town for supplies and mail. There were two letters from Charlotte. Charlie put them in his saddlebag and headed back to the cabin. His sister had cautioned him to be discrete with her news. Once he reached the cabin, Charlie bedded down his horse in the barn and settled himself in front of the fire to read. The earlier letter was short.

"I am well and will write more about the details of my moving to Colorado later. My work as a law clerk keeps me busy and I have been saving as much of my salary as I can. It will take time to get established in Soda Flats, so I need to be able to cover my expenses for a few months, until I have some paying clients.

The second letter, which had only been waiting at the post office for a few days, was much longer. Charlie put on a pot of coffee and when it was done, he settled back in his chair with a steaming cup. Opening the letter he read:

"I trust you are managing the winter weather. On the colder days, I try to imagine that you are warmed by a roaring fire and enjoying a good book. I am likewise keeping warm, but generally busy with work.

"I do so look forward to coming out to Colorado in the spring, but watch your words when you speak of me to others. I beg you not to tell anyone the whole truth about me. Simply say that I am a widow who lost her husband to the influenza last year, barely a week after the wedding. Being a widow is much more respectable than being jilted. I'm so ashamed that I could be taken in like that."

Charlie put down the letter and rubbed the bridge of his nose. *Why couldn't she have met someone like Niels? That fellow she was involved with was a snake. If there were any justice, the influenza should have taken her erstwhile beau, instead of one of the many others less deserving to die.* He sighed and continued on with the letter. There was some general news about the weather, her work and her thoughts about moving and opening her law practice. He continued to the heart of the letter.

She wrote: "Of course, you can and should feel free to tell the truth about our parents, who they were and how they died, working at the furniture store, my going off to school, passing the bar and so forth. And do refrain from being too modest about your own achievements. Going out on your own to help me is an extraordinary undertaking. And all the things you have learned and done! How to ride a horse, how to build the cabin, getting the office set up and so many other things. I can only hope to be worthy of your efforts."

Charlie shook his head and got up out of his chair. Picking a log from the pile near the hearth, he tossed it on the fire and watched the flames catch it. He thought about all of the things in Charlotte's letter. He had never had any intention of saying much about Charlotte other than her coming out to Colorado and how she came to have a career in the law. As far as her personal life was concerned, she would have to handle that. What she decided to say and whom she decided to share her story with was up to her. Still, he hoped that Charlotte wouldn't regret her ruse. Small lies had a way of getting bigger and spinning a web around a person. It could be a big problem. Best not to worry about it now. Spring still seemed a long way off.

After re-reading the letter and spending another half-hour turning over everything in his mind, he felt more conflicted. The weather was holding so he decided to go outside and split some wood. Physical activity usually settled him. As he swung the ax, he thought about what Charlotte's impressions would be of the people in Soda Flats. He was sure that she would find a kindred spirit in Harriet Parker. And how could she not like Ward? His two friends were so warm and open.

Buck was a devil in a way, but ran an honest business. The one he really wondered about was Niels. He would be good for her. But in the end, all Charlie wanted was for his sister to be happy.

After perhaps an hour of work, Charlie had split most of the odd pieces of wood and felt that he had worked off the demons. Winter wasn't so much worse in Soda Flats than back East, he decided. There was just more of it. And you couldn't argue that it wasn't peaceful. He had never heard of anyone causing trouble in the winter. It was too damned cold for that.

Chapter Fourteen

Charlie had finished a total of six chairs. It was the middle of April, but he continued to work on furniture. Even though he could easily venture out, he found that he enjoyed making things, not just redoing them. He enlisted help from Ward to finish the table and the bed frame. Ward added some nice flourishes to the headboard that Charlie was sure Charlotte would appreciate. The carvings were simple but added such a fine touch that the bed looked like something one would find in a store back East.

When Ward was finishing the details on the headboard, Niels came by to view the stonework. "I wanted to check over the chimney and hearth, now that you have been through a winter," he said. "Make sure there are no problems. You can't have cracks or smoke coming into the cabin."

"Everything worked well." Charlie coughed and cleared his throat. "Kept warm all winter." Charlie put his hand on the mantle and nodded. "This is well done, Niels. It will please Charlotte."

"Yes, indeed. It's the perfect place for family portraits or other mementoes." Ward grinned. "Harriet has our wedding picture and the one of her medical college class on ours."

"Charlotte might prefer a picture of our parents," Charlie replied.

"Of course. Have you heard from your sister lately?" Ward asked. "When do you expect her?"

Charlie nodded. "In about a month."

"I hear from Buck that she's your twin," Ward ventured.

"True, Ward, but she's the better looking one." This got a laugh from Ward and a slight grin from Niels.

Niels cleared his throat and focused on his feet before he spoke. "Charlie, is Charlotte bringing anyone with her?"

"What?" Charlie said.

"He means," Ward elaborated, "is she married?" He grinned and nudged Niels. "Right?" Niels nodded sheepishly.

Charlie had been expecting this question and was thankful he had been able to avoid it for so long. It had given him the time to consider his response. "Not now. She's a widow, though she wasn't married long. It's a painful subject."

Niels exhaled and looked up at Charlie. "I understand how she must feel." He paused for so long, Charlie thought he'd killed the group's conversation. Then Niels spoke again. "I lost my wife to the influenza five years ago." He looked away, clearly not wishing to say more.

Charlie did not know what to say. He simply nodded sympathetically. He decided that Charlotte's cover story would hurt no one and should help her standing in the town. Perhaps after people knew her, she could tell them the truth, in her own way. Soda Flats had good people. Surely, they would understand. Fortunately, Ward spoke up and changed the subject.

"Charlie, do you need more help with the cabin? Looks ready to me." He gathered up his tools and prepared to leave.

"No. What's left I can do myself." Charlie coughed. "Could not have done this on my own."

"Glad to help." Ward put out his hand to Charlie. "I think all Niels is waiting for is to meet your sister." They shared a laugh as Ward and Niels left.

As Charlie surveyed the interior of the cabin, he smiled. The living area was a decent size, given what he had seen in Soda Flats and it was starting to look like a home. He had tried to strike a balance between basic rustic and eastern decorator. For the time being, Charlie placed all of the chairs around the table. They could be moved into other areas as his sister might wish. The table was rectangular and solid. The chairs were likewise simple and sturdy. Not as fancy as the headboard Ward had finished, they were, after all, for sitting on. Charlotte could add more pieces later, but Charlie knew she was one who always chose practicality over appearance. She would probably settle for putting her things in place and using what was there.

Charlotte had not been able to stay in Pittsburg long. After reading of Benjamin Walker's death, she watched the news reports in the *Post* carefully and considered her options. The situation was getting dangerous and she did not feel far enough away from Philadelphia. She contacted Charlie, who advised her to follow her instincts and go West. He had volunteered to go out ahead for her if she wished. She left for Chicago and said she'd send word of her plans from there. The plan turned out to be Soda Flats. Arranging for her possessions to be sent was easy: she mostly had books, including the additional volumes she acquired before leaving Pittsburg.

Now that she would finally be arriving in Soda Flats, she thought about the journey West. The trip started out on a part of the Pennsylvania Railroad, the Pittsburg, Cincinnati, Chicago and St, Louis Railway, which took her as far as Chicago. She dressed modestly in black and hadn't wanted to speak to anyone on her way there. She was simply too anxious that such contact might give her away. Travel across Ohio and Indiana into Illinois went through towns and past farms, but mainly the landscape was the same flat view, mile after mile. Once in Chicago, she felt safe. The more distance from Conrad, the better.

The sight of the railway station in Chicago was enough to make her gasp in awe over the sheer size and opulence. Pittsburg had a smaller station, though she had heard about plans for something more ambitious. Chicago's station had a high Victorian gothic style, with arches and a large central pavilion. It also featured a number of small businesses, including gift shops, a shoeshine stand and a small bookstall. There, she purchased a copy of The Time Machine by H.G. Wells. She wanted to read something that would be completely apart from her own life. The idea of time travel was fascinating. Would life be different in the future? Might someone like her father be more accepted for his ideas? She fervently wished this would be true.

When she saw the Chicago posting for the opening in Colorado, she immediately sent a telegram and awaited a reply. It hadn't been long in coming. Being accepted for the position meant she had a destination. Charlotte assembled the paperwork to present her credentials to the bar in Colorado. She forwarded her academic records, letters and proof of her graduation from the University of Pennsylvania to open her application. She would sit for the examination later in Denver. As women were now ceasing to be an oddity among the ranks of the legal profession in the major cities, she felt she could concentrate on the process and the exam, not being any sort of trailblazer.

Charlie went out in advance as promised and she gave him her copy of The Time Machine to read. He could return it later when she reached Soda Flats. To aid her travel, he left her a detailed listing of the train routes he had booked. The Chicago, Burlington and Quincy Railroad was the best way to reach Denver. She also wanted to stay safe. To do so, the plan was that when sitting in the dining car, if contact with fellow travelers was unavoidable, conversation would remain simple: the view, the weather, the food. It would not be wise to discuss anything related to the purpose of the trip or who might be interested in knowing about Charlotte Baker.

From the information she gathered at the Chicago train station, she knew travelers would reach Denver in a matter of days. The first part of the trip offered more flat land, though as the train passed through northern Missouri and into Nebraska, there were endless miles of farms with huge stretches of wheat and cornfields and fewer and smaller towns. Midway across Nebraska, the terrain began to be more elevated.

The farther west the train pushed, the higher the elevation became until it reached Denver, said to be a mile above the level of the oceans. With the higher elevations came a much more varied and interesting view from the train. Flats gave way to hills, which then became mountains. She had never seen such wide-open beautiful spaces. No wonder there were so many tales about the West. Were any of them true? Certainly stories of open country were inspiring. Those tired of the crowded conditions of the Eastern cities read them and left the confines of their smoky homes for the hope of a new life and clear air.

The last portion of her journey was a relatively short one: the stagecoach to Soda Flats. As the coach got closer to her destination, she wondered what her new hometown would be like. Charlie was not much of a writer. She knew he had settled in and was building a cabin and finding her office space. His letters had basic descriptions of the buildings and people, but she would have to see for herself. Approaching the town, she was both excited and afraid. She was ready to start a new life, so far from Conrad that he would never find her, but would she be accepted?

Ten days after he last spoke with Ward and Niels at the cabin, Charlie was as ready as he could be for Charlotte's arrival, but he had to make a trip first. He sought out Ward to give him the news.

"There are boxes and trunks coming to Denver for Charlotte. I have to be there to check the cargo. Then, they can be delivered to Soda Flats before she arrives in three weeks."

"You will be back to greet her, won't you?" Ward asked.

"I'll try, but I have to take the train out to San Francisco after I make certain her crates get sent here."

"San Francisco? Why so far?"

"Got a letter from a family friend," he explained. "Things are booming out there. He's pushing me to join him. I said I'd go out and talk to him. Can you meet the stagecoach?" Charlie asked.

"Of course, my friend, though I think Niels would rather be the one to be there," Ward replied.

"Sure. Tell him to look for a tall gal who looks a little like me."

On the third Friday in May, Charlotte Ann "Walker" arrived by stagecoach to Soda Flats, having taken the train from Denver to Colorado Springs. She dressed tastefully in black, and couldn't wait to see all the things Charlie had written about. It had been a long year since her life had changed direction. She noticed a man at the depot who was looking over the passengers as they disembarked. As she stepped off the train, she realized that he was waiting for her.

The man approached her and smiled in greeting. "Charlotte Walker?" She nodded. "I'm Niels Sorensen." He took off his hat to her.

Her mouth went dry. His slight accent, which Charlie had

mentioned, was very interesting and attractive. However, Charlie never mentioned how devastatingly handsome the man was. Maybe he never saw Niels all dressed up. But of course, another man would not take notice. *This must be his Sunday best.* He had a pressed shirt and suit, and was clean-shaven. Charlotte lost her concentration and tripped over her own feet. Niels caught her. When she looked up, she got a direct look into the bluest eyes she had ever seen.

As Charlotte regained her composure, another man rushed up and smiled. "Well, Mrs. Walker, I see you've met."

"Please, just Charlotte. It seems so...awkward to be called Mrs. Walker." Charlotte took a step back and composed herself as the other man spoke.

"Very well, then...Charlotte. I'm Ward Parker, and this," he motioned to the woman walking up to join them, "is my wife, Harriet, the town doc."

She smiled slightly at the Parkers and put out her hand. Charlie's descriptions had been accurate. They made a handsome couple, though she knew they must be close to fifty. "A pleasure to meet you both, and Niels, of course." Niels smiled. "Charlie wrote me about how helpful all of you have been." She craned her head about to look around the center of the town. "May I ask, where is he?"

"He really wanted to be here to meet you," Niels offered. "Ward?"

"Your crates came through on the last stage, but without Charlie. He had to go through on the train to San Francisco," Ward answered.

"San Francisco?"

"Yes, but he sent this letter for you." He handed it to Charlotte.

Chapter Fifteen

"A letter?" Charlotte accepted the envelope pressed into her hand. "But why isn't he here? When he last wrote, he promised to meet the coach."

Ward Parker shrugged. "Best you read his note, then. Would you like us to take you out to the cabin first?"

"No, thank you. Allow me to read this and then I would like to see the town. Afterwards, you can show me out to the cabin." She let out a deep breath. "It has been a long journey." There was no reason to elaborate on the timing or the stages of her trip.

Niels offered a sympathetic look. "We brought a wagon. We can get your bags from the coach while your read Charlie's letter."

"And I need to see to a patient," Harriet said. "Come with me to the clinic, Charlotte. You can sit and rest while you read your letter. Let the fellows get your bags. They can pick you up later."

"Oh! Yes, that sounds like a wonderful idea. And thank you, Mr. Sorensen. How good of you gentlemen to bring a wagon." She pointed out which were her bags and as Ward and Niels saw to her things, she walked over to a nearby building with the older woman. She saw a sign in the front reading, "Dr. Harriet Ward, Physician and Surgeon." She stopped and stared at the sign.

"Surely you have seen much more impressive clinics, back East, Charlotte." Harriet chuckled and led Charlotte inside.

"But I have seen few that have a woman's name so proudly displayed. I hope to do as well."

"And you shall," Harriet asserted. "Give it time. Have a seat in the parlor area and see to your letter. I'm going to check on my patient upstairs. He should be able to go home tomorrow."

When Harriet left the room, Charlotte settled into a comfortable chair and opened the letter. It was written in a familiar hand. She took a deep breath and read.

"Dear Charlotte,

"So sorry I could not come to meet you, but remember my friend, Edward Paige? He went out to San Francisco a few years ago and he has done well for himself. He's heading up his own furniture company and wants me to join him. He's a business whiz but says he needs a guy who knows about furniture and upholstery. He also wants to have a partner he can trust. It's too good an opportunity to pass up.

"You are most welcome to come and visit San Francisco, but first do make yourself at home among the best friends a man could have. Ward and Harriet Parker and their children have a fine home outside of town, and Niels Sorensen rents a room in town.

"The cabin is ready for you and the office has your crates. You can unpack as you like. By the way, the owner of the saloon, Buck Larson, is your landlord and in need of some good legal advice. Look him up.

"I'll try to visit, but my friends will see that you get what you need. The Wards have been anxious to meet you and have you out for dinner and Niels has been most curious about my sister. I suggested he should judge for himself.

Take care,
Charlie"

Charlotte took a deep breath and held the letter close to her chest. All in a matter of minutes, there was so much to absorb. Charlie was not in Soda Flats, nor would he be for the foreseeable future. The cabin was ready for her and her office was nearly so. All she had to do was unpack and arrange everything. Then she would be open for business. Would Soda Flats be ready for her?

And this fellow, Niels Sorensen. He was so... Charlie's letters had mentioned the people he had met, but she was unprepared for her reactions. Ward and Harriet were a strong and stable force in the community and she could feel the warmth in their welcome immediately. She waited for the men to return to give her the tour of the town.

Minutes later, she heard male voices and the sound of people coming into the clinic. "I still say it seems too familiar to call her Charlotte," she heard Niels say. "We have just met."

"I say we respect her wishes," she heard Ward Parker reply. "Because we know Charlie. I'm sure that she'll be more formal with anyone who sees her for legal advice." As they entered the room, Ward saw her sitting in the chair and laughed, knowing she likely heard them. "Okay, cat's out of the bag. Is it Charlotte or Mrs. Walker or…?"

It was Charlotte's turn to laugh. "You were more right than you knew, Ward. It's Charlotte to my friends and Mrs. Walker to clients, or at least clients who are not also friends. I think that would work."

"Only if you call me Niels and not Mr. Sorensen," Niels replied.

"Agreed." Charlotte felt her face flush. This Niels Sorensen was so distracting and strong...and, no, she was not going there.

"Okay, then. What did Charlie say?" Ward asked.

Charlotte gave them a quick summary of Charlie's plan. The men nodded.

"I always thought he was itching to move on. What about you, Ward?" Niels asked.

"He did give me the sense of wanting more. I'm sure he'll visit later, Charlotte. Wait 'til you see what all he's done to make Soda Flats feel like home. You'll never want to leave," Ward proclaimed. "But first, let's show you the town."

They started with Harriet leading a tour of her clinic. The waiting area was in the front, and resembled a fancy parlor, the rest of the downstairs consisted of her office, a room for files and two examination rooms. The larger examination room was also used for any surgeries. Harriet begged off from following the others to view the rest of the town. "I've seen it and I need to watch my patient for a while. How about you get your things to your cabin and have Ward bring you to our place for dinner tonight?"

"That would be wonderful, if it's not too much trouble," Charlotte replied.

"Nonsense," Harriet said. "What's one more when there's a houseful already? Now, gentleman, please finish guiding our newest resident before the day gets any later."

Ward and Niels spent the next hour showing Charlotte around the town. They pointed out where her office would be, not far from Doc Harriet's, and Ward handed her the keys. They went inside. "In a few days, you can start putting things where you want them," he said.

"We can help with some of the heavier crates," Niels said. "I know Charlie assured us you can do most of what he does, but some of the furniture needs at least two people to move."

"Thank you, Niels. I am certainly not above accepting help and Charlie warned me that the bookshelves he ordered were rather... substantial. After all, a lawyer has to have a lot of books." Charlotte was impressed by the amount of work that had already been done. Her office was taking shape nicely. There were tall bookshelves across the back wall and there was space on the adjacent one to hang her diplomas. A chair was placed opposite.

"Your other crates are upstairs with the rest of the bookshelves," Ward explained. "And there are a few more pieces coming."

"This is...more than I could ever have hoped for." She paused. "You best show me the rest of the town now or I'll just stay here." Charlotte laughed lightly, but was serious. After the travel and the past year of trying to start her life over, this was a dream come true. She would have to tear herself away while she could.

The men walked her through the main street of the town, past the general store. "They may not have as much merchandise as the stores back East, but they can order in anything you want," Ward told her. They pointed out the newspaper office, the telegraph office, the barbershop, the town café, the livery, the bank, and lastly, the saloon.

At the saloon, Ward told her, "This is the main gathering spot for the men in town. You can drink, play cards, and yes, there are ladies who 'entertain,' but Buck keeps things orderly. He gets enough business without anyone having to hustle, and he doesn't put up with any trouble in his place. As long as the customers behave, he stays out of their way."

Charlotte found herself liking Buck already and they hadn't met. He would seem to have quite the cosmopolitan outlook here in the middle of, well maybe not nowhere, but it wasn't Boston or Philadelphia or Pittsburg by a long stretch.

"I see there is a sign for a hotel as well," Charlotte observed.

"The rooms are upstairs. Since nearly all of the visitors to town are men, it suits."

"I think that's all we can show you," Niels said. "We should get you and your baggage out to the cabin."

Niels decided that Charlie certainly underestimated his sister's impact. Sure, they were twins, and yes, their faces were very similar, but Charlotte was so much taller than the other women he had seen in Colorado. He liked that. She reminded him some of the women back in Norway, though her hair was dark, not blond. The biggest difference that he noticed immediately, besides the obvious, was her voice. It was clear and sultry, not damaged like Charlie's. Just the sound of her words was fascinating, so he had to pay extra attention to hear what she was saying.

She had dark eyes like Charlie, but hers seemed...softer. Her hair was so much longer than his. It probably reached to...well, not something he was going to think about. Her skin was smooth and creamy. She clearly did not spend much time out in the sun. And her figure... she was not as buxom as those saloon girls, and her clothes were modest, but there was no mistaking her for anything but a very appealing woman.

Niels shook himself and tried to clear his mind. His life had been lonely since his wife was gone. He had met her after he came to America, when he was eighteen and she had helped him with his English. Later, it became more. It had been a good marriage until her tragic death. He knew that he wanted to marry again someday, if he could find the right woman. He had needed time to mourn, to work and to move on. Maybe now it was time to think about his personal future, not only his work.

On the ride out to the cabin, Charlotte thought about the eyes of Niels: so blue, so pure, so captivating. And he had a long mane of golden hair, pulled back the way Charlie wore his. If she didn't have her twin vouching for him, she'd be wary of this good-looking man. After all, Conrad was attractive on the outside and a lout on the inside. After that experience, it was going to be hard to trust any man completely.

While her life was not following the course she had anticipated, for the first time in a year she truly felt good about the future. Soda Flats was a small western town, but after everything she had experienced, she was glad to be settling in it and be away from the reach of the Walkers. She had half-expected the town to be a few ramshackle buildings with nothing but mud for roads and piles of horse droppings everywhere, but it was much more.

In minutes, she and the men pulled up in front of what was now *her* cabin. Charlotte was impressed. It was fairly large and she could see the other buildings Charlie had mentioned: the barn and the woodshed. The men helped her unload the wagon and put her baggage inside. Whenever Niels looked at her, she felt flustered. She soon noticed that he turned away whenever their eyes met. Did he feel as awkward as she?

Ward turned to her as he was ready to leave. "I'll be back at six, Charlotte."

"Oh, thank you, Ward. You really don't have to," she said.

"Really? There are some basic provisions here, but by the time you unpack a few things, it will be tomorrow. Besides, dinner at our house is always an adventure." He nudged Niels, who laughed knowingly.

"I accept. I don't mind cooking, but it has been a long day and this is all so new. Now, get out, both of you, so I can start unpacking."

Chapter Sixteen

When the men left, Charlotte opened one of the boxes she had brought and took out candles and candlesticks. She set them around the cabin, to be ready for the evening. She placed a box of matches on the mantle. Then she noted that there was an oil lamp next to the bed and one on the table in the dining area. She was in luck. The lamps were full of oil. With Charlie's sudden departure, she was not sure what she would find. On closer inspection, there was wood in the fireplace ready to light, but she doubted that it would be needed tonight.

What to put away first? She decided that she should start by taking an inventory of what was in the cabin. In the front room, there was an impressive fireplace and hearth set into the back wall. To the left as she walked in, there was a table and chairs, with the oil lamp she had seen set in the center. Against the front wall by the table was a modest hutch with dishes stacked neatly. What a nice touch, she thought. There were windows on both sides of the front room. In the middle of the large room was a comfortable chair by the fireplace.

To the right was the kitchen area with a cast iron stove and a pump for water in the sink. She had sent money specifically for this item. The stove she had selected was the latest model out of Chicago with an oven and cooktop, a side firebox and a vent to the outside wall. While she considered this somewhat of a luxury, it was the one special item she wanted. She looked through the stove and found pots stored in a lower drawer, a coffeepot on the cooktop and some baking pans on a small table to the side.

As she checked around, she opened the few cabinets in the kitchen area and found canned goods. With these, she found a note. "There is a small supply of salted and smoked meats out in the woodshed. You can get more at the general store or talk to Ward." From what she could see, the cabin was well equipped with general household items. She had brought a few things with her, mainly some utensils that had been in the family, and bottles of spices purchased in Denver.

Going into the second room, the bedroom, she noted that the fireplace was built to provide warmth for both rooms as it had two sides set into the wall. She admired the clever design and was even more impressed with Niels. Charlie had told her that his friend had done the stonework. What a brilliant idea to have the chimney accommodate two fireplaces! She turned her attention to the furnishings. There was a bed with a handsome headboard and a long low chest of drawers. A mirror hung above the chest of drawers to double as a dressing table.

Her hope chest, which she had shipped out from Chicago, was at the foot of the bed. On top of it she found a handsome pair of beaded leather gloves and another note. "I bought two pairs of gloves at an Indian trading post on my way out to Colorado. They are comfortable but will serve you well with the necessary outdoor chores and protect your hands. The workmanship is beyond anything I have seen in the East. Yours are more decorative than the pair I chose for myself, but no less serviceable. The more you wear them, the more comfortable they will feel."

She unpacked her small valise of personal items. Inside were the brush and tortoise shell comb her aunt had given her when she went off to college, two decorative hair combs and a few smaller items including a bottle of French perfume that Conrad had given her. She kept this not because she cared about *him*, but she saw no reason to waste the nice things he had bought for her. It was the least he could do, considering. Any day now, the armoire that she ordered in Denver should arrive. Yes, this cabin would definitely do. A few added touches and it would be home. Still, it would remain simple and practical.

Charlotte went out to the front room and carried her other valises into the bedroom. She placed most of her clothing into the dresser drawers, carefully folding them and placing them with like items together, to make it as easy as possible to locate any particular article of clothing in a hurry. She moved one of the chairs with the dining table into the bedroom and placed it next to the dresser. Pulling out the few dresses she brought, she draped them over the chair. When the armoire arrived, she would hang them. There were a few wall pegs, but these she would use for her coat, hat and other outer garments.

Opening the hope chest, she looked inside. There were extra blankets, and the tablecloth her grandmother had crocheted. Underneath, she had placed the wedding gown she had never worn. She considered leaving that behind, but even though she hated Conrad, she did love the dress. There were other items, also delivered to her boarding house in Philadelphia with her gown, and she was not about to return those, either. She closed the lid and took a deep breath. No, she had no desire to look at any of it.

Days after the wedding clothes arrived, the engagement was off and she packed everything into the hope chest. Though it seemed odd to still have them, their possession would make it easier for people to believe that she was a bereaved widow. She also had a black dress, but felt that enough time had passed that she need not wear it. Charlie assured her that folks in the West moved on with their lives faster. Maybe it was because of the many additional hazards. Not only did they face the same illnesses as those in the Eastern cities, but life was harder. Farmers, miners and loggers led hazardous lives. There was less access to medical care and many lived well outside of the towns. If some untoward event occurred, these people had limited means of summoning what help there was.

Charlotte drummed her fingers on the top of the chest as she thought. Best to leave the wedding finery under the blankets, perhaps forever. She turned her attention to the intricate carvings on the headboard. She knew that Ward had carved this. Running her hands over the smoothed wood, she thought of the skill it took to do this. The beautiful wood grain had a rich dark color, which was only enhanced by the carving of a cluster of acorns. There was a handmade quilt on the bed and she wondered who had made this. She would ask Harriet. A plump feather pillow looked inviting. She would likely collapse into deep sleep after she returned from dinner.

Done with the immediate unpacking in the bedroom, Charlotte

returned to the front room and continued her inventory. All of the dishes, table linens and cookware she had ordered was present and everywhere she looked, there were welcome extras that Charlie had left for her—the oil lamps, a pitcher and wash basin in the kitchen, a carved wooden salt and pepper set and so on. She reached into another box and pulled out a photo of herself with Conrad. They had the photo done for the society pages. One of the last things she did before leaving was to have a print made to fit a frame. At the time, it was because she treasured the photo. Now, it served another purpose.

She walked over to the mantle, and placed the framed picture squarely in the center. Then, she pulled a chain from her pocket. It held the ring she was to place on Conrad's hand. She hung the chain over the picture, the ring covering his face. She felt a deep pang of guilt for embellishing her story, but Conrad *was* dead to her and this exhibit was not a shrine to him, as others might assume. It was a visible symbol of her freedom and a reminder of the hell that might have been.

Charlotte mulled this over, and realized that she was twisting the rings on her finger. She recalled the day she picked them up at the jewelers. Conrad had off-handedly told her to hold on to them until the wedding. The wedding! One of the smartest things she did as their relationship crumbled was to hold on to the rings. They were valuable on so many levels: they helped her establish her story and if everything went bad, she could always sell them. With her gift from Conrad's uncle, that was unlikely, but it was always good to have an alternative. She found herself thinking about handsome Niels and cursing herself for being unable to stop her very unchaste thoughts. She needed a distraction.

Going out to the barn to continue her inspection, she saw a wagon. Was there a horse? She looked about and saw no animals. She knew Charlie has been riding to and from town. Well, something to ask the Parkers about later. She walked over to the woodshed and peered in far enough to see that it was nearly full. All of the buildings were connected with thick rope. She hoped the winter would not be so severe that this would be her only way to find her way back to the house, but Charlie had made sure she would be prepared for anything Old Man Winter dealt.

Done with her inspection, she returned to the house to wash her hands and face and brush out her hair. She did not feel the need to dress up. Soda Flats did not seem to be a place that stood on any kind of formality. Minutes after she went out to the front room again, she heard a knock at her door and a voice calling out to her.

"Charlotte? It's Ward. Can I come in?"

She crossed quickly to the door and opened it. "Ward! Of course. I'm ready to go."

"Okay. Come on then. I brought a wagon." The two went outside and got aboard. Ward signaled the horse and they headed off.

"Oh, yes, that reminds me. I noticed a wagon in my barn, but where's Charlie's horse?"

Ward laughed. "Sorry, I forgot about the animals. I took them over to our place when Charlie left. He wasn't sure how long he would be gone and exactly when you would arrive. It was easier than caring for them here." He pulled up on the reins a bit. "My son and I will bring them over as soon as you are ready to have them."

Within minutes, they pulled up to the Parker's home. Theirs was a much larger cabin than hers, with two floors, and a lovely leaded glass window set into the front. As they went up the front steps, Charlotte asked about the window.

"Harriet admired the big mansions back in New York and Philadelphia, but it would be crazy to build something like that out here, let alone how much it would cost. But a fancy window? That we could do and it makes her smile, so it's worth it to me." Ward smiled. "Enough of that. Come on in. Dinner's about ready."

They entered the house and were greeted by Harriet. Charlotte saw two children, a boy and a girl. These must be Victoria and Joseph. The oldest child was off at college, according to Charlie. Introductions were made all around and indeed, she learned that Victoria was twelve and Joseph would soon be sixteen.

Over dinner of chicken, potatoes, biscuits and vegetables,

conversation was animated. Joseph wanted to know more about what lawyers did and asked when Charlie would be back.

"He hasn't said, Joseph," Charlotte answered. "He was offered a great opportunity in San Francisco, and I hope he does well, but I understand that people will miss him," Charlotte replied. She was truly conflicted. On the one hand, the fact that Charlie was so well liked made her happy, but his success meant he would not return for a long time, if ever. She sighed inwardly. It would be easier that way.

"Did Ward tell you we have Charlie's horse?" Harriet asked. Charlotte nodded. "Do you know how to ride?"

Charlotte smiled. "Charlie *did* warn me about that. Said I'd best learn before I got here or I'd spend a lot of time having a sore backside." This got a laugh from Joseph and giggles from Victoria. "I hear there are other animals as well?"

"Goodness, yes!" Harriet exclaimed. "There are two cows and a bunch of chickens, Charlotte. I'll have Joseph help you get them over to your place. If you need him to, he can show you how to take care of them."

"Thanks. I have the general idea, but I could use some help finding where everything is in that barn."

"You have ten acres of land behind the house, too," Ward added. "Doubt you'll want to farm it, but it'll keep any neighbors from bein' too close."

"Charlie and I agree on that." After the crowded neighborhoods of the East, she savored the wide-open spaces she had seen as she crossed the country. Ward offered her a ride back to her place. She thought a minute. "How about you let me ride Charlie's horse back?"

"Only if you let me ride with you to show you the way. It's dark out and Charlie would never forgive me if we let you get lost."

Chapter Seventeen

Charlotte was right. After the enjoyable meal and conversation at the Parkers' home and the ride back on Charlie's horse, she collapsed into her bed. With the travel, the excitement and the long day, she slept well into the morning. Her dreams were filled with possibilities for the future but there was an element of hesitation. Would the memories of her last meeting with Conrad forever dull her sense of hope for better things to come? Would she always suspect that someone who professed to love her and promise her a life of companionship had an ulterior motive? Would she be so afraid that another man would cruelly use her and cast her aside like rubbish that she would be afraid to love again?

How could she have fallen so easily for the charming Conrad? Then again, how could she not? Everything seemed to be looking up during the second part of her first year: the scholarship, the friendship and then courtship, the promise of a place in a prestigious law firm. The dream lasted long enough that she truly believed it would happen. It made the loss so much deeper, so much more raw. A part of her had died and she doubted whether she could trust again. She still wanted the dream, but no longer believed it could happen. She shook herself and tried to clear her head of all of these muddling thoughts. Not one of them was of use to her. Her best course was to concentrate on getting her new home completed and setting up her office.

Part of settling into life in Soda Flats meant getting her financial affairs in order. Charlie had assured her that the local banker was stable and honest, even if rather stuffy. Harriet opined that the man had a high sense of entitlement. Charlotte did not ask more, deciding to see for herself and went into town, taking some of her cash. She had deposited a sizeable amount of her funds in a Denver bank, but had kept this amount for starting her practice. The box, with the jewels and remaining cash, she placed in a hiding place under the floor in her bedroom. No need to let anyone know about it. Should she feel the need to sell the gems, she would take the train into Denver and do so where she would both fetch a good price and avoid any talk in Soda Flats.

Riding into town, she went over to the bank and hitched up her horse. She went in and asked the teller if she could speak with the banker about opening an account. The teller had her wait a moment, then ushered her into an office area.

"Mr. Bradwell, this is the lady who wishes to see you," the teller announced, then turned and left.

Mr. Bradwell was Winston Bradwell, she had been told, and he came from a very wealthy family. This would explain why he headed a bank at this age. He looked to be in his mid-thirties. He stood as she entered and put out his hand. He was average height, trim and extremely well-dressed. "Always a pleasure to welcome a new customer, Mrs. Walker."

He knows me? "Why, thank you, Mr. Bradwell. I had no idea you knew who I was." Bradwell smiled. While he was pleasing-looking, and dressed well, no amount of packaging could achieve the outstanding good looks of other men such as Conrad Walker or Niels Sorensen. No matter. She was here to do business, not look for a mate.

"I find it is good for me to know who is moving in and out of this town, and having another professional person is welcome, even if you are not quite what one would expect." Bradwell offered a disarming smile.

"Oh." Charlotte paused. She wasn't sure how to respond. "I plan to be what the town *needs*. Now, sir, I wish to open an account."

"Very good. And will your husband be coming in to sign the papers?" Bradwell's tone was pleasant, but Charlotte detected a note of condescension.

"I am a widow, Mr. Bradwell." He nodded. "Even if I were not, there should be no reason for anyone else to sign." She sensed some quiet disagreement from the banker. Best to move on to something that would appeal to him. "I have come prepared to make a deposit."

Clearing his throat, the banker seemed to relax a bit. "Of course, Mrs. Walker. How much would you like to open your account with?"

Charlotte passed him a slip of paper with the figure and then the envelope with the cash. As he read the number and looked into the envelope, she could sense his surprise. "I had an...inheritance, sir, and I worked at a firm in Pennsylvania before I came to Colorado."

"Well, then." He got up and opened his office door. "Miss Stone, can you bring me a new depositor contract, please?" In a moment, the teller returned with papers and Charlotte read them over. Apparently, he had not expected her to do so. "I assure you, Mrs. Walker, these are standard forms."

She decided the best course was to be gracious. "Of course, Mr. Bradwell, but you have to understand that as a lawyer, I am trained to read any paper I am asked to sign." He smiled indulgently. She determined that these were the same basic forms she had seen in Philadelphia. No surprises. "These appear to be in order." She signed and put out her hand to the banker. "A pleasure to do business with you, sir." She rose. "Now, I have other things to attend to, so do excuse me."

Charlotte untied her horse and walked him down the street to her office. She planned to meet with Ward and Niels to discuss finishing the interior. She looked at the front. She would need a sign, of course. As she went inside, she tried to decide how to word it. Charlotte, Walker, Attorney at Law? C. Walker? Or should she 'retake' her maiden name? No, that would be hard enough back East. Best to keep the Walker, no matter how much she hated the name. It gave her credibility and made it all the less likely that anyone from Conrad's family would ever try to find her. If they did not assume her dead, they would be looking for Charlotte *Baker*. "C. Walker, Attorney at Law" would be best. No reason to throw her gender in anyone's face.

Her thoughts were interrupted by the sound of a wagon pulling up. She looked outside. It was Ward and Niels. And what was this? They were unloading a desk. The two carried it to the front and she held open the door for them. They moved the desk inside to her consulting room. The desk was beautiful, fashioned in heavy oak, polished to a modest shine and as she examined it, also very practical, with plenty of drawers and a slide out writing area above the drawers.

"Ward! This is gorgeous! You said you would make something for me but this! This is a work of art!" She put her hand to her chest as she admired it.

Ward shrugged. "It's been a while since I made a desk. I enjoyed doing it. Harriet loves hers. It's a bit different, as her needs are not the same."

"Ward is too modest, Miss Charlotte," Niels said. "Making a desk is complicated."

"No more so than making a double-sided hearth for the chimney, I'd say," Ward returned.

"Okay, gentlemen. Let's agree that there is an impressive amount of talent in this room." They all laughed. "By the way, what's your take on Bradwell? I assume you and Doc Harriet do business with him."

Ward rubbed his chin. "Well, we do now, but at first, he was not so interested."

"I heard him say that if women want to work, there are only a few suitable jobs for them," Niels added.

"Oh?" Charlotte raised a brow.

Ward nodded. "We got that speech from him when he hit town. They can be spinster teachers, as he grudgingly respects them and understands their necessity, or housemaids and cooks. He's a spoiled rich city boy who grew up with a lot of servants."

"Or they can be saloon girls," Niels said. He wagged his head. "He says bad things about them, but that does not keep him away. If he feels that way, why is he over there so much?"

"Our banker has very strong ideas about a woman's place," Ward told her. "I'd avoid debating that subject with him. It won't get you anywhere."

"Really?" Charlotte replied. "I'd like to think I could change his mind."

"He's a tough one, Miss Charlotte," Niels warned. "He was against women voting in the territory. He'll smile at you if you have money in his bank, but he'd rather you had no say in what goes on in the town."

As Charlotte pondered their opinions, Ward had more to say. "He has grudging respect for Doc Harriet. You see, she saved him from his case of appendicitis. He would never have made it to Denver. Let him figure you out for himself, when he sees the advantages to your being here."

"Which are?" she asked.

"Bradwell spends a lot of time going to Denver to see his lawyer. Would be a lot easier for him to hire you," Ward said. "But don't expect him to consult you anytime soon...unless he wants to court you," he chuckled.

"Now, Ward, don't go embarrassing her," Niels said.

"I'm not embarrassed," Charlotte assured him. "After...all that has happened to me, I just want to start over and get my practice established."

Ward remembered that he had another piece on the wagon and went out to get it. Niels looked at her and then looked away. He spoke quietly to her. "Miss Charlotte?"

"Yes, Niels? And you can call me Charlotte."

"Charlotte, then. Might *I* call on you? I mean, when you are ready?"

Charlotte nearly gasped. She had been able to think of little else since arriving in Soda Flats. All she could manage to say was, "I would like that, thank you." Niels bade his leave.

Ward came back in with a chair for the desk. "You might have your first client."

"And that would be?"

"Buck Larson, the saloon owner. He's across the street. I'll introduce you."

At the saloon, Charlotte noted that the front was well done, with a fancy, but tasteful sign. The décor inside was much more upscale than the tales of the sleazy Western saloons told in dime novels. There were tables and chairs set up throughout the room, a long bar with a brass rail, a mirror on the back wall of the bar and an assortment of bottles on display. There were a half-dozen customers around the bar that afternoon and two ladies in fancy dress. Their outfits were flashy, and somewhat provocative, but she did not find their appearance offensive. They were just playing a part.

Ward led her over to a man standing by the bar. He was tall and lanky with long, light brown hair, a mustache and a nicely trimmed beard. She estimated that he was in his late thirties. The fellow was good-looking in a rough sort of way. When he smiled at Ward, she noticed a deep scar on his left cheek. He exuded an easy sense of charm. Ward opened his mouth to speak, but Larson spoke first.

"Well, I see that Charlie's sister has come to call. Nice to meet you." He put out his hand. "I'm Buck Larson."

Charlotte shook his hand as Ward chuckled. "Okay, Buck, guess you didn't need me to make the introductions."

"Hell, no. She's a lady and all, but they *are* twins." He smiled. "The height and the features gave her away."

Ward shrugged. "I brought her here because you said you had some legal issues you wanted to discuss."

"Later," Buck said. "First, I want her to meet one of my girls." Ward raised an eyebrow, but Charlotte waved him off.

"It's fine, Ward. Thanks for escorting me."

Ward left and Buck motioned to the older of the two saloon girls. She walked over and smiled. Charlotte towered over the other woman, who was several years older and had jet black hair, dark eyes, and a beauty mark on her left cheek.

"Charlotte Walker, this is Pearl Hudson. Charlie said you might want to talk with her about a different line of work." Pearl was curvy, much more the Victorian hourglass ideal, compared to Charlotte, who was tall and slender like Charlie.

"Thank you, Buck," Charlotte said. "Can we talk over at a table?"

"Sure, go ahead," he replied. "It's the slow time of the day. Can I offer you ladies a drink?"

"Two sarsaparillas, Buck," Pearl said. "We've got some serious talkin' to do." She led Charlotte over to a table in the back and they sat. She smiled at Charlotte. "I have a feeling we're going to get along just fine."

"Oh?" Charlotte asked.

"Charlie's a straight-up kind of guy. He said if I liked him, I'd like you even better." The other saloon girl brought their drinks and left.

Charlotte smiled back as she lifted her glass. "Well then, to the future!"

Chapter Eighteen

After the toast, Charlotte got to the point of their conversation. "Pearl, Charlie wrote me. He speaks highly of you. He considers you a friend. I hope that we can be friends, too."

The saloon gal smiled and took a sip of her drink. "I see no reason why we shouldn't. What do you want to know?"

"Charlie thinks you might be the right person to work for me. Can you tell me a little about yourself?" Charlotte took a sip of her drink. Pearl was a beautiful woman, she thought. She didn't need all the makeup, even though it was expected of her here.

"Ask me anything. I have no secrets anymore."

"Let's start with simple things. Charlie says you're from Philadelphia and went to finishing school. How did you end up in Soda Flats?"

She smiled and took a drink. "My family was fairly well-off, but there were four of us girls. I was the youngest. They hoped that I'd snag a rich husband, but I couldn't stand the stuck-up rich boys they introduced me to. I did well with my studies, but I didn't see myself as a teacher. I'd read about the West and thought, there's a place where I could make my mark."

Charlotte nodded. "I felt the same when I read of it myself."

"So, I packed up and headed west." Pearl smiled and had a wistful look. "I was going to set the world on fire."

Charlotte smiled back and sipped her drink. They had more in common than most would guess. She moved on with her interview. "How long have you known Buck Larson?"

"I met him when I was nineteen. I'm thirty-four now, so I've known him fifteen years. I made it as far as Denver on the train, and by the time I got there, I realized my choices were not quite as broad as I had imagined. I met Buck there and was drawn to him like a magnet. He has that great hair, those hazel eyes, and his scar. It's one of those manly-looking things." She paused. "Well, he didn't have it when we met. He got it from breaking up a bar fight. It only increased his appeal."

"Tell me more about him, if you would."

"Well, first of all, he hasn't had a lot of formal education, but he's very sharp." Pearl lowered her voice to just above a whisper. "He asked me to help him learn more. Now, he likes to read anything he can get his hands on. Don't tell anyone that. He enjoys being the tough guy."

"I sensed that."

"He's a good man, Charlotte. Buck can talk with anyone. He's able to keep order without getting physical, unless someone asks for it. He's fair and practical, regardless of what some people think of his business. This is a place that gives its customers a good time, whether they want to play cards, have some female company or only get a drink. I've seen similar establishments in other towns and they are often horrible places." She paused. "Buck treats us well and keeps out the riff-raff."

"How did you come to work for him?" Charlotte picked up her drink and took a sip. Then she waved her hand. "I mean no insult. It just seems a strange vocation for one with your education."

This comment made Pearl shrug. "True, but as I said, I came to realize that my choices were limited. I was not prepared to become a farmer's or rancher's wife, nor be a spinster schoolteacher. I'm also practical. I've done well with Buck and saved some money. I'm at an age where it's time to move on, but I like the idea of staying here in Soda Flats."

"Would there be a problem with the townspeople knowing your former employment?" Charlotte asked.

She shrugged. "Charlie says you need someone as a clerk and secretary. I would hardly be on public display. I expect many of your clients will be from the surrounding towns, and the ones from here would not be in a position to discuss the details of my former employment."

"Quite so," Charlotte said. "Well, I think we should try working together. Now as to the terms..." After some discussion they agreed on salary and responsibilities. They would give the arrangement three months and then decide whether to make it more long-term.

"What about Buck?" Charlotte asked. "How does he feel about your leaving him?"

"He's okay with it," Pearl responded. "We've already talked about my moving on someday and when Charlie said you might want to hire me, it sounded like a good idea. Buck wants to be sure that I have somewhere to go. As I said, we've been together a lot of years. I'll still help him out from time to time."

"Oh? I thought you weren't going to entertain anymore." It wouldn't do to have her secretary doing so.

Pearl laughed. "I'm not. Truthfully, most of what I do now is serve drinks and make the card players feel better whether they win or lose. They enjoy having a pretty gal flirt with them." She laughed. "I'm going to help Buck find new girls and get them settled in. He needs a certain type. They have to be able to handle a lot of different kinds of men and they have to understand what they are getting into. It helps that some of the towns we go to have the kind of places the girls want to get out of." She smiled. "I guess, in a way, I became a kind of teacher after all."

The more they talked, the most impressed Charlotte was with Pearl. Charlie was right. This was a lucky break for them both. "By the way, do you know Winston Bradwell?"

"The bank president? Are you kidding?" Pearl stopped and shook her head. "He spends a lot of time here at the saloon. He likes to keep the gals close by." She paused. "He doesn't often go to the private rooms, but he loves to play the big shot. He tips well, but he's small-minded."

"I'm not surprised, but with all these wide open spaces, there should be more free thinking as well, don't you agree?" Charlotte asked.

Pearl nodded. "There is a good bit of that, but not with him. He has very strong ideas about a woman's place. If you don't work here at the saloon or teach school, you'd better be an obedient wife."

"I gathered as much." Charlotte took a drink. "Good thing for me that he cares more about a person's money than their occupation."

"Whatever you do, Charlotte, don't cross him." She leaned forward in emphasis. "He tried his best to get rid of Doc Harriet, but she has Ward to back her up. Besides, she'd hardly been here a year when she'd saved a bunch of people, including the big ingrate himself. He's likely to be twice as hard on you. He has his own lawyer in Denver and can afford to bring him here, if need be." She shook her head. "He's nice to us because he feels so superior, not because he really likes us."

Charlotte pressed her lips together slightly but made no comment. She would deal with the banker at a distance until she could know where she stood. "Well, Pearl, we'd both best get back to work. When can you start at my office? I'll need another week or so to get the place in order. I have no idea when I'll get any business."

Pearl smiled and finished her drink. "Sooner than you think, I expect."

Charlotte walked over to her office space and unpacked a crate of her books. She thought about her chat with Pearl. It had been most enlightening and the trial period would allow them both to decide if Pearl would make a good secretary for her. She had a lot of work to do for the opening of her office. At least she had made a huge first step. She had hired Pearl.

Over the next week, Charlotte continued to unpack and organize her books after she received another crate from Denver. Pearl came by at the end of the week and the two made a list of the additional items Charlotte needed. They acquired a second, smaller desk and a set of shelves for her clerk's office. Pearl was delighted that her space had a window, albeit facing the alleyway. She wasted no time getting both work areas organized and had a number of useful suggestions. She knew more about what might impress the clients in the West than did Charlotte. It soon became apparent that their experiences both in and out of school were complimentary rather than contradictory.

"Charlotte, how should I address you in the office? Mrs. Walker? Attorney Walker? Miss Charlotte? Something else?"

Charlotte pondered. She had never thought about this. Opening her office was becoming more real now. "Hmm...I like Attorney Walker. Let's try that for now."

Three days after Pearl had first started in the office, she came into Charlotte's consulting room. "Attorney Walker, you have a client to see you."

"Oh? Do we know this person?"

"I'd say. It's Buck, or should I say, Mr. Larson." She smiled.

"Did he say on what type of matter he wished to consult me?"

"Something about a property dispute. He can give you the details."

"Please, show him in, Pearl."

She left and a few moments later, returned with Buck. She gave him a quick smile, and left the room, closing the door behind her.

Charlotte motioned toward the client chairs opposite her desk "Please, sit, sir. How can I help you?"

Buck pulled the chair out a bit, sat, and crossed his legs. He had an old leather folio with him. "Before we get to that, how's Pearl doin'?"

Charlotte considered. Buck seemed truly concerned. "She is working out quite well, Mr. Larson. I feel fortunate to have her. No hard feelings for losing an employee, I trust?"

"Remember, it's Buck." She nodded in acquiescence. "Like she told you, it's time for a change." He cleared his throat. "Glad to see she found something here in Soda Flats. We go back a long time. I'd kinda miss her if she left."

After a moment, Charlotte spoke. "Now, to the reason you wished to consult me. What sort of legal problem do you have?"

He nodded. "A former partner of mine claims that he owns all my property. He's demanding that I pay him an outrageous amount of money, in cash no less, or he'll lay claim to the saloon *and* the hotel. He's a crook, a liar and he hopes to be a thief." Buck narrowed his eyes. "You have to stop him." He gritted his teeth. "If I thought I could get away with it, I'd have half a mind to have him disappear...permanently." He took a deep breath.

Charlotte waited a moment for the mood to lighten. Indeed, Buck's expression soon softened to more of a smirk and he shook his head. She thought she heard him mutter, "Scum's not worth the effort."

"What papers do you have to support your position, Buck? A deed?

A contract?" She eyed the leather folder. "I see that you brought some things with you."

He shifted his weight and opened the leather folio. "I have the original deed." He passed it to her. "You can see that it names me and Jess Gillis as co-owners."

"I assume he is the former associate that is now suing you?" He nodded. She looked over the document. It was duly drawn up, signed and sealed. It also bore the signatures of two witnesses. "Looks good to me. I assume the two of you voided the agreement at some point?"

His answer was a snort. "We had a falling out and I bought out his share years ago." He pulled another paper from the file. "This is the agreement we drew up and both signed." He handed the second document to her.

This paper was different. It was handwritten in a much cruder hand, though legible. It had the two signatures of the partners, but only one witness, not the same as either of those on the first document. "This also seems to be in order. What makes this Mr. Gillis think he has a claim?"

"He says that this surrender agreement is a fake. Unfortunately, the man who witnessed it died two years ago. Now it's only his word against mine."

Charlotte shook her head. "Maybe that's what he thinks, but not in a court of law. I'll telegraph the circuit judge to arrange a hearing."

"But what if the judge believes Jess?"

"It's my job to see that he doesn't. I'll check every detail and present your case." Charlotte was warming to the prospect of a good fight and was confident in her abilities, regardless of what anyone else thought. "Now, tell me everything about your partnership. Start at the beginning and don't leave out a thing."

Chapter Ninteen

As promised, Charlotte walked over to the telegraph office the following day and sent a message to the circuit judge. She requested a hearing on the matter of Buck's claim of sole ownership of the land on which the saloon and hotel were built, as well as said buildings thereon. In the meantime, she went over the papers Buck had entrusted to her and planned her strategy. She assumed that his former business associate was prepared to lie, so Charlotte needed to find a way to expose him.

Two weeks later, on the day of the hearing, Charlotte gathered her papers and left her office, accompanied by Pearl. They made their way over to the saloon. The tables had been pushed aside and the chairs rearranged to provide one table towards the front for the judge and one for each side of the dispute. A man she presumed to be Jess Gillis sat alone at one. Charlotte joined Buck at the other. Pearl had a sheaf of papers and sat behind Charlotte. There were quite a number of the townspeople gathered to observe the proceedings. Charlotte knew that an appearance by the circuit judge was infrequent and doubtless, this had raised their curiosity. In a small town, this was a big event.

A man seated near the judge stood and called the crowd to order. "Hear, ye! This is the court of Circuit Judge Abner Cole. The court is now in session. Please remain in your seats unless you are called upon to testify."

Judge Cole nodded. "I see both of the parties involved are present." He pointed over at the table across from Charlotte. "Mr. Gillis, are you represented by an attorney in this matter?"

Jess Gillis rose. His demeanor was that of a man who felt that the outcome of the hearing was a foregone conclusion in his favor. "Hardly saw the need, as I have a clear claim. Besides, I don't see no lawyer here for Buck." A commotion arose in the room with much muttering.

The judge banged for order. "Mr. Larson?"

Charlotte motioned to Buck to stay seated. She rose to address the judge. "Judge Cole, I am Attorney Charlotte Walker. I am the one who requested this hearing."

Over at the other table, Jess Gillis could not stay still. He coughed loudly. "As I said, judge, Buck don't have no one here for him neither. Who ever heard of a lady lawyer? Might as well just hand over the property to me now." A smattering of laughter passed through the assemblage. Many seemed to be of the same opinion.

Judge Cole banged loudly. "Mr. Gillis! I will have no such outbursts in my court. Whether you agree or not, Attorney Walker is a member of the Colorado Bar and duly qualified to represent Mr. Larson. As to the matter of who gets the disputed property, you are reminded to leave that to me."

At first it appeared that Jess Gillis had a lot more to say, but a stern look from the judge prompted him to merely mutter, "Guess the rev's right. The world is going to Hell."

"Mr. Gillis!" The judge banged his gavel. "Do you have something you wish to tell the court?"

He made a face and shifted his weight. He no longer looked so confident. "No, Judge."

"Very well, let us proceed. Mr. Gillis, as you initiated this action, please present your evidence."

Gillis straightened up and regained some of his prior bravado. "Judge, it's pretty simple." He got up and approached the judge. "We signed this here paper that we were partners." He passed his copy of the deed and partnership agreement to the judge. "Even Buck ain't dumb enough to argue that." He looked back at Buck and sneered. Charlotte put her hand on Buck's arm to restrain him. "That means I own half of everything he had. Buck has to pay up or sell and give me half."

For several minutes, Judge Cole studied the documents. "Yes, I had notice of these prior to the hearing. Is there any dispute as to their validity, Attorney Walker?"

Charlotte stood to address the judge. “No, Your Honor. The dispute is not with the original partnership. We contend that Mr. Gillis has already received compensation for his share of the property and therefore has relinquished all subsequent claim.”

“What proof do you offer?” Judge Cole asked.

“I have this handwritten document, duly witnessed, signed by both parties, dated November 12, 1890. I would ask that you compare the signatures on the two documents.” She passed it to the judge’s assistant, who handed it to the judge. “It states that in return for the sum stated, Jess Gillis surrenders all claim to any partnership property. His signature acknowledges said payment and agreement.”

“That’s a lie!” Jess yelled. “He made this all up and forged my signature to cheat me!” He jumped to his feet.

Judge Cole banged his gavel louder than he had before. “Mister Gillis! Please refrain from such outbursts.” Gillis sat and looked sullen. “Now, Mr. Gillis, it is your turn to present your evidence.”

Gillis started to smile. “Thanks, Judge.”

“I will remind you, Mr. Gillis, that this is a court of law. You must swear to tell the truth. Do you so swear?”

The feuding partner got back to his feet, happier than he had been moments before. “Yes, judge, I do.” He took on a serious look. “First of all, that paper is a fake.”

“What about the witness?” Judge Cole asked.

Gillis grinned. “He’s very conveniently dead.”

“Attorney Walker?” the judge asked.

Charlotte rose. “Unfortunately, the witness, while well known in this town to be a fine and upstanding citizen, is indeed deceased.”

“Well, then, that does complicate matters,” the judge opined. “And you say you did not sign it, Mr. Gillis? Please, come and examine this.”

“Hell, no!” Gillis yelled. The judge glared at him. “I mean, no judge.” He came forward and looked over the document. “That’s Buck’s handwriting stating the terms, all right, but I never saw this before. He’s made this all up to cheat me. I’d never sell out that low.”

“Attorney Walker, have you witnesses or evidence to present?

“Yes, Your Honor. I wish to call Mr. Buck Larson.” The judge nodded. Charlotte turned to Buck. "Mr. Larson, What have you to say in this matter?"

Buck stood and took a deep breath. "I drew up that agreement when Jess needed money and wanted out. He didn't want to go to Denver. That's where the nearest lawyer used to be. Jess said he needed the cash, right then, so he could clear out of town."

Charlotte nodded and continued. "Did he say why he needed the money? And in cash on the spot?"

"Look, Jess, I never meant to bring this up, but you started it." He turned to the judge. "Jess is lousy at cards but he won't accept that. He'd gotten deep in debt with some sharp card players passing through Cedar Springs. Jess swore to me that if he didn't pay them that day, they were going to break both his legs and dump him outside of town."

This brought Gillis to his feet. "That's a damn lie! You can't prove a line of bull like that!"

The judge banged again. "Mr. Gillis! Remember what I told you. One more outburst and you'll cool off in jail."

"Did he give you this man's name, Mr. Larson?" Charlotte asked.

"William Faris."

"Judge!" Gillis got to his feet. "May I say something?" The judge nodded. "This is a cheap attempt to smear me. Faris is a known criminal, serving a sentence in Denver."

"Attorney Walker?" the judge asked.

"This is true, Your Honor. However, I went to Denver last week and spoke with Mr. Faris, in the presence of the warden and a notary. I have here that statement." She handed it over to the judge's table to be given to the judge. Gillis sat slowly and started to visibly sweat.

After several minutes of reading, the judge looked up. "Mr. Gillis, Mr. Faris supports the testimony of Mr. Larson." When Gillis started to open his mouth, the judge waved him off. "Now, ordinarily, the testimony of a convicted criminal isn't worth much, but it appears that you were the key witness in the case that sent him to jail. They agreed to not prosecute you in another matter if you testified. In your sworn statement in court, in addition to naming him as the culprit, you stated that you sold your interest in your property in order to pay Mr. Faris for a gambling debt. Does that refresh your memory, Mr. Gillis?"

"Oh, all right, Judge." Jess muttered, "Never thought Buck would find out. Leave it to a meddlin' woman."

Judge Cole banged his gavel. "Judgment for Mr. Larson. Mr. Gillis, you are fortunate indeed that I loathe needless paperwork. If you leave this town in twenty-four hours and do not return, I will not jail you for perjury. Court adjourned."

Gillis fairly ran out of the saloon. Buck and Charlotte stood. He hugged her impulsively, then stepped away. "Never saw Jess move so fast. Thanks."

"Glad to be of help, Buck. How about you come by the office later? Pearl and I have some ideas to help your business."

"Sounds good. By the way, she needs to make a trip with me next week to hire on some new employees."

As Charlotte disengaged herself from Buck, she spotted Ward and Niels in the group leaving the saloon. Ward gave her a salute and Niels doffed his hat and lowered his head. When he looked up he was smiling. Seemed both of her friends were pleased with the verdict. She walked over and Ward stopped the group of men with him. "Attorney Walker, let me introduce you to the powers of Soda Flats." This elicited a laugh from all the men. "You already know our town's minister, the Reverend Bob Miller." He motioned to the man on his right, who was in his sixties, with a very fatherly appearance. He had crinkly eyes and had an open, trusting face.

"Yes," Charlotte acknowledged. "It is good to see you here, Reverend."

"Our church has been blessed to have you join our number since your move to Soda Flats," the clergyman responded.

"You can thank Harriet and Ward for that, Reverend. They have been kind enough to have me sit with their family."

"And this," Ward pointed to the man on his left, "is our esteemed mayor, Ed Lowell." Lowell doffed his hat. He was in his forties, average looking with a pock-marked face, but a winning smile. "And last of all, is our Sheriff, Grant Turner." Turner put out his hand for her to shake. She took his. The grip was firm. He was also in his mid-forties, ruggedly handsome with a deep cleft in his chin. The men and Charlotte all exchanged greetings and then went their separate ways.

When Buck came to her office later, Charlotte proposed a number of marketing ideas to expand his business. She and Pearl had discussed a long list of possibilities and then chose the most promising to present to Buck.

He sat and listened, then rubbed his chin. "I think you have something with this 'ladies night' at the saloon. I could use a bit of goodwill with the proper folk in this town and it wouldn't hurt to sell more drinks, even those of the non-alcoholic variety." He chuckled. "Might show the church ladies that my place is more than merely 'entertainment' for the men."

"Exactly. Actually, I have to credit Pearl with that one. She told me some of the regular card players wished they could convince their wives that there were other reasons to be in the saloon besides the 'fancy ladies.'" She smiled. "So, she figured why not bring them in to see for themselves?"

Charlotte and Buck worked on drawing up contracts between Buck and his new employees.

"I'm a bit surprised that certain aspects of my...business don't seem to bother you," Buck said. "Guess it's from bein' around Pearl, eh?"

She nodded. "I appreciate your efforts to maintain a balance between providing...services out here in the West and enforcing reasonable rules of conduct."

"I keep tellin' you. It's good business to have the customers park their firearms at the door, and toss out anyone who beats up on my girls, or cheats at cards."

Charlotte had also spoken with Doc Harriet, who stressed that the saloon girls needed to maintain minimal levels of cleanliness and have access to her clinic whenever needed. Buck agreed, again on the grounds of this being to his benefit.

"I'm going to promote Belle to help supervise any issues with the newer girls. Pearl's been kinda doin' this for me on her own and I can see how it helps keep things running smoothly. Now that she's workin' for you, she won't have time for that."

Charlotte had to admit that her heart did flip-flops whenever she saw Niels. Since meeting him on her arrival and having him help with her cabin and office, she thought about him more than she dared admit. She wondered what it might be like to be closer to him. Could she really move on? She had worn regular clothes to the hearing. It was time to put aside her "widow's" black for good. She removed her wedding rings and placed them on the chain with Conrad's hung over the photo on the mantle. Maybe she would sell them when an appropriate amount of time had passed. She hoped that Niels would ask again about calling on her. She could hardly bring up the subject before he did so. Her emotions were in turmoil. They hadn't kissed or even held hands, but she felt more heat from being near him that she ever did with Conrad.

Each day in Soda Flats brought her more happiness, more interesting stories, and more guilt. Though it was true that, like any widow, she was no longer a virgin, she had never *married* Conrad, and he was far from dead. As long as he stayed in Philadelphia, all would be well. She could not imagine Conrad having any desire to leave the protection and wealth of his father's law firm. He had ordered her to leave town, and she had. He would never have to see her again. What else could he ever want from her?

Chapter Twenty

The day after the hearing to settle the ownership of Buck's establishment, Charlotte accepted a dinner invitation from the Parkers. When she came into their home, Harriet fairly scooped her into her arms in greeting. "My dear Charlotte! Ward tells me that you were masterful in the courtroom...even if it was the saloon." Charlotte tried to dismiss this, but Harriet would have none if it. "Buck and I have had our differences," Harriet continued, "but he's a straight shooter. If he says he'll do something for you, he does and if he disagrees with you, he says so and tells you why. I was happy to see Jess put in his place. Him I never liked. A man who drinks that much should never own a saloon."

"Buck never mentioned that his former partner was a drunk," Charlotte noted.

"He probably saw no reason to mention it." Ward replied. "It wasn't going to make a difference."

At that moment another guest arrived. Charlotte turned and saw Niels. She had been hoping that he would be there. Secretly, she would like to have dinner with him many more nights.

He smiled at her and bowed slightly. "Miss Charlotte, pardon, Attorney Walker, should I ever find myself in trouble with the law, I would hope to have you on my side."

Charlotte felt herself flush. She tried to retain her composure and react to this as merely an endorsement of her professional acumen, not a flirtation. "Why, of course, sir. I hope to be of great service to this town."

"And you shall." Harriet smiled. "Come, dinner is ready and best eaten while hot." Charlotte relaxed as her friend's comments diffused the situation.

Since her rather public victory for Buck, Charlotte had acquired several additional clients, or potential clients. So far, these were all for small matters such as composing wills, verifying deeds for transfers of real estate or drawing up contracts. Any business was good. She saw these small transactions and the various inquiries as a positive sign that the town would eventually accept her and she could make a respectable living. While money was not an immediate concern, she wanted to reserve the bulk of her gift from Conrad's uncle for emergencies. It was her security and the way she could avoid any possibility of having to go back East.

Charlotte was at the café in town, seated at an outdoor table having a quick lunch. She was reading over a brief when she heard a voice.

"Miss Charlotte?"

She looked up and saw Niels Sorensen. He held a cup of coffee in his right hand. She hurriedly pushed her papers into a pile and put them into a leather folder. "Oh! Mr. Sorensen! What can I do for you?"

"Please, it's Niels." He spoke quietly and looked a bit nervous to her.

She took a deep breath. What should she say next? She tried to be nonchalant. "Of course, as long as you call me Charlotte...at least outside of the courtroom."

Her response seemed to make him relax. "May I sit?" he asked. She motioned him to do so. He placed his coffee cup on the table and joined her. "I am sorry to interrupt your lunch."

"Hardly. As you can see, I have nearly finished."

"Well, then." He cleared his throat and shifted his weight in his chair. Charlotte waited to see what he would say. Every second seemed like long minutes. "Nice weather today."

He has come to sit with me to discuss the weather? Charlotte tried to conceal her disappointment. "It is. Is the weather often this nice here?"

Niels smiled slightly. "It is so beautiful in Colorado. Much of the landscape reminds me of what I remember of Norway."

"Does it often rain more here than it has recently? We get a lot of rain back East in late spring." *I can't believe this. I am sitting here talking about the weather and the sound of his voice is making my insides feel like jelly. What is the matter with me?* Her musings were interrupted by the sound of his voice.

"Perhaps, but it has been enough. I have heard no complaints about the farms." Niels took a sip of his coffee. He shifted his weight again and looked down at his hands. "Pardon, I did not come to discuss the rain."

"Oh?" Would he finally get to whatever was on his mind? Charlotte wondered.

"Do you like our town? It is not nearly as big as those I saw when I first came to this country." Niels lifted his coffee cup.

The town? "Well, I find it pleasant. But a town is more the people in it than the number of streets or the height of the buildings."

This brought a smile to his face. "Or even the size of the mountains. Though they are very impressive here."

"The open spaces make me feel so...free." She took a deep breath and exhaled. "Everyone seems to be more cross when they are crowded together in a big city."

"So...everyone here is nicer?" Niels raised an eyebrow. He lifted his cup in a mock toast.

Charlotte had to laugh. "Not exactly, but even the ones that are less than cordial are easier to deal with. Like our banker. I imagine he would be even more of a...well, he would be more unpleasant had I met him in Philadelphia."

Niels did not reply immediately. "Is that possible?"

They laughed.

"Can you tell me more about the other leaders of the town? I was introduced at the hearing, but that's it."

"Well, they are an interesting bunch. Reverend Bob could never be a farmer. Everything green gives him a rash. Ed Lowell ran for mayor after he was thrown from a horse and hurt his shoulder. He used to be a cattle rancher. Grant Turner has been sheriff for oh, more than ten years. Ward told me Grant didn't want the job, but everyone in town agreed he was the best man for it and now he's used to it. He's fair, and has a great respect for the law, so criminals beware." He paused. "And they're all married."

Charlotte nodded. It was helpful to know more about these key figures of the town. "Thanks. Good to know those details." She laughed and got Niels to smile.

"Charlotte, there was something else."

"I suspected as much. What is it?"

After another awkward pause, he spoke. "I wished to ask if I could call on you now. Would that be agreeable?"

Agreeable? It was far more than agreeable. This was what she had been hoping for. Still, she did not wish to appear too eager. "I suppose so, yes. When would you wish to do so?" She searched his face, not wishing to miss any clues as to his thoughts.

"I would like to take supper with you at the hotel. You can pick the day."

Dinner? With Niels? At the hotel? The fact that this was something she could barely imagine or hope for stunned her into silence. Her throat was dry as dust.

"Charlotte? If I have overstepped..."

She waved him off and took a gulp of her tea. "No, no, not at all." She took a deep breath. Niels looked anxious. "I would love to." The next few minutes were a blur and she vaguely recalled agreeing to meeting him the following Tuesday. He was to call at her office and take her to the hotel for their dinner. Niels touched her hand as he left the table, or at least she thought he did. She was in a happy fog the rest of the day. Pearl shot her a few odd looks, but said nothing about her boss's mood. Charlotte figured that she had learned a long time ago when not to ask questions.

Charlotte spent much of the week researching a thorny matter of property lines in order to issue a clear deed for an upcoming sale. Due to poor record keeping and five changes of ownership, as well as the selling of portions of the total acreage, the boundaries had come under dispute. Charlotte had to go back to the original deed and find the surveyor's diagrams to follow the evolution of the tract and determine the correct placement of the current property lines. It had been time-consuming and sometimes dusty work. She had made three trips to neighboring towns and one to Denver to find the documents she required. At least it kept her mind off her dinner with Niels. She had little social experience and none of it in a small town in the West.

As she sat at her desk, a jumble of thoughts swirled through her mind. Pearl came in with a sheaf of papers. Her assistant must have sensed her tension. "Charlotte, I know you focus on your work and all, but it's like you're driving yourself extra hard. Is something bothering you? I don't want to pry, but..."

"No, Pearl, you aren't prying." Charlotte heaved a sigh. "Truthfully, I've been trying to find a way to ask you something."

"Me? Have you a problem with my work?" Pearl looked anxious. She put the papers down on the far end of Charlotte's desk.

Charlotte shook her head. "No, not at all. I wouldn't be able to run this office without you." She motioned for Pearl to sit. "No, it has nothing to do with work." She took a deep breath. She hardly knew how to begin. Having someone to discuss her personal life with was new to her. She did not have many friends in college and fewer still in law school. Thanks to Conrad, she had to leave behind any she had.

"You haven't had much life outside of your work. I don't see how you have time. What is it?" Pearl seemed genuinely confused.

Charlotte laced her fingers together and tapped her knuckle against her lip as she gathered her words. "Niels Sorensen asked me to join him for supper at the hotel."

"And? I thought you liked him."

"I...I do. But I have so little experience with men."

Pearl blinked. "You *were* married."

"But he was the only man I was ever with and he died just weeks after we got married."

"Oh. I assumed it was longer than that." She paused. "What are you worried about?"

"Where do I begin? I'm not sure what to wear, how to act, what to say, whether I should wear any lipstick or rouge..." She laid her face in her hands. "I'm hopeless." She finally admitted it. When it came to solving the thorny problems with the property lines or clearing Buck's claim to his saloon, she was confident and in control. With this dinner, she was completely at a loss.

Pearl reached across the desk and touched her arm. "Charlotte, it's okay. You'll be fine."

Charlotte looked up. "You think so?"

"I do. Look, I can help you with what to wear and so forth. All you have to do after that is relax and let him take the lead. Get him to talk about himself. Ask him about his work. Getting him to guide the conversation should make it easier for you."

This seemed like good advice. "I'll try that. You would help me decide what to wear?"

"Why not? And don't worry, I won't make you look like you're working for Buck."

Charlotte laughed. The humor made her feel a lot better. "Agreed. Now, I'll get to that stack of documents you brought. Where should I start?"

"This pile." She handed Charlotte a bundle of papers. "On another subject, there is going to be a special event this year on the Fourth of July."

"Oh? What kind of event? A band concert? Fireworks? A parade perhaps? Though I have no idea how they would round up the people for one."

"No, no, nothing like that. Better." Pearl sat in the chair opposite Charlotte. "It's a Tug of War contest. Mayor Lowell challenged the mayor of Cedar Springs. Each town has to put together a team."

"What's the prize?"

"Mostly bragging rights, I suspect, and some silly thing like having to dress up and appear in the other's town." They laughed. "Buck is signing up people to participate."

"Sounds like a great way to celebrate the day," Charlotte commented. "I should go over and see who is going to represent the town."

"Time for that later. Now we work."

That evening, Charlotte went through her wardrobe trunks, trying to decide what to wear for her dinner with Niels. She wanted to make the right impression. While she secretly liked the flashy dresses and bright colors the saloon "ladies" wore, that attire would hardly be appropriate for any other woman in public. The plain brown and grey dresses she had for court were practical and appropriate, but they made her feel so...matronly. She had lessened this effect by eschewing some of the traditional extra layers and hoops that society women of the time favored, but she was well aware of the limits. Charlotte tried to achieve as much comfort as she could without being scandalous.

Well, then, none of the dresses for court would do. What else did she have? The black dress? She had packed that up a month ago and did not intend to wear again soon. She also had a fancy blue satin and velvet gown she had worn to the engagement gala at Conrad's family estate. While it was the perfect outfit for a high society event, it was too extravagant for a dinner in Soda Flats.

As she mentally ticked off all of the clothing in her possession, it was hard to forget one item. Her wedding gown. When it had been mistakenly delivered to her in Philadelphia after the broken engagement, she had hidden it away, and taken it with her on each step of her journey West. What she kept in her trunks in her room remained safe from the Walker family.

What was left for her to wear? Would she have to look for a dress at the local mercantile? That store catered to the farm wives and she was not fond of calico. She thought for a minute and realized she had never unpacked the smaller trunk of things she had bought in New York. Charlotte had traveled there with Conrad and other honored students to conduct mock trials at the University. Of course! Conrad had given her an enormous sum of cash and encouraged her to shop for the upcoming social season. She had done so and shipped it home, put it with her larger trunk, then forgot about it with all of the later drama. To Conrad, the purchase of some fancy clothes was nothing. In hindsight, it certainly kept her from being suspicious of what he was doing in New York while she shopped. She had splurged by purchasing dresses, hats, gloves and a small handbag decorated with imitation jewels. Knowing now what she did about Conrad, she was certain that while she shopped, he had an intimate rendezvous with a very attractive female.

Before she pulled out the shopping spree trunk, she packed away the other clothes, and a flash of glass caught her eye. She pulled it out. It was a framed picture of Conrad. Lord, she thought she burnt that! Her first impulse was to smash it to bits. She hated him so much, hated him with more passion than she felt when she believed he loved her. She opened the back of the frame and pulled out the photo. She crumpled it up. It did not satisfy her. Her hatred was an unquenchable fire. She walked over to the mantel and reached for the framed engagement photo on the mantel.

Chapter Twenty-One

Charlotte removed the chain with rings from the portrait of her with Conrad and placed it around the vase set next to it. In the photo, Conrad looked every bit the adoring mate. She raised the framed photograph over her head and prepared to smash it against the stone mantelpiece. The mental image of the glass shattering and the photograph being ruined rose in her mind. It promised a moment of satisfying revenge against her hated ex-fiancé. As she hefted the frame over her head, reason prevailed. No, she could not afford to smash this yet. Not until she felt entirely free of the past and was prepared to confess. She had to be ready to tell someone, especially Niels and the Parkers, at the very least, and beg them to forgive her for her lies. This was not the time.

What would they think of her when they knew? It was so much more than the truth of her marital status. While she was truthful about not being married at present, it was because she was *never* married, not because she was a widow. But even this lie was not all. She did not wish to think about the stack of lies, one built upon the last. They kept her from planning her life too far ahead. They kept her from hoping for much happiness in her life,

Lowering the photo and replacing it on the mantel, she thought about what she had nearly done. How would she ever explain smashing her "beloved" husband's picture? That she hated him for dying? At least she had put away the damned widow's weeds. All the while she had worn the black dress, it reminded her of Conrad. Now all she wanted to do was to forget him forever. Could she?

On the sixteenth of June, Charlotte made a visit to the bank. She needed to set up a second account for her law office, now that she had a few clients. She had mentioned this to the banker recently, saying she would be in that week to complete the transaction.

The clerk ushered her into the banker's office and motioned her to a chair.

"Mr. Bradwell, I wish to have two accounts— one for my household expenses and one for my practice. It is most important that I keep careful books."

Winston Bradwell cleared his throat and sat with his arms crossed. "Standard business practice, of course. But, this is a rather unusual request from a lady." He paused and Charlotte waited to see what he would say. "Now, since you came to town, I have been checking up on you. What I have found out is most interesting."

It was all she could do to keep her composure. What in the world did he know? Could he possibly realize her true situation? That she was no real widow? That the Walkers would be looking for her if they suspected she were still alive? With effort, she kept her face neutral. All she could manage to say was, "Indeed."

"Yes, well, then." Bradwell pressed his fingertips together and tapped his nose as he considered what to say next. "Your credit is very sound, actually outstanding. I have to say I am rather surprised. Your husband provided well for you."

Charlotte stifled a cough. *My husband?* She decided it was best to say nothing about that. "I am glad that you were able to confirm my finances. Can we discuss the account then?"

"Yes, of course. I have prepared some papers for you, as requested."

Charlotte blinked. Money did indeed speak. Her secrets were safe. With her degree, well-educated speaking, and the impressive sum of cash, it was clear that banks did not probe deeply. Probably few businesses did, as long as there was enough money involved.

Returning to her office, she looked over the framed documents displayed on the wall. She had her college degree, her law degree and her certificate for passing the bar. Hopefully these were impressive enough that no one would take notice that she had cleverly covered her maiden name with a piece of parchment with "Walker" in precise calligraphy. She had done this in such a way as to be able to remove it without damage, as she planned to later remove all reminders of him by "resuming" her maiden name.

Even if Bradwell or another banker or an especially nosy legal adversary would check up on Charlotte *Walker* from Pittsburg, she doubted that person would find anything. They would have no reason and no means to track her farther back. She made a mental note not to invite Bradwell to her office to allow him close examination of her documents, and not to incite him. She was not concerned about using her "married" name, as she reasoned that Conrad would look for Charlotte *Baker.* As Conrad knew how much she loathed him, it seemed logical to assume that he would never think that she would take his name. She planned to quietly resume her birth name in a year or two. Even Conrad had limits as to how long he would pursue a vendetta. More so, as he surely believed her dead.

The day of her dinner with Niels, Charlotte closed up her office an hour early and let Pearl help her change for the occasion. She had brought her dinner dress and hairbrush to the office and Pearl contributed a pot of rouge and her assistance with applying the right touch of it.

Pearl stepped back and looked at her. "We have to do something about your hair."

"My hair? What's wrong with it?"

"Nothing, when you are at work or in court, or working in the library. This is dinner with a man you care for."

"I never said.."

"You didn't have to. If you didn't feel that way, you'd never have asked for my help. Now, let's take down that bun and make a nice braid. It's soft and feminine, but still proper."

When Pearl was done, she had Charlotte inspect herself in the hand mirror. "Well?"

Charlotte was amazed. She looked...pretty. She stood with her mouth open and did not know quite what to say. She heard Pearl clear her throat. "Oh! I hardly recognize myself."

Pearl laughed lightly. "It's still you, Charlotte. Now, take a deep breath and have a wonderful evening. Niels should be here soon."

Indeed, only a few minutes after Pearl pronounced her "done," Niels came to the office to escort her to the hotel. He was dressed in a dark brown suit and seemed ill at ease. Charlotte thought he was the most handsome man she had ever seen. His blond hair shone in contrast to the dark suit and those eyes...

"Charlotte? Is there something the matter?" He asked. "Is my tie crooked?" His expression softened. "You look...nice."

"Oh! Thank you. I didn't mean to stare, Niels. It's just...been a long time since I've gone to dinner." She could hardly tell him the truth. How could she tell him that he was the most handsome sight she had ever seen?

"Even longer for me, I'd say. Britta has been gone..." He paused. "Enough of that." He put out his arm to her. "Shall we go to dinner?"

Seated at a corner table in the hotel dining room, Charlotte and Niels ordered their meals and Charlotte found herself relaxing. Niels was easy to be around. She remembered what Pearl had said and decided to find out more about him. "How long have you been in America?"

He smiled. "I came over before I turned seventeen, so more than a dozen years."

"Did you come with your family?" She assumed that leaving so young to go so far, he must have come because his entire family had made the decision to seek their fortune elsewhere.

"No, with a group of other adventurous fellows."

"Why did you leave, then?"

Niels drank from his glass. "My parents died in an epidemic when I was very young. I barely remember them. My grandparents raised me. They told me stories about this strange and wonderful place called America. They said a man could become anything he wanted to be there. When they died, I decided I would go."

"How in the world did you manage to do that?"

"I had some inheritance and sold what I could not take with me. That paid my passage. I found work when I got to New York." The waiter came with their meals, and for a few minutes, they turned their attention to the food.

There was so much about him she wanted to know. She would try to keep her questions simple. "How did you learn such good English?"

"From someone I met in New York. She was a relative of one of the fellows from Norway. She had been in America since she was a little girl and helped all of us to learn English. It was important if we wanted to succeed here."

Now she knew why he spoke so well, especially compared to others she had met back East who had immigrated. He had a fine teacher who had a personal interest in him and his friends. "Is New York where you met...Britta?" Charlotte had wondered if she should ask about this but could not help herself. The more she learned about him, the more she felt drawn to him. She had come a long distance to leave her past, but Niels left his home country and crossed an ocean.

"No, I met her in Chicago. I went out there for a job doing stonework for some of the great buildings. We were only married for two years before she died of the influenza."

"So, how did you come to Soda Flats?"

Niels' bright expression faded. "When Britta died, I wanted to go far away. I even thought of returning to Norway. Then, I heard that there were great mountains in America. I traveled West until I found them. When I met Ward and his family, I knew this was where I wanted to stay." He ate more of his dinner, then looked up at Charlotte. "Enough about me. What about you? We are not so different, I think, at least how we grew up. Charlie said your aunt and uncle raised you after your parents died."

Charlotte wiped her mouth as she considered how much to say. Niels was right. They had much in common, and it was more important than the things she had shared with Conrad. That had only been the study of law. Otherwise, they could not have been more different. Niels understood what it was like to strike out on one's own, and to have lost people you loved. Both had lost their parents. And though her break with Conrad could not be compared to his loss of Britta, the effect was the same. They were alone.

She gave him a brief telling of her upbringing, going off to college and then law school. She told him that her husband was also a lawyer, but left out the details of the scholarship, his being in school with her, and the fact that his family controlled great wealth. She never said his name and Niels did not ask. In short, she said as little as possible about the things she feared most and talked more about her studies and her desire to emulate her father. She could not afford to say more. Not yet. "Where did you learn how to do stonework?"

"I learned much from my grandfather. More when I came to America and worked on the huge buildings. I always wished I could carve the stone like some, but I got very good at putting up walls."

"And building fireplaces," Charlotte added.

"Yes, and fireplaces."

"The stone mantel you built for my cabin could rival any I have seen in the fancy houses back East. It's a work of art."

Niels smiled slightly and looked down at his plate. He seemed unaccustomed to praise. "It is enough that it pleases *you*."

Their pleasant conversation continued throughout dinner, which for Charlotte was over all too soon. They left the dining room and headed out to his wagon, hitching her horse behind. She hoped they would be having more such times together. She wondered what Niels thought of her. She certainly liked him more every time she saw him.

When they arrived at her cabin, he helped her down from the wagon. "I...had a most pleasant evening." He touched her face. "May I call on you again?"

"I'd like that." She yearned to be kissed, but had no idea whether the social etiquette here was any different than in Philadelphia. A decent woman certainly did not wish this early in a courtship, if this even *was* a courtship. She wasn't sure, having so little experience. All she knew was that she had no clue as to how to deal with the strong pull she felt towards him. Being near Conrad was never like this, even when she truly believed they were in love.

Niels was still standing close. He did not move to kiss her but she sensed that he would like to. Why didn't he? *Am I not attractive to him?* Then he leaned closer. Would he kiss her after all?

Chapter Twenty-Two

Niels leaned to kiss her, but before he touched her lips, he pulled away. "I...should be going." He looked at her for what seemed like the longest time, as if neither of them knew what to do next. Before Charlotte could form a thought or suggest he come in, he turned and got into his wagon. She watched him drive away. After he vanished into the night, she put her horse in the barn.

Charlotte was trembling just from the possibility of a kiss. She couldn't imagine how thrilling it would be to really kiss him, touch him, feel his face against hers... She had to focus. Maybe he didn't feel the same sparks. Maybe he was planning to kiss her as an expected part of going out for dinner and then decided that he didn't find her attractive enough to bother. He was too polite of a fellow to say it. No, he would do as he did—leave quietly.

There was another issue as well. Even if Niels did want a lasting relationship with her, she had to make peace with her own past before she could build a future. With even the slightest possibility that could include Niels, she would work twice as hard to banish her demons and assure that neither Conrad nor his family would ever know that she lived, let alone where.

Two days later, as Charlotte walked into the saloon, she nearly bumped into Niels and Ward coming out. "Did Buck get either of you to sign up for the Tug of War?"

Ward nodded. "Buck talked *both* of us into it. The mayor is taking this far too seriously."

"He'd better," Niels added. "If our team loses, he has to put on a dress, wear a sign saying he'd rather be in Cedar Springs and sit in front of their city hall for an entire day."

"That would be a big motivation, all right," Charlotte agreed. "Well, we'll see. Good day to you both." The two men left and Charlotte walked over to Buck. "Getting plenty of strong volunteers?"

He smiled at Charlotte and said, "Well, we need a few more. How about you?"

Charlotte laughed. "Me? Why? Isn't it for men only?"

"Nope. Only requirement is to live in Soda Flats. No one said nothin' about men only. Though they probably assumed..."

"Again, Buck. Why me?"

"I figure it this way," Buck continued in his characteristic drawl. "We'd have Charlie, if he were here. He was a lot stronger than he looked and there's real money to be made on the bets. That's what this is really about, you know. It's not the stupid wager between the mayors and it's not the event. It's the money to be made on the *bets*."

"Seriously?" This was a whole new angle for Charlotte.

Buck shook his head and laughed. "You have no idea. Anyways, Charlie said you're 'bout as strong as he is, and he was no pantywaist. Besides, we'd get a lot of money bet on Cedar Springs for havin' a lady on our side. No offense, you understand. It's that you'd be sort of a... ringer, in a dress."

Charlotte started to open her mouth to protest, then stopped herself. She liked the idea. It was just this side of cheating and deliciously fun. Her protest turned into a grin. "Why, Buck, I'd be honored. Where do I sign up?"

Buck presented her with the list and bowed to her. "This," he announced, "will be some event. Like takin' candy from a baby."

"Are you that confident?"

"Ask me after I collect the bets. And, you, Madame Attorney, should get in some extra exercise." Charlotte raised a brow. "Never hurts to ensure the outcome." Buck grinned and she returned to her office.

The Monday before the big competition, Pearl entered Charlotte's consulting room at the office. "Mayor Lowell says he has an important matter to discuss with you."

"Did he say anything to indicate what it was about?"

"Something to do with property. Must be important." Charlotte looked up. Pearl shrugged. "He looks worried."

"Show him in and then get another chair. I think you should make some notes."

"Of course." Pearl glided out of the room and soon reappeared with Mayor Ed Lowell behind her. "Mayor, have a seat, please. Can I get you some coffee? I just put a pot on the stove."

"Why, yes, thank you." Pearl went out and shortly returned with a tray bearing three cups and a pot of hot coffee. She poured and than drew up a chair to the side of Charlotte's desk. She had a pen and paper at hand.

Charlotte gave them all a moment to take a sip of their coffee. "What can I do for you, mayor?"

"Ed, please." She gestured and he continued. "Seems the town has a very serious problem. It's a disaster."

"I assumed it had to be for you to come in today."

Mayor Lowell nodded. "Quite a weekend the town has coming up. Rumor has it that you are participating."

"True, but that is not why you are here, is it?" Charlotte wondered how long it would be before he got to his issue.

"No, but I did want to tell you how impressed we all are with you. Charlie was not exaggerating. You were masterful at the hearing over Buck's partnership."

"Thank you, but please, what is the problem that you came to see me about?"

"Well, this turned up the day after we made the bet with Cedar Springs. Hellish bad timing."

"Oh?"

"It has to do with the land that the town is built on." When he stopped, she motioned for him to continue. "It seems that there were some, er... irregularities with the charter for the town."

Not a good thing. "What kind of irregularities? And exactly how much land is in question?

"Nearly the entire town, other than the private homes and farms." The mayor shook his head.

"What is the allegation?"

"Some fellow named Vernon Price claims the papers were not filed properly so the charter was not legal. Therefore the town does not own the land it sits on. He claims that he has a proper deed that predates ours and he is the legal owner."

Charlotte glanced at Pearl. Her clerk was making copious notes on her paper. "What does Mr. Price plan to do? Do you know?"

"He wants the buildings removed or vacated so he can build a hotel and design his own main street. He'd like to get a trunk line for the railroad once he re-builds the town." The major lifted his coffee cup to take a drink but then put it down without bringing it to his lips. "Probably will name it after himself," he muttered. He took out a handkerchief and wiped his brow.

"And the buildings involved?"

The mayor shifted his weight in the chair and rubbed his chin anxiously. "The main street, the school and even the church. He also claims the school yard and half of the cemetery."

Charlotte blinked. This *was* a big problem. The area he described encompassed most of the town's major buildings.

"Did this man produce any documents?"

"He waved some things at me, but the only thing he gave me was this." He passed over a paper. "It's some kind of legal nonsense saying that we have to vacate the property within ninety days."

Charlotte unfolded it and read. It indeed was a request to vacate, signed by a judge in Denver.

"Is there more to this?"

"Well, this Price, the one who produced the order, came around last year wanting to buy the same land. The council told him it was not for sale. Now, he turns up with this...horse crap, claiming it was never ours to begin with and that he has exercised his right to file for ownership.

A stretch of homesteading, I gather. Never heard of such a thing, but there's that paper from a judge..." He wiped his forehead again.

Charlotte nodded. "First, we need to see whether there is any validity to this claim. I need to see all of the papers relating to the town's deeds, as well as any documents Mr. Price gave you. I'll also need to speak with the persons who filed for the original charter, if they are still living and in the territory."

"Yes, yes, of course." The mayor seemed a trifle calmer. "Well now, I shall be on my way and gather up those papers."

When he left, Pearl closed up her notebook and looked over at Charlotte. "That's a kettle of fish. Can you figure a way out?"

"I'll need to examine all the relevant documents and talk to some people, but I certainly hope so. It wouldn't do for the town to be taken over like that." She finished her coffee. "What can you tell me about our mayor? Does he often get this nervous?"

"No, he's usually a very calm fellow. Not much flusters him. That's why I knew you had to see him right away." She paused for a moment. "What can I tell you about him? He's married, has a couple of kids. He does his best. Seems to me that he sees his job as helping the town prosper while offending as few citizens as possible." She thought a moment. "About the only thing I've seen that bothers him is his bad shoulder. When it rains, he rubs it a lot."

Charlotte nodded. "I heard something about that." She thought a moment. "After the mayor gets me all the papers he can find, I'll need to take a trip to Denver and see what documents are on file there. We'll need to request a hearing before the judge that granted the order to vacate."

"What can I do? The thought of having the town torn up...it's not right." Pearl had a determined look about her. She was not to be trifled with.

Charlotte thought for a minute. Pearl *did* know a lot of people in the area. How, did not matter. "Find out what you can about Vernon Price. See if he has been trying to buy up land in the neighboring towns. I'll check the Denver newspaper files."

Later that week, Charlotte was at the Parkers for one of her frequent dinners. She had brought a pan of cornbread as her contribution to the meal. Niels was also there and the topic soon turned to the Tug of War challenge. "I heard a rumor that Buck signed you up, Charlotte," Ward said.

"Guilty as charged," she replied. "He says that the event is all about the bets. He has an angle and is convinced he can make a killing if we win."

"*When* we win," Niels opined. "If you are half as strong as Charlie claimed, Cedar Springs has no chance."

"Here, here!" Harriet raised her glass of cold tea. "And I'll be there to tend to the sprains and bruises on the Cedar Springs team." They all did a mock toast. "Whatever the outcome, it should be great fun and a memorable day."

After the meal, Charlotte helped clean up and the men stayed in the great room, to check the fireplace. Niels thought he spotted a loose stone. It turned out to be a minor issue, but Niels was a perfectionist.

When they left the Parkers, Charlotte pulled Niels aside for a moment. "Are you really okay with my being in this Tug of War?"

Niels did not answer immediately. "Only if you promise me one thing."

"And that would be?"

"You must promise to stand in front of me in the line."

"Of course, but why?"

"I do not wish you to fall on top of anyone else after we pull Cedar Springs over the line." He grinned. "You remind me of the women back in Norway. They are also very strong. That is a good thing to be."

Charlotte smiled. The event would be memorable, no matter the outcome.

Chapter Twenty-Three

The weather on the Fourth was about as perfect as it could have been: sunny and warm but not blazing hot. The sky was as blue as Charlotte had ever seen. It was a good day to be alive. There were sack races, pie-eating contests and even a parade of sorts, with prizes for the best entries. The parade consisted of children from both towns and many of their parents, dressed to portray famous Americans or represent events in American history. Charlotte could recognize several "Washingtons" and "Lincolns", some reenactments of the War Between the States and one of the Boston Tea Party but some of the portrayals were more difficult to recognize. Still, the great enthusiasm displayed by all the participants, win or lose, was infectious.

The Tug of War was the final contest of the afternoon and was set up on the edge of town. There was a hefty rope complete with flag in the center, a line drawn in the center of a pit, and eighteen participants on each side. Cedar Springs put one of their largest men in front. Soda Flats put Charlotte in the front, followed by Niels, Ward, a collection of farmers and ranch hands, two of Buck's bouncers, Sheriff Turner, and at the rear, Buck Larson.

Charlotte wore her lucky gloves, at least she considered them lucky. Charlie had left her this wonderful pair of Indian decorated buckskin gloves. She liked using these for the heavier chores around her cabin. For this contest, they helped her not only grip the thick cord, but also avoid rope burns on her forearms. She had found a dark skirt that was divided for riding, rather like wide trousers, and this would give her better mobility, as well as modesty.

The two teams took their places. Mayor Edward Lowell had the honor of calling the participants to order. He raised his arm and shouted, "Get ready, get set, pull!" He dropped his arm dramatically. Both teams set to the earnest task of trying to drag the other across the centerline. Grunts, yowls and shouts rose from either side. The crowd around the teams screamed and shouted for their town and tried to add to their strength by the sheer force of their voices.

The balance of strength shifted from one team to the other and back again. Clearly, neither side was going to quickly drag the other across the center. Charlotte and her teammates were pulled a few steps over to the Cedar Springs side, then the Soda Flats team surged and pulled the Cedar Springs team back and past the center. Back and forth, the center flag moved, from one side to the next. The crowd roared. How would it go? The men on the Cedar Springs team hurled insults at Soda Flats. "Have you no real men?" they accused. "Is that why you have to resort to having a woman at the front?" The insults became more heated with each shift of the lead.

The Soda Flats team had planned their strategy before the contest. It was time to implement it. The key had been to put Charlotte in the front. With the contest growing more intense by the second, she returned the taunts of the man on the front of the other line. "Hey! Want to feel what it's like to lose?" Some of the men on the other side laughed. "Want to find out who the real men are?" More laughter. She could feel a shift in the rope. "Want to lose to a woman? Get ready to go down!" When the lead men from Cedar Springs laughed again to the point of tears, the whole Soda Flats line pulled with all their might and dragged the Cedar Springs team so far over that they could not recover. With one more hefty pull, the last man from Cedar Springs was dragged across. Mayor Lawson declared Soda Flats the winner and the crowd went wild.

With the contest over, the members of the Soda Flats team, a few from the Cedar Springs team and many of the onlookers swarmed into the Soda Flats Saloon for a noisy celebration. The men from Cedar Springs that chose to attend grudgingly gave the team from Soda Flats their due. The strategy had been unusual, but effective. Many of the people of Soda Flats, particularly Buck, and even Charlotte, had won varying amounts of money with their wagers. Charlotte suspected that the biggest winner was Buck. Not only had he won money betting on the outcome of the contest, the beer and whiskey was flowing freely at his saloon.

Charlotte sat at a table with Niels, Ward and Sheriff Turner. After they shared a round of toasts to their team victory, Ward and Sheriff Turner left to speak to the others in the room. She and Niels shared more of their earlier lives and she carefully selected those parts that she could relate truthfully, mostly the stories of her parents and her days in college. Niels told her that the only thing keeping this from being a perfect day was that Charlie was not with them to see this.

"Do you suppose you could write to Charlie and ask if he could come out for a visit?" Niels asked.

Charlotte coughed. She tried to look calm and then said simply, "I will write." She then changed the subject. "I wonder whether Buck made more money on his bets or on the business here in the saloon? I've never seen such a crowd."

Niels shrugged. There was no further discussion of Charlie and after another round of toasts, he escorted her home. When they got out of his wagon, he pulled her close and hugged her. This was nice enough, but as he moved to release her, he leaned in to kiss her. The kiss was tentative at first, but then deepened for a few moments. She kissed him back with more passion than she thought she had. She did not wish for it to end, but Niels pulled away all too soon.

"I do not wish to rush, Charlotte. We have both been through much. You were married for such a short time. I have been long alone." He gave her a look that told her that he would prefer to be otherwise.

Charlotte was in heaven and in such a haze, that when Niels mentioned coming over for supper later that week and suggested a few other plans, she merely murmured agreement. One idea was to visit San Francisco to see Charlie. When he left, her dreamy high later confronted reality. *What have I done? I have all but promised to get Charlie here or go visit him there. How can I expect him to understand this is not possible?*

Charlotte spent the next day in a state of perpetual daydreaming. She was glad that the great contest had been staged on Saturday, so that she had a day of rest before returning to her office. In the town church Sunday morning, she sat quietly in a pew behind the Parkers. She gave thanks for their win and for Niels wanting to seriously court her. It was difficult for her to conceal how happy she was about Niels kissing her, but she contained her joy to the extent that she showed only a usual level of outward happiness. Fortunately, with all of the celebrating the day before, most of those she saw were more concerned with how they felt than with how anyone else appeared.

She said nothing to anyone about the events after the celebration of the Tug of War victory, but the images crowded her mind. The kiss had been quite unexpected, no matter how desired on her part. She had only been in Soda Flats since May, but when she was with Niels, she felt as if she had known him for years. While he focused on the differences in their educational background, it was the number of similarities in their personal lives that struck home with her. They had both been orphaned in childhood and had to become independent earlier than their peers. They both had taken great leaps of faith to pursue their dreams. She was a woman who went to law school and he was a man who had sailed across the ocean to find his fortune. Both paths required a certain type of drive and inner strength, she reflected. She recognized these qualities in him on hearing his story, but only now considered herself in a similar light.

After the night Niels kissed her, she began to have strange dreams. At first, it was the pleasant haze of the kiss and her impressions. She had an increasingly vivid sense of how she felt being close to him and the taste of his lips. How she wanted to experience this again! She also dreamed about the night she spent with Conrad. It was meaningful to her at the time, but the kiss from Niels was far more stirring. Now, in her dreams, Conrad's face was gone. No matter where the dream went, she saw only Niels.

The dream started the same way each time and then went further each time it came to her. With limited experience to draw from, she had to fill in the details with her imagination. With what she had heard from others, Charlotte stretched the memories and made them all the more fulfilling. Could the real thing be even better? Would she ever find out? Still, the very thought of being with Niels in that way made her heart skip a beat. She had to put these thoughts aside. Everything would come in its due time, if it was meant to be. Patience was her ally. She had to let any closer relationship with Niels develop on its own. Forcing things might ruin any chance for making her dream happen.

The week after the contest, with her dreams ever more intimate, Charlotte felt that that she needed some serious advice and sought Doc Harriet's counsel. She made a formal appointment at Doc's office to ensure privacy. After all, she had not seen a doctor for any reason in years, so she had a good excuse to go. All she had said was she had "female issues" to discuss. What could be less suspicious than that?

She went into the office and Doc Harriet's assistant took her to the examination room. Soon, Doc Harriet came breezing in. "Well, Charlotte, what seems to be the problem?"

Charlotte was reluctant to get to what was on her mind. "I thought I should see you about my general health. I have not had the counsel of a physician since I was a child."

"And that was for?"

"When so many of us had the influenza, my parents had the doctor come. I only remember having a fever and not feeling well for a few days. A few of our neighbors were laid up for a long time and two of them died."

"Have you had any problems since then? Any difficulty with breathing or other illness?"

"No, I have been well."

"I assumed as much. You were quite the phenomenon at the Tug of War. I certainly never had such strength, even at your age."

"I was only a part of a clever strategy." Charlotte explained. Praise was always somewhat difficult for her to accept.

"Nonsense. The strategy would never have succeeded were you not much more capable than the men from Cedar Springs suspected," Harriet insisted.

"I suppose."

"Now, as to why you are here to see me today."

"Well, as I said, I just wanted to discuss health issues and...female problems."

"Are your monthlies regular?" Charlotte nodded. "Have you had other symptoms or complaints of pain?" Charlotte shook her head. "Any changes in digestion? Unusual spots or swellings?" Again, Charlotte indicated she had not. "Charlotte, what's really on your mind? I can tell that something bothers you." Doc Harriet paused and leaned on her desk. "You know that anything you tell me is in strict confidence."

Charlotte took a deep breath. *Where to start?* "I...wanted to ask you about something I never got a chance to find out about." Harriet raised a brow. "I don't know much about well, relations between men and women."

Harriet was quiet for a minute then asked, "There's more on your mind, isn't there? You were married, you must know a little."

Charlotte covered her face with her hands. She tried not to cry, but there was no helping it. She was holding in so much. Harriet got up and walked around her desk. She put her arm around Charlotte's shoulders. Charlotte waited a moment, then regained her composure and motioned for Harriet to go back to her chair. "I wasn't married. I was deceived and seduced by a man who used me to get through law school, and then broke our engagement after we passed the bar."

"Charlotte! My God!"

"I felt that being a 'widow' was a safer way to come West alone. It was also a way not to have to explain my...situation. I'm used goods, Harriet. As a widow, I'm respectable." She paused. "Please, you mustn't tell anyone."

Harriet nodded. "The way people view women is sad. Don't worry. I won't say a word, not even to Ward. So, what did you really want to see me for?"

"I wanted to ask you about ways to avoid, well, ways to avoid getting pregnant. After...after, what happened to me, I realized I was lucky. Whatever else happens in my life, I don't want to trust to luck."

"Very wise. There are several reliable methods available. I will warn you, however, that you best refer to them as ways to promote feminine hygiene, not as ways to avoid pregnancy. Those silly men in Washington have made it illegal to sell any devices that could prevent conception. I cannot believe that if Congress were made up of women, it would ever be so foolish." She went on to explain the procurement and use of the more popular methods. Condoms had been in wide use for years, though now these products had to be sold without any mention of their most popular use.

Charlotte listened and considered. All of this was fine information, but would she ever even need it? Was she simply letting her fantasies take hold of her reason?

Chapter Twenty-Four

On the fourteenth, Niels stopped at her office late in the afternoon. She was about to close up for the day. They started to chat and he suggested that they take a walk while they talked. "I must go to my boarding house and get my wagon at the livery. I'd like to ride with you back to your cabin. We can talk more."

Once at the boarding house, they went into the parlor. "I won't be long. Maybe a minute." Niels said and went upstairs. He returned in not more than that and then smiled at her as he looked around. He pulled her into a corner and was about to kiss her when they heard a voice.

"Mr. Sorensen! Is that you?"

Charlotte quickly moved a step away from Niels and caught sight of a stout middle-aged woman whose stern face said she took no guff from anyone. Niels motioned her to move back further and he stepped forward.

"Yes, what do you want, Mrs. Mowser?"

"This week's rent. I know you have another day, but since I'm here..." She raised an eyebrow.

Niels paid his rent and Mrs. Mowser left. He motioned to Charlotte and they quickly departed from the boarding house. Charlotte was disappointed that the moment was gone, but hoped for another soon.

When she was alone with her thoughts and her guilt, Charlotte pondered the situation that bothered her more than anything else in her life. She had her reasons for doing as she did and saying the things she said. It wasn't *all* a lie. She had confessed her non-widowhood to Doc Harriet, but stopped short of telling all. Neither did she wish anyone else to know even as much as she had said to Harriet.

Harriet had understood her reasons for that falsehood. It might be almost the twentieth century, but it was still not safe for a woman to travel for great distances alone and single, nor was that a secure way to live out in the West in particular, where there were still many more men than women. This was acceptable if one sought a life as a saloon girl, or a dance hall partner. However, if you strove to be more, especially in a traditionally male profession, you had to have a husband, have *had* a husband by virtue of being a widow, or at the very least have a steady beau, a father, a brother or some other male that could intercede when there was unwanted or inappropriate male attention.

She tried to focus on the parts of her story that were true. So much of it was, she reminded herself. She had told the truth about her parents' lives and deaths, her schooling, her desire to follow her father's path into the law, her broken heart, her desire to start her life in a new place. She did have proof to back up her tales. The rings were hers, after all, and the relationship with Conrad *had* ended as abruptly as it would have had Conrad truly died. The difference was that she was *glad* to be done with him. While she had truly had her heart broken, it was by his deceit, not by his death.

Charlie was always the one who backed her emotionally after Father died. He kept her company when their parents were gone, supported her causes, helped her get enough money for school by working in the furniture store, defended her to her uncle when she decided to go to law school, and came to her rescue when she had to get out of Pittsburg. Regardless, Charlotte faced an unsolvable conundrum. All of Soda Flats believed that Charlie was in San Francisco. Niels had suggested she invite him to visit. A fine idea. But how could Charlie visit when not only was he not in San Francisco, there *was* no Charlie, only a very deceitful Charlotte?

Charlotte was in a pickle. Charlie had been born out of her need to cope with the loss of her parents. *Charlie* could protect her. He could show her how to be strong in the face of adversity and loss, to gain physical strength with her work in the furniture store and to follow her dream to be a lawyer like her father. But Charlie was only an extension of Charlotte, an aspect of her own personality. When Charlotte "died" in Pittsburg, she disguised herself and hid her face when she boarded the train out of town. Her only thought was to get away as quickly as possible. But even Chicago was not enough distance from Conrad. To gain her freedom, she made Charlie into a *physical* alter ego. It was necessary for safe travel and to accomplish her escape. So, *Charlie* made the journey West to Soda Flats.

The trouble started when she had to physically remain as Charlie for months. In her need to escape Conrad and all the pain he had inflicted upon her, she had buried herself so deeply into the character that Charlotte did not consciously exist. She had been able to deny any attraction to Niels until she returned from Denver as Charlotte. As Charlie, she thought of Niels as a brother and the idea of him being a couple with Charlotte was a concept outside herself, truly as a brother would screen potential suitors. Charlie had bonded with Ward as a son would to a father and had felt chivalrous towards Pearl when he had recognized her as an educated woman who might make a good assistant for his "sister."

Charlotte hung her head and wept softly. Would she ever get out of this mess she had created? How did she let her life get so complicated? Was there a way out without having people hate her? Most importantly, without Niels hating her? Would anyone suspect the truth on their own without her owning up to it? They hadn't seemed to as yet...or at least they had chosen not to speak to her of their suspicions.

Mayor Lowell sent word that the documents of interest for the case of Vernon Price vs. Soda Flats would be at the bank. When Charlotte went to collect the papers, she happened to see Winston Bradwell. "This is everything we could find, Counselor. Ed tells me it looked to be in order when the land was deeded, though I was not in Soda Flats then." He gave her the oddest look when he handed her the folder.

"Thank you." She wondered. She appreciated his respectful tone, but was suspicious. Did he know something? Had he been doing more checking up on her? If so, he did not say anything about it.

"Good luck, Counselor. None of us want to see the town lose its charter, least of all, me."

Charlotte spent the next week working on the town's case. She studied the documents and traveled to Denver to delve into the courthouse records and the newspaper archives. The trip was enlightening. On return, she spoke with Pearl.

"Find anything of interest?" she asked her assistant.

Pearl smiled. "You might say that. Our Mr. Price has been a very busy man." Charlotte motioned for her to continue. "He visited a number of towns in this part of the state and expressed interest in buying land. In every one, he was told that none was for sale. I couldn't get anyone to give me specifics, but several men expressed the opinion that there was something off about Mr. Price."

Charlotte nodded. In conjunction with her research in Denver, she sent out a number of telegrams to pursue some of the information she had uncovered and to confirm her growing suspicions about the true nature of Mr. Price's operation. She filed suit demanding that Price appear before a judge to prove his case. She would leave nothing to chance when the time came for the hearing before the Denver judge. In her prepared brief, she meticulously, yet succinctly, outlined her arguments. She sent it on ahead for the judge's review. Her opposing counsel was presumably in the process of doing the same.

After some delay, The hearing was scheduled for the last Wednesday in July. A contingent from Soda Flats comprised of Mayor Lowell, Ward Parker, and Rev. Miller accompanied Charlotte and Pearl for the day's activities.

Charlotte and Pearl seated themselves at the table across from the prosecutors. Charlotte was ready to prove that Vernon Price had no claim to any land in Soda Flats. She had her stack of papers with lists of witnesses and arguments. Pearl brought another stack of corroborating documents. The courtroom was less than half-filled with spectators. Those gathered included the group that had accompanied Charlotte, and a few others from Soda Flats that had come on their own. As to the rest, Charlotte had no idea who they were. They could have been potential witnesses for Price, or simply interested citizens. She glanced at the opposing counsel table. There was a stack of papers, but no sign of Vernon Price or his lawyer.

Fifteen minutes later, with still no sign of Price or his lawyer, the judge entered the courtroom. An aide made an announcement. "Please rise for the Honorable Judge Grover."

Judge Grover was a tall, broad gentleman of about fifty, with an impressive head of thick grey hair. "Attorney Walker, would you and your assistant please come into my chambers?"

Charlotte glanced at Pearl and shrugged. This was highly unusual. Had Price or his lawyer had an unavoidable delay? Had one of them fallen ill or met with foul play? They picked up their papers and went into chambers.

The judge's aide motioned them to chairs. There was no sign of the opposing counsel. "Attorney Walker, Mr. Price's counsel has chosen not to appear or oppose your suit." Charlotte's eyes widened. She opened her mouth to speak, but the judge motioned for her to remain silent. "The reason he gave me was that he refused to try a case against a woman, that he did not feel you should be allowed to appear." He paused. "Off the record, I can tell you that the real reason he declined to oppose your action was that he wanted to save face by not losing to you, a woman, in open court."

"Pardon, judge, but if he was so dismissal of my qualifications, why would he concede defeat?"

The judge suppressed a smile. "Seems he read a copy of your brief and his client was unable to refute the charges. The arguments set forth made the outcome a non-decision. Vernon Price is clearly an unscrupulous land speculator who has forged deeds in the past and has done so again. I suspect that if the district attorney wishes to bring charges that he will find that Mr. Price has left the state."

Pearl smiled and hugged Charlotte. "Sorry, Your Honor. I knew she'd win, but this was unexpected."

"I daresay that some of my colleagues do not welcome the new faces in our profession." He shook his head. "I suggest that you write an article about this case for the Denver law journal. Maybe it will stop other clever schemes."

"Thank you, Your Honor."

"Now, I have some papers to sign for your town and then you may all go."

On the train trip back to Soda Flats, Charlotte explained what had transpired in the judge's chambers. Rev. Miller had more questions. "So, what did you find out about Price?"

"He's a con artist and Vernon Price was only one of the many names he has used. He's an expert at forging documents and started with small properties, then worked his way into bolder schemes. Soda Flats was his first attempt at taking possession of an entire *town.* He would pass himself off as an investor who had proof that he was the true owner. By appearing generous and sympathetic, he would add to his credibility. After all, he a businessman. He would offer a token amount of money to the hapless "former" owners to ease their loss, then make a hefty profit on the land he swindled them out of."

When she went over to the saloon with Rev. Miller and Ward for a celebratory drink, Buck pulled her aside. He wanted to speak privately with her for a moment.

"I know why Charlie hasn't come back for a visit." He grinned. "Or, should I say, why he *can't* come for a visit."

She gripped her drink and tried to look calm. "Oh?"

Chapter Twenty-Five

Charlotte tried her best not to let Buck see how nervous she was. What did he know?

Buck smiled. He really could be charming when he wanted to be, Charlotte realized. "In my business I have to be able to size up potential employees. Sometimes, I have to do that in spite of layers of drab clothing."

"And what does this have to do with Charlie?" Though she suspected his meaning, she would make him say it straight out.

"Well, I'll grant you that I never suspected Charlie was a woman, only that when you came to town I recognized after a time that you and he were the same person."

"What gave me away?"

"Oh, a lot of things, after I put 'em together. Watchin' you talk with Pearl started me thinkin'. I saw some of the same mannerisms and expressions. This was more than bein' twins. The more I thought about it, the more sure I was. I realized I'd never seen Charlie's hands, and never really heard Charlie's voice, supposedly because of an injury. Also, I never saw Charlie with a clean face. Thought it was the stubble and dirt from buildin' the house. Not to mention that Charlie never paid to take one of the ladies upstairs for more than a chat. Again, at the time, I didn't question anything, but once the thought was there, it fell into place for me."

Charlotte tried to slow her breathing. Her secret was about to be exposed. Now was not the time for this. "Please, Buck, don't tell anyone. Not yet. I want to tell people myself, later."

He grinned. "Hell, I owe ya one, and I rather like knowin' something no one else does. Pearl know?"

Charlotte shook her head. "Not that she'd ever say."

Buck laughed. "In her former line of work, she learned to recognize all sorts of things and to keep quiet about it. Not askin' too many questions makes for a happier customer, and happy customers are good business."

Before Charlotte could ask Buck any more questions,

Ward came over and asked what they were so intent about.

"Just tellin' the legal lady here how lucky we are to have her in Soda Flats." Buck raised his glass to her and then drained the last of his beer.

"Very true," Ward agreed. "If she hadn't dug up all the dirt on Price, we'd be out looking for a new place to put the town." Ward supplied the details about how Price had pulled his swindles on increasingly larger marks and thought that he could get his biggest score of all by taking over Soda Flats. "Not only was Price a smooth talker, he was an expert forger. One of the reasons he got away with as many scams as he did was that he was a one-man operation. The fewer people who know about what you're up to, the less likely you are to get caught."

Charlotte could only hope this was true for her.

For much of the first week of August, Charlotte was hard at work on her paper for the law journal in Denver. Her proposed article discussed the points of property rights covered in the town's lawsuit and how the principles that she researched had broader implications across the West. She detailed the methods by which Price had perpetrated his swindles, so that others would be alerted to similar tactics.

Price promoted himself as a successful landowner, investor and developer, when he was none of these. Many of his marks never checked his claims and this was his key to success. Since he looked and acted the part, he was often accepted at face value. On occasion, he wasn't. The wily Price was shrewd enough not to try another scam too close to any failure, lest they be able to warn them off. What worked most in Price's favor was that the West was still full of wide-open territory. It attracted those who hoped for a chance at a quick buck and a smooth talker like Price fed right into their greed.

This project energized her, as it made her stretch her brain. She had handled some interesting cases since coming to Soda Flats, but she missed the stimulus of the academic world and wanted to bring a piece of that learned life to Colorado. She craved that sort of challenge and set her mind to pen the best paper she could. Her hope was that by having it accepted and recognized, she would not only be helping to thwart future scam artists, but prove that women belonged in the law.

Her other focus was undeniably Niels. Any occasion that she could see him, and any moment she could be alone with him was a treasure. She thought about when she went over to the Parkers, only days after the Tug of War. She joined them for dinner and later, there was another guest.

"Hello, Charlotte," Niels said. Had he known she would be there?

Hearing his voice made her stomach do flip flops. Why had Conrad never affected her this way? She had loved him, hadn't she? "Good to see you, Niels," she replied as calmly as she could. She hoped that the heat she felt in her face did not show.

Harriet offered a bemused look, but said only, "I'm so glad that you could join us, Niels." She indicated the chair next to Charlotte. "I trust you'll be comfortable there."

Niels grinned. "I think I can manage."

Charlotte smiled slightly but tried not to react too much. She was not up for a lot of probing questions from the Parkers and kept the conversation to topics involving what Vernon Price did and the town celebration. After dinner was over, Niels offered to see her back to her cabin. "I rode my horse over, but if you want to ride along with me, why not? You have to go that way to get back to town." She did not wish to appear too eager, no matter how she felt. She merely smiled.

At her cabin, Niels bid her good night. While he did not get down from his horse, he did ask her to join him for dinner again at the hotel in another week.

Working hard made the time pass more quickly and soon it was the day to be sharing supper with Niels at the hotel. When they returned from their meal, the evening was still very warm and pleasant. Charlotte and Niels sat on the benches in front of her cabin, enjoying the night air and each other's company, though not saying much. Niels took her hand and seemed to be about to speak. At that moment, there was the sound of a horse and wagon approaching her cabin. Who would be coming at this hour? It was Harriet Parker. She stopped her wagon and rushed up to the couple.

"So sorry to interrupt, but Charlotte, I need you to come along with me to the Lane homestead. Lillian Lane is ready to deliver and my usual helpers are all away."

"Harriet, I don't have any experience…"

"What I need most is another pair of hands and the ability to be calm in any situation. You fit the bill." Harriet waited a moment. "Coming?"

"If you really think I can help." She turned to Niels.

Before Charlotte could even speak, Niels squeezed her hand. "Go ahead. I'll stop by your office tomorrow."

So, Charlotte's evening took an unexpected turn. She had never seen a baby born before, but she was good at following directions. Doc Harriet coached Lillian Lane to push and Charlotte offered moral support and wiped Lillian's forehead. Soon, it was clear that the baby was coming and Charlotte heard a lusty cry.

Harriet smiled. "Great job, Lillian. You have a daughter."

Harriet passed Charlotte a small blanket. "I'm going to hand you the baby now. Don't be nervous. She's a bit slippery." She placed the baby in Charlotte's blanket-covered arms. "Now, give me a moment." Doc clipped the cord. "There you go. Now, wipe her off and wrap her in that other blanket. She needs to stay warm."

Charlotte accepted the wet, squirming infant girl and as she wiped her dry, marveled at this perfect little being. She counted ten fingers and ten toes and touched the cute little nose. Doc Harriet turned her attention to seeing that all was well with the mother. Charlotte was overwhelmed and relieved.

She left an hour later with Doc Harriet and was soon back to her cabin. She thought about the lovely evening with Niels, and though it had not ended as she had anticipated, it had been a revelation. She did have several points in her week to look forward to, times to see Niels.

She sat with him at church on Sunday, saw him almost every week at the Parkers for a meal and when he had work in town, he came by her office every now and then to join her for lunch at the cafe. There would be other opportunities to get closer.

On August twenty-eighth, Charlotte received a letter at the office from the *Denver Law Review*. She held it in her hands and hesitated.

Pearl nudged her. "Well, go ahead and open it. It won't bite."

Charlotte did so and when she read the enclosed letter, she smiled. "They've accepted my article for the *Denver Law Review*."

"I never doubted it for a minute." Pearl clapped her hands. "The way you exposed that snake oil salesman Price! That was brilliant."

"Why, Pearl! What brought this on?"

"You don't give yourself much credit for what you do, so I figured I'd have to do it for you." She smiled. "We'll have to have an article in *The Observer*."

The Observer was the weekly paper in Soda Flats. Anything and everything that happened in town appeared in its few pages: births, deaths, weddings, arrests, petty thefts and so on. Charlotte nodded. This would be big news in this small town. "Okay, but let me tell Doc Harriet first."

"And Niels Sorensen, perhaps?" Pearl winked at her.

"Pearl! Well, of course, I would want all my friends to know."

"Friends? Are you sure that's all he is to you, hmm?" Pearl arched an eyebrow.

"All I'm willing to discuss. Now, back to the rest of the mail and that contract I was working on."

Pearl sighed and shook her head, but pulled out the stack of mail and resumed sorting.

The *Denver Law Review* was the most prestigious legal publication in the state, and perhaps the West. Charlotte was undeniably pleased with this achievement, but she was equally proud of her contribution to reducing the amount of land fraud. After she had submitted her paper, she had heard of others with similar, though perhaps not as successful, scams. Her hope was that as more read her paper or heard her talk, the level of awareness would thwart all but the most sophisticated plans before they could be implemented.

She felt a sense of accomplishment that her article had been accepted, but when the news came out in *The Observer*, it seemed that everyone in town had to stop and offer their congratulations. She was unaccustomed to all of the attention and was a bit uncomfortable with her new found fame. Her focus for the last year had been to keep out of the sight and sound of the Walker family and now she was the most popular topic of conversation wherever she went.

Following church that Sunday, Niels walked along with her and asked how she felt about all of the attention.

"It's...strange." How could she explain how she felt without telling everything? "I feel a bit overwhelmed by the attention."

"Ward said you must go to Denver to speak about it. Are you worried about speaking in front of all those other lawyers?"

She shook her head. "It's not that. I feel honored to have my article published and I look forward to presenting it in Denver." She sighed. "It's...hard to explain. It's just a feeling." She felt awkward having everyone know so much about her. It was disconcerting to think that they might know where she was, as well.

Two days later, Winston Bradwell dropped into her office. "You should be pleased to know that I have contacted the Denver papers to interview you about your article in the law review."

Charlotte desperately wanted to decline, but could not think of a convenient excuse that would not make him more suspicious. "Why, Mr. Bradwell, how kind of you, though I doubt they wish to bother themselves with such minor things."

"Tsk, tsk, Counselor. Is there some reason you wish to avoid having your fame spread across Colorado?" He gave her the oddest look. She could not get past the thought that he knew something she did not wish him to know.

"Don't be silly. I would not wish to take up their time, or mine, without good reason." She offered him a smile and acted as calm as she could. "Now, I am sure you have other things to do today, as do I. Good day."

With Charlotte spending more time with Niels, she had several uncomfortable moments as well as the memorable ones. More than once, she nearly confessed her secret. Worst was when Niels said, "It is so odd that you look so much like your brother. Of course, I didn't feel the same way about him," he laughed.

Each time they had a chance for a stolen kiss, the act became more serious and Charlotte felt herself slipping deeper into something she could not control. Why was it so hard to tell the truth? The more she cared for Niels, the higher the stakes became. She had to find a way to keep her deceptions hidden, just a bit longer.

Chapter Twenty-Six

On the third of September, Charlotte returned to her office after visiting with a client at an outlying property. Pearl was waiting for her with an anxious expression. Bradwell had come to the office while she was out.

"Our friendly bank president wanted me to tell you that he has heard from the Denver newspaper about your article."

Charlotte rolled her eyes. "How nice. And what else did he say?"

"They're sending out a reporter next week to interview you. I'm impressed." Pearl gave her a slight nod. "We haven't had a paper from Denver out here to cover anything since the train came through Cedar Springs."

"Well, I did say that I would agree to this. Did he say anything else?" Charlotte wondered aloud.

Pearl made a face and thought a minute. "No, but he did spend a lot of time looking over your diplomas. It seemed like he was trying to memorize them. Is there some secret writing on them or something?"

Charlotte laughed nervously. It didn't help make her feel better. "No, Pearl. They're only diplomas. Regular, plain old diplomas like everyone else who has been to a school has." This behavior by Bradwell was disturbing. What was he looking for? Had he found it? Was he planning to use whatever it was against her?

"That's what I thought." Pearl put her hand on Charlotte's arm. "He's envious that you got here on your own. I heard that his father put him through school and set him up in business."

"I suppose." Charlotte decided there was no use in wondering. The best she could do was to be wary and prepare a counter plan, should she need one.

"Oh, there is one other thing. You had another visitor. I left his note on top of your papers on your desk." Pearl smiled and gave her a wink.

This was more pleasant news. Pearl was telling her that Niels had come by. He could not wait until she returned and instead, left a note for Charlotte. She opened it before starting on her stack of papers.

"Please join me for a picnic after church on Sunday. I will get food from the café."

She sighed. A picnic with Niels was just what she needed. She would bring a blanket and maybe some wine. These pleasant thoughts got her through her days and past the possible problems with Bradwell or the Denver reporter.

Sunday could not come soon enough. She filled her days with her work. She prepared two deeds for filing, drew up a will and caught up on her law journals that had arrived on the last coach. It had taken her some time to arrange for these, but now that she had them, she would read between cases. Studying decisions and the reasoning behind them had always fascinated her and having re-established connections with her eastern law journals was important. Yes, she was in Colorado, but changes in the law in the eastern states would lead to similar changes in the West, eventually. She was not about miss any important rulings.

Charlotte dressed for church with a special sense of anticipation. For the last several weeks she had met Niels and the Parkers every Sunday and sat with them during the service, but today she and Niels had special plans. Niels was waiting for her at the church and offered his arm. Dressed in his Sunday best with the sun highlighting his golden hair, he was so handsome that Charlotte had to calm herself. Her thoughts were not the kind one should have in church. They walked in and sat together behind the Parker family. Knowing they would be spending the afternoon together made it hard for her to focus on the service. She recalled that the minister's message was nice, but could not for the life of her recall any specifics.

Finally, the small choir led the congregants in the benediction and everyone filed out, greeting Reverend Bob Miller as they left. He put his hand out to Charlotte. "Always good to see you, Counselor. I can't tell you enough times how grateful I am that we did not have to lose the church we worked so hard to build or move the graveyard."

She smiled. "Even in court, Good usually wins over Evil."

"Especially if Good has a better lawyer on its side," Niels added.

Charlotte tried not to laugh but this did not stop Rev. Miller from doing so. "God does wish us to be active in doing good, not merely pray for it to happen," the pastor added. He smiled and moved on to the next wave of people exiting the church.

Niels walked Charlotte over to his wagon. "I need to stop and pick up our basket."

"And I have a few things at the office to get." Niels raised an eyebrow. "Relax, Niels. It's not papers." He chuckled, but Charlotte noted a hint of relief in his expression.

A half-hour later, they had their picnic lunch, the blanket Charlotte had left at the office and a pretty bunch of flowers that Niels had surprised her with. Niels drove his wagon to a spot outside of town overlooking the water. She had never been there before, but heard mention that many local couples enjoyed taking a picnic lunch "up to the lake." This must be where they were talking about. She could not imagine that there was another spot this picturesque so close to town. The day was perfect, with bright sun, a blue sky, and a gentle breeze. There were shady trees and lush fields of clover.

They unloaded the wagon and Charlotte spread out the blanket. Niels brought out the picnic basket. From it, he produced cold chicken, a vegetable plate and a fresh apple pie. The basket had plates, silverware and napkins.

"The café packed all of this?" Charlotte asked.

"It's their Sunday special. Big picnic day for them. All I had to do was get a basket and they put everything in."

The two settled into the tasty lunch and talked about the weather, the service and, as they packed up the plates, Charlotte's upcoming interview. "I know it's supposed to be an honor, but I don't want to say the wrong thing."

"They are going to ask how you kept Price from taking over the town. What can you say wrong?"

"I hope they don't ask many personal questions. I don't wish to talk about myself."

Niels smiled. "Not even when you are the most fascinating person I know?" He put the last of the lunch debris into the basket.

"Niels! That's nice of you to say, but you are a very interesting person. Tell me more about your work. Ward said you were up for a big contract."

Niels got very quiet, then replied, "Yes, very big. I got the job. It's a lot of stonework and good money. Steady work for weeks, maybe for months."

Charlotte wondered why he did not seem very excited about this. It sounded like a dream job for a stonemason. "Is there a problem? Do you have to work for someone you don't like?"

"No, nothing like that." He waited a moment. "It's that it is in Denver."

"Oh." *Denver.* Niels would be gone. Was he trying to break it to her gently? "It's a wonderful opportunity. You should be congratulated."

He smiled slightly. "I will have Sundays off." He turned away to cover the basket. "I...could come to visit you, if you wished it." He turned back to her and waited.

Charlotte felt her heart pound. "I would like that."

Niels moved closer and touched her face. "I do not welcome being apart from you."

Even this slight touch gave her shivers. As he closed the small space to kiss her, he had barely touched her lips when the noise of approaching horses interrupted the moment. He quickly moved back, as did she, with reluctance. She was not one for public displays. She looked about and saw three young riders, full of high spirits. They slowed as they passed, but continued on to the lake. They were gone, but the moment was as well. It would have been nice if it had lasted longer. Maybe another time, she thought. Instead, she helped Niels pack up the wagon and they returned to town.

At her cabin that night, Charlotte sat by her lamp and read but her thoughts returned to the fine picnic and the brief kiss. How she craved more! She sighed. She had to be patient. Her feelings about Niels and his new project were at odds. While she was thrilled for him that he had been hired for this prestigious and well paying project, she selfishly wished this opportunity was in Soda Flats and not Denver. Still, his being away so much might help her be more patient. She would have no other choice.

The newspaper interview took place on the twelfth of September. A tall, husky man of about thirty-five presented himself to her office and produced his credentials to Pearl. She ushered him into Charlotte's consulting room.

"Mr. Johns, may I present Attorney Charlotte Walker. Counselor, this is Mr. Herbert Johns of the Denver Post."

She passed over his credentials to her boss. Charlotte saw that he was the head features writer for the Denver Post. She had no idea she was such big news. "Mr. Johns, please, have a seat."

The reporter did so. He pulled out a small notebook and opened it. "Well, Counselor, tell me about yourself. Where are you from? Where did you go to school?"

Charlotte pasted a calm smile on her face. "For the purposes of this interview, please call me Charlotte. It's much simpler." The reporter smiled and nodded. She proceeded to give him a basic outline of her education, how she had been on the law review and that she had been inspired by the work of a family member who had been in the law. She carefully avoided any personal details, not specifying that the family member was her father, or that her "late" husband had been in law school with her.

"That's impressive, but can you tell me more about your family? Your background?"

She smiled and did her best to be charming. "Sir, I doubt if your readers are that interested in *me*. What they want to know is how to avoid getting taken by a slick con in a suit like Vernon Price."

He nodded. "I'll concede that point for now. So, what advice can you offer?"

"First, an honest man wishing to do business with you will not be afraid to give you references or have you check his background. He will not try to rush you into a deal that can only be done that day. The bigger the deal, the more you have to be sure the person you are dealing with is on the square." She continued with some of the details and asked if the reporter had read her article.

Mr. Johns said that he had. "It's impressive. I would think it would have wide appeal, well beyond Colorado."

"Thank you. Did you have any other questions for me?" She thought. *Would* her piece make the grade back East? No matter. She was here.

"How about a tour of your town. My readers enjoy getting a sense of the places we visit for our interviews."

"Certainly." She rose and led the reporter out. "Pearl? I'll be back in a half-hour. Mr. Johns wants to see the town."

When Charlotte returned to the office, she was much calmer than when Herbert Johns had come in. The interview had a few scary moments, but she felt that she had managed to bring it off and not give herself away. She kept the reporter mostly on topic with the article and the issues that it raised and he had not pressed for more personal information. Charlotte breathed a sigh of relief. She had avoided the most obvious chances to trap herself, but it taught her a very important lesson. It would be too easy for her to slip and allow her house of cards to collapse around her.

CHAPTER TWENTY-SEVEN

Niels had only been gone a week and a half. He'd had to continue with the masonry work the first Sunday on the new job, but sent a telegram telling Charlotte he would be in town the following week. To her, it seemed like months. She missed him already, more than she would ever have thought. There was no possibility for a last-minute invitation to lunch or an accidental meeting in town or a chance to sit with him for dinner at the Parkers. She tried to remind herself that they had no defined relationship and no agreement to meeting at any set interval. Still, she could not silence her sense of loss and felt even more compelled to keep busy with work. Being busy was the only way for her to suppress thoughts of being closer to Niels. While they had only shared a few stolen kisses, she had experienced more thrills from this brief contact than anything with Conrad. Simply being in the same room with Niels made her feel more alive.

Charlotte had asked Herbert Johns about how to obtain copies of the article when it was printed. He advised her that the *Denver Post* would send her ten copies of the paper for that day in appreciation for her time. True to their word, a bundle of papers arrived at her office two weeks after the reporter interviewed her. She was cutting the twine when Niels came into her office. She was so surprised, she nearly dropped the bundle on her foot.

"What are you doing here?" It was the first thing that popped into her head, but it sounded silly as she said it. She could not help herself. The words came tumbling out before she could stop them. "I didn't think you would have a day off from your new job until Sunday."

Niels grinned. "Plans changed. We need another load of block.

Won't be in for another three days." He pointed to the papers. "Taking a second job delivering papers?" His expression was far from serious.

Charlotte wanted to laugh, but was too surprised and nervous at seeing Niels. He was here, in her office. "Thought I'd try it out and see." When Niels shook his head, she continued. "Hardly. These are copies of the paper with my interview. I haven't even had a chance to read it yet," She pulled off the last of the twine and handed him a copy.

He nodded in appreciation. "I'll read it later."

"Not impressed by my new-found fame?"

"I already know how amazing you are." He moved in close and put an arm around her. As he moved to kiss her, there was the sound of footsteps rapidly approaching. They sprang apart and Charlotte busied herself with her papers. Niels folded the one he had given her.

Pearl's voice accompanied the sound of more footsteps. She spoke rapidly as she entered ahead of a familiar tall, sandy-haired man. "Attorney Walker, Sheriff Turner is here for his appointment." When she saw Charlotte, and Niels, she stopped. "Oh! I didn't know you had company."

"It's okay, Pearl. Niels was helping me with these papers. Here, Grant, I'd like you to have a copy, too. It has the interview I did with the *Denver Post*."

"Hello, Grant," Niels said. And to Charlotte, "I'll be going, now." He saluted her with his paper. "Can't wait to read this."

Niels returned to the office as Charlotte was about to close up. "Care to join me for supper tonight? I know it's not Sunday, but it seems this job will depend more on the deliveries of our materials than the days of the week."

"Yes, I would love to," she replied quietly. Charlotte never knew what to say to his invitations. She wanted to scream, "Of course!" but that would not be terribly lady-like and she was not sure enough of where their relationship was going to act too forward. While she often defied social convention, there *was* an acceptable limit. She smiled and took his arm. They walked down the street to the hotel and into the restaurant. Niels pulled out her chair and Charlotte took her seat. They both decided to have the special of the day, which was roast chicken and potatoes.

Charlotte was still trying to realize that she was sitting down at a meal with Niels, after wishing so hard for it. "Tell me more about this job in Denver, Niels. It must be quite an undertaking." She had more of her chicken.

Niels finished his bite and took a drink. "It's going to be the finest building in Denver, Charlotte. The entire project will take two years to finish, but my part will be done in a few months."

"What part is that?"

He smiled. "I am with the men laying the foundation blocks and doing the masonry for the first level." Niels beamed with pride. "We are also responsible for the detail work above that. The bricklayers and ironworkers will do most of the basic structure. The parts that most people will see, that is ours."

"I must go and admire it when it's done. You can show me your handiwork." She smiled. "You said you started learning about stonework in Norway. Did any of your family come to America with you?"

He shook his head. "No, but my uncle came over later. He's the one who arranged for a few English lessons before I left."

"Oh, yes. You did tell me that you had learned some English before you even got to New York."

"Only enough to ask directions." This made Charlotte laugh. "Well, maybe a little more than that. But it was our friends here and also, Britta, who taught me more. They insisted that I learn to speak well. Then I would have better opportunities." He paused. "They were right. I would not have this job in Denver otherwise. I would not have even known of it."

"Oh?"

"I answered a newspaper ad. Yes, I had heard something about a big project, but I learned more about it in the *Chronicle*."

After they finished their dinner, they lingered in the lobby and found a darkened corner. Niels put his arms around her and leaned in for a kiss. The contact was delicious, but momentary. A moment after their lips touched, a noisy group of perhaps ten burst into the hotel lobby, laughing, talking loudly and spreading out into all parts of the lobby. No longer alone, Niels and Charlotte took a step apart. Niels held onto her hand and kissed it.

Charlotte sighed deeply. Another opportunity lost. Niels shrugged, and kept hold of her hand as they walked out of the hotel to the livery. There were other people there as well, also fetching their horses. Again, Niels looked as if he had more to say but said simply, "Supper tomorrow? Ward asked me over to the house. He said he planned to mention it to you." He hinted that he had some very important things on his mind, but said nothing more. He bade her goodnight.

Charlotte was left wondering what he wanted to say, but thought that she would have to wait. She felt frustrated not knowing. Their time together was limited, and too public for Charlotte's liking. Worse, their attempt at being alone had again been thwarted. They were never *really* alone long, and tonight was yet another lost moment. It seemed to be their pattern. Many furtive glances, interrupted talks and near clinches. She was left wondering where things might go if they were alone for an entire evening. She trembled at the thought, but this was a good kind of scary. The kind that excited, that drove people to a wonderful sort of madness.

Indeed, the following evening at the Parkers' house, Niels was pleasant and polite, though he managed to hold her hand for a minute under the table and walk out to the front porch with her after the meal. The burning look in his eyes said that he planned to kiss her. Charlotte's heart pounded. She wanted this so much. He pulled her in close and she could feel the warmth of his breath.

Then, the Parkers' youngest child burst out of the house. "Miss Charlotte? I wanted to give you something before you leave."

Charlotte moved away from Niels. "Yes, Victoria, what is it?" The child had flowers and held them out to her. Charlotte smiled and accepted them, but cursed the timing.

During the month of October, Charlotte saw Niels almost every Sunday. Though she tried to downplay her feelings, this was the high point of her week. She was hesitant to admit how much she cared. The last time she had given her heart, it had been torn out and thrown in her face. Why risk that again? The hard part was that Niels did not act like Conrad. He seemed to be a good man inside and out. Not only that, other people whom she trusted also thought well of him.

Niels suggested to Charlotte that they could have supper at her house, if it would not be too unseemly. They couldn't find anywhere else to be alone and he was tired of worrying about what other people might think. She agreed and they decided on the last Sunday in October.

Niels asked her to ride in for church with the Parkers so he could meet her there. After the service, they had lunch with the Parker family and then went for a long walk.

"We'd best get out to the house if I am to get supper on," Charlotte told him.

"We have time," he assured her. "Let us enjoy the day."

"Alright. Another half hour and then we really have to go."

Later, Niels rode her out to the house. When they went in, Charlotte stopped still. The table was set for two and fresh flowers were in a vase.

"What's all this?"

"Dinner. Harriet came and set up the table and the hotel will be bringing out our dinner shortly."

"Really? How did you arrange all this?"

"It's not hard." He smiled and pulled her close. "You only must know who to ask." He touched her face and tilted her chin up. When he kissed her, she felt hot down to her toes. As she gave into the wonderful sensations, she was aware of a knock on the door. *Not again…*

Niels smiled and released her, then answered the door. It was, indeed, their dinner. Two employees from the hotel brought in covered dishes and Niels motioned for them to set them on the table.

"You can return the dishes tomorrow, folks. Have a good evening." The men from the hotel nodded to Charlotte and Niels and left. They sat at the table to enjoy the delicious meal while it was hot.

The evening was magical. As it grew darker, they turned up the lamps and Niels lit the fire in the fireplace. Niels poured wine for them and set chairs by the fire. He sat in the upholstered chair and took Charlotte by the hand, gently pulling her onto his lap. He slid his arms around her.

Charlotte's first impulse was to object, but being wrapped in his arms in the chair was so nice, she laid her head on his shoulder and sighed contentedly.

"Charlotte," he said and lifted her head so he could look into her eyes. "Charlotte, I have to tell you. I've been waiting for the perfect moment." He paused and took a deep breath. "It has been hard to find it." Touching her face, he continued, his voice soft. "I love you. I cannot imagine spending the rest of my life without you. I do not have a fancy education, but I promise to stand by you and make you happy. Would you...would you marry me?"

Niels was proposing to her? That Charlotte was surprised was a major understatement. She was also equally overjoyed. "I...I...don't know what to say." She saw the hope in his eyes. "I do love you, Niels. I just hadn't thought..."

He smiled and put his hand behind her head and closed the clinch to kiss her more passionately than he ever had. Charlotte was caught in a storm and her lips parted on their own. All she wanted was to be with Niels, in every way. Now. She didn't want to think about answering, or about talking. Was that a mistake, she wondered? With his being away so much, she didn't care. He was here now and he loved her. That was what mattered.

She returned his kiss with more passion than she dreamed she possessed and as he slid his hands down her back she did the same to him. Everything was a blur to her. All she wanted was to have him, all of him. Now. For once, they were not interrupted. When she tried later to recreate every detail in her mind, she could not recall how they had gotten to the bed, or how much of their clothing was lost along the way. She did remember the advice Harriet had given her about taking precautions. When she and Niels made love, it was everything she could have imagined and more. Nothing like her night with Conrad. Niels was big and hard and knew how to bring her a kind of pleasure she had never experienced, or ever thought she *could* experience. She was in heaven, but had not given Niels an answer. How did she let things get so far out of hand?

When they were done and both breathing heavily, Niels tried to assure her that he had not proposed to her simply to take advantage. He apologized for pushing her too far, too quickly. He had to return to Denver for his stonework job, but promised her that everything would be fine. They would talk more the next week when they met again. Charlotte was at war with herself. She could not accept his proposal without telling him the truth, but if she did tell him, would he still wish to marry her? The perfectly fine mess she had made was now even worse.

Days after their rendezvous at her cabin, Charlotte received another letter, forwarded from Denver. Someone had submitted a copy of her article in the *Denver Law Review* to the *University of Pennsylvania Law Review*. Well, that was interesting, but did not explain the letter. She continued on to the following paragraphs. Her article had been accepted for the next edition of the Review. She smiled. She really *was* "good enough for the East." Attorneys from across the country would read about her work to thwart fraud. She sighed. Her father would be so proud. Then her smile faded.

Chapter Twenty-Eight

Charlotte's initial wave of pride from reading the letter faded into a cold chill. Soon, it became controlled panic. There was an aspect to having her article published in such a prestigious journal that she had not considered. Everything had come full circle. Was this some weird twist of fate? A perverse kind of payback for the things she had done to start her life over? She feared from the first that her lies would extract their payment. Was this the time for her to ante up? Could she face the possible consequences?

What was it that she feared from such a great honor? There was certainly benefit to derive from it. Publication would mean more respect from the lawyers in Denver as well as the people in Soda Flats. It also made it less likely that she would win a case because the opposing attorney refused to appear in court against a female colleague. But there was another point to consider, one that could have serious consequences for Charlotte. Conrad and his family never missed an issue of the *Law Review*. They prided themselves on the number of articles that the family firm had placed in the publication. There was not a chance in a million they would miss an article penned by "Charlotte Walker."

This was a huge problem. The entire Walker family was supposed to believe she was dead. As long as they did, she was safe from further recriminations from Conrad or his relatives. However, it was clear that the events in the article had occurred *after* her supposed death. Worse, the article not only identified her as Charlotte Ann *Walker*; it gave her date of graduation from the University of Pennsylvania. There was no way the Walkers would miss the connection and fail to realize that Charlotte had either faked her death or that another person had assumed her identity. Either way, she feared that someone would come to Soda Flats to find the author. If so, she was sunk. She could hardly deny her identity to them.

She wondered if the University of Pennsylvania had ever been notified of her "death." She knew that she had not done so. Had someone sent them the newspaper account? Had this been printed in any of the school publications? She had not dared give them a direct forwarding address, only a roundabout alias. What *would* Conrad's family do when they saw the article? They would not only suspect that she might be *alive,* but they would also know where to look. How long would it take for them to investigate?

The letter she was holding had been forwarded three times to get to her. Had her article already appeared? The postmark was twenty days past. Her only chance to counter this threat was to tell her story first, and this had to begin with Niels. He said he loved her and she believed him. Because of this, she fervently hoped that if he heard her side of the events in Philadelphia from her own lips, before his ears were fed poison by the Walkers, he would understand and stand by her against Conrad and his family. Niels would be back Sunday. She would talk to him then.

While she waited out the days, she had work to do. She had given a passing thought to speaking with Harriet about her concerns with the article, but that would require a lot of explaining, explaining she was not ready for. True, Harriet knew some of her story, the part that had not been of her making. On the other hand, her method of getting away was far from honest, and she felt awkward justifying what she had done. When no one else knew, she could pretend that none of it had happened. She had never met Conrad, never been humiliated, never had to go the extreme of faking her death to escape him. She would never have to explain what did not happen. She could just be Charlotte. If someone had to know the unadulterated truth, it had to be Niels.

C. Walker, Attorney at Law was not the only business in town with news. Soda Flats was growing rapidly, which had prompted the ad leading to her own relocation here. The bank was expanding to meet the needs of the number of new merchants, the local newspaper was considering a change to twice weekly publication, the barbershop had added a second chair and Pearl had made a trip to Denver with Buck to interview new "employees." One of Charlotte's current projects was drawing up contracts for many of these ventures.

Buck came into the office to work out the details of the contracts for his new hires. "All this legal stuff, Charlotte." He shook his head. "I know we need this, but there are so many details I'd never thought of." He ran his hand through his hair, then made himself comfortable in the upholstered chair opposite her and chewed on a small cigar.

"These details are important. They serve to protect *you* as much as your employees," she explained. "This way, any disagreements can be handled in a civilized manner. Having everything spelled out on paper will also make it easier for you to hire when you need to. Or fire, as the case may be."

Buck nodded and took the cigar from his mouth. "I did have some trouble that time I had to get one of the girls to leave. She was stealing from customers and complained that my turning her in was going to make it hard for her to find other work, but that was not my problem. She kept waving the old contract in my face, telling me I couldn't do that."

"So, what did you do?"

"The last thing I wanted to do. Had to call Sheriff Turner to haul her off to jail. It was the only way to protect the customers and my business."

"How did that go over with the other ladies?" Charlotte could never bring herself to call them "girls." If they were old enough to be in the world's oldest profession, they were old enough to be "women" or "ladies."

Buck grinned. "Not so bad after Grant talked me out of arresting her. He had a better idea."

"Oh?"

"He suggested I talk with my other..." he nodded to Charlotte, "*employees* and let them work out a solution." Buck shrugged his shoulders. "Don't know what they said to her, but she quit and left town the next day. Upset a few of the others that were left for a while. So, I'm happy to avoid a situation like that again."

"And your *employees* will be happy knowing that you are watching out for their health and safety." One of the provisions in the updated contracts was having regular visits with Doc Harriet. Charlotte had pointed out that this was good business. He could attract more of the higher-class customers passing through town by having the reputation of running a clean establishment. These customers would spend more and would likely return to tell their well-heeled friends about the good times in Soda Flats. "Okay, Buck, I think we have it worked out. You and Pearl can handle explaining the terms of the contracts to the new ladies."

Of course, besides the worry over the repercussions of her law review article, the other thing on Charlotte's mind was the passionate night with Niels. It seemed that the most unlikely things would remind her of how she had felt when he touched her. Certain words, a scent that reminded her of the dinner, seeing another couple kissing in an alley—all of these triggered images in her mind so strong that she almost felt his presence. She was still trying to understand how things had gotten out of hand that night at the cabin. The dinner had been lovely and she had assumed they would finish the wine and Niels would go home. Having him kiss her that way and then... It had been wonderful, but what did he really think about what they had done? That she would fall into bed with anyone? No, she doubted that. This was a small town. Everyone knew that she had not given a second look to any man but Niels. And he *had* proposed to her. She would have to give him an answer eventually. Still, he did not know the truth about her life before Soda Flats. He did not know that she had never been married. Instead, she had surrendered her virginity to a lying swine with a smooth line.

She had to talk to Niels. It was hard waiting until Sunday, but he was out of town on his important stone job. The thought of seeing him again and having the chance to unburden herself consumed her. She could barely eat or sleep. He would also expect an answer to his proposal, if not immediately on his return, surely soon thereafter. She tried to calm herself. It was only three more days until his weekly visit. She could barely concentrate on work.

On Friday, Pearl came into her office with a telegram. Niels could not come this Sunday. His team was on a rush job for the project and would be paid extra to stay. As a result, he could not make the trip to Soda Flats until the following week. Charlotte's hands shook as she put down the telegram.

Pearl rushed over and took her arm. "Bad news?" she asked. "Has Niels been injured at that building site? It's a big project and must be dangerous." She waited. "Charlotte? Did you hear me? Is he hurt?"

Charlotte shook herself and refocused on Pearl. "Oh! No, no, he's fine. It's...they have to meet a deadline and he can't come into town this Sunday. I was so hoping to talk to him."

"Talk?" Pearl shook her head. "I would think there would be more on your mind than that, the way you've been acting lately. Is that what happens when you have so much education? You forget about... pleasure?"

Her assistant's tone was teasing and Charlotte could see the trace of a smile on her face. Pearl had cut to the heart of the matter. Charlotte had to talk to Niels to have a chance of sharing another passionate evening with him. "Well, some talk first, then we'll see."

Pearl grinned. "That's better. I see how he looks at you. You have him on the hook. All you have to do is reel him in."

The following Sunday, the second one in November, Charlotte waited for Niels at the stagecoach station near the center of town. Until the railroads expanded to smaller towns like Soda Flats, these coaches would continue to provide the link to the rails. The coach stopped. She could tell by the amount of luggage stacked on the top that the coach was full today. Niels was the first to disembark. Charlotte rushed towards him. She was bursting to tell him everything. If he understood, she was ready to accept his proposal. Then she would feel safe from any future threat from the Walkers. If he believed her, he would defend her. She was sure of that.

Niels opened his arms to her. She went to him immediately. When she hugged him, she whispered in his ear. "I must speak to you. Privately."

Niels pushed her back enough to look at her. "Now?"

"Yes, now. Please." She tried to urge him to come with her.

He did not move. He merely smiled and pulled her back into the circle of his arms as he whispered to her. "I presume you wish to tell me yes to something?" He hugged her. "Be patient, my love. I missed you, too."

Charlotte closed her eyes for a moment and savored the feel of being in his arms. She did not care who saw them like this. She did not wish to be anywhere else in the world. As she sighed in contentment, she opened her eyes for a moment. She pushed back from Niels, hoping she was having a passion-induced hallucination. For as she stared, she saw another familiar face stepping out from the coach. It was one she never thought she would see again.

Chapter Twenty-Nine

Charlotte clung to Niels urging him away from the coach. She whispered urgently. "Niels! We need to talk. I'm serious. It must be now."

"What has you so upset?" Niels was clearly perplexed.

"Please, come with me and I can explain everything."

"Now, Charlotte, that isn't necessary. We can talk later," he replied. "Let's get settled in first. I'll get my bag off the coach."

"No, Niels, please." She looked past him and the man getting out of the coach got closer. Charlotte's blood ran cold. "We have to go."

"In a minute. There's someone you should meet." Niels was clearly excited. She wondered who this was. "He says he read your article. He's very impressed with you."

Charlotte tugged at Niels. She simply had to get him to leave this place and let her speak to him privately.

Then she heard a voice she had hoped never to hear again. "What's your hurry, Charlotte?"

She thought she might faint. The man who had alighted from the coach was none other than Conrad Walker III. Charlotte tried one last time to pull Niels closer and get away from the station, but he was in no rush. "Please, Niels."

Niels gave her a short kiss on the cheek. "Whatever it is, it can wait." He smiled. "I want to introduce you to this man. I met him while I was waiting for the coach." He took a step away from Charlotte to shake hands with Conrad. The sight of him made her skin crawl.

Conrad stepped forward. As Niels started to introduce him, he said, "Oh, she knows very well who I am, don't you Charlotte, my pet?" Niels looked confused. "Please, Charlotte, don't be shy. It's really not in you. Tell this gentleman who I am."

Charlotte took a deep breath. She would try her best to remain civil. It would be a challenge. "Why, Conrad, I had no idea you could find your way out of Philadelphia. I hope you left a trail of breadcrumbs to find your way back." Sarcasm was the only way to mask her terror at seeing him. She could imagine any number of bad motives and worse outcomes from his being here. There was a chance that she could salvage this. She had never mentioned her "husband's" name. Maybe she could get rid of the big blowhard before anyone made the connection.

"Now, now, Charlotte," Conrad purred. "I'm perfectly capable of finding my way back, but you're coming with me."

"A generous offer, to be sure, but not even if Hell freezes over, *sir*." She narrowed her eyes to slits. "I'm not going anywhere with you."

"Oh, I think you will, my sweet. You have no idea what I can do." Conrad smiled as he said this.

"Charlotte? What's all this about? Clearly you know this man, this Conrad." Niels looked from one to the other and back. "Why are you acting like this? I've never seen you talk like that to anyone, not even Bradwell."

"I have my reasons, Niels. I want him to get back in the coach and return from whence he came." With great difficulty, Charlotte tried to control her rage.

"Hardly hospitable of you, Charlotte," Conrad countered.

Charlotte stood her ground and kept her chin up. "We have nothing to discuss, so I would not wish to waste your valuable time."

Conrad shook his head slowly. "Again, I think we have much to discuss. Perhaps, you would wish to do that in a less public setting."

What she wished was not to be speaking with him at all. She now noticed that while the coach had emptied, the passengers had not dispersed. Would it be advisable to let Conrad have his say elsewhere? She was reluctant to be anywhere with him, much less alone with the man she hated most in the world.

"Charlotte! Please, what is going on here?" Niels pleaded with her. "Why would you consider going off with him? What could he possibly have to discuss with you?"

"Nothing. I have nothing to say to him." Charlotte was not looking at Niels. She was looking right at Conrad, doing her best to reel in her hatred.

Conrad whispered to a man with him. He had left the coach after Conrad. The man nodded and scurried off. He was on a mission. The problem for Charlotte was that she had no idea what it was. Conrad then smiled and said, "Now, Charlotte, is that any way to greet your dead husband?" Everyone around them gasped. She could hear murmurs through the crowd. Reactions were mixed: shock, disbelief, horror, and condemnation.

Niels could not keep silent. He took her by the arm and turned her towards him. His face reflected a bit of everything she had seen in the surrounding crowd. "This man is your *husband*? Please, Charlotte, I need to know." The crowd was getting larger and louder.

Conrad's smirk was even more pronounced. "Yes, Charlotte, on our way from Denver, I had a most delightful conversation with Mr. Sorensen. He informed me that you were a widow. Oh, and even sadder, that your husband died only weeks into the marriage! How very tragic! I nearly cried." Conrad dramatically wiped his eyes. "Shouldn't you be overjoyed to see me alive, my sweet?" He opened his arms to her with a sweeping gesture. In response, she turned away, not facing him or Niels, who still held her arm. She said nothing and tried to keep her expression neutral.

The crowd murmured a sentiment similar to Conrad's. Yes, if Charlotte had indeed loved and lost Conrad in the way she had told everyone, she would be sobbing with joy and throwing herself into his arms. If it were not for Niels, she might have tried faking it to save face and having it out with Conrad later. What in blazes did he want with her anyway? Yes, she had been afraid he would send someone out to find her, but why would he want to drag her back to Philadelphia? He had his pick of women and she was not his problem anymore.

The delay in response from Charlotte was making the crowd restive. She could feel the accusations being whispered among the people gathering by the coach. The coachmen finished unloading the baggage from the arrivals. They were now loading again and waiting to leave with those making the trip back to the train. Charlotte did not know what to do. She glanced at Niels. He was standing next to her, holding her arm, apparently not willing to let go yet. However, the shock and disbelief showing on his face meant that Charlotte needed to explain a lot to keep him there. Conrad was in front of her and his smirk said he had more to throw at her. She was cornered. Was there any way out of this?

Conrad's words meant there was not. "Is that any way to welcome me, Charlotte? Of course not. But you see, my dear, I do understand. I'm not dead, nor were we ever married."

Niels pulled Charlotte a bit closer. "Then you have no claim on her. She does not wish you here. Leave."

Conrad was enjoying every second of his big moment. He shook his head and wagged a finger at Charlotte. "Tsk. Tsk. No, it never got as far as marriage, though I must say, the preview of the wedding night *was* entertaining."

Niels lifted Charlotte's chin so that she had to look directly at him. He spoke softly. "Is this true?" Charlotte could only nod. She felt numb.

Conrad's smirk was even more confident, if that were possible.

Niels was angry, as evidenced by his red face, but his anger was not directed at her. "You can stop right there, Conrad. I will hear no more from you. Charlotte, I'm going to wire your brother in San Francisco. He can deal with Conrad."

Conrad raised an eyebrow. "Brother? She has no brother."

"What do you mean?" Niels responded. "Her twin brother Charlie was here for almost a year. Ward and I helped him build his cabin. Nearly everyone in town knows him." He looked from Conrad to Charlotte to the crowd and back at Charlotte. He was at a loss. He appealed to the crowd. "Don't we? Most of you met him." There was a murmur of agreement. Charlotte hoped this was a good sign.

Conrad started to laugh. "Charlotte, Charlotte. I had no idea you carried that brother fantasy so far. You see, folks, there's no Charlie. There's only Charlotte. What did you do, dear? Play dress-up again so you could do things you're not supposed to?"

The tone of the crowd turned to surprise and shock. Niels stared at Charlotte. "He's lying isn't he? Tell me he's lying!"

Charlotte sadly shook her head. Niels dropped her arm and stepped away from her. Conrad's traveling companion returned, with Sheriff Turner in tow.

Conrad greeted the men. "The town sheriff, I presume?"

"Yes, sir. I'm Sheriff Grant Turner. What in blazes is all this commotion about? Your friend here said you would explain." Sheriff Turner looked seriously annoyed. Charlotte hoped this might work in her favor.

Conrad put out his hand to the sheriff. "So good to meet you, Sheriff Turner. I'm sure you do a fine job keeping order in this town." Conrad looked especially pleased. Charlotte knew that look. It was never good. Conrad pulled a paper from his inside pocket and held it up. He was trying for the most dramatic effect possible. In her opinion, he was all show with minimal substance. "I have here a writ issued by Judge Lothrop in Philadelphia ordering Charlotte Ann Baker to return with me to face charges of theft and conspiracy." There was a cry of horror from the crowd. Charlotte felt the blood drain from her face.

"Charlotte *Baker*? But this is Charlotte Walker!" Sheriff Turner scratched his head.

"Sorry, Sheriff. You missed that part." He put his hand to his chest in a gesture of attempted sincerity. "I'm Conrad Walker, her very much un-dead and never-was husband. The lady here, and I hesitate to call her that, is Charlotte Ann Baker. Ask her."

"Is this true, Charlotte?" Sheriff Turner looked right at her. The walls were closing in.

Charlotte nodded in shame. She could not speak. It took all of her control not to cry.

"Oh and one more thing, Charlotte," Conrad added.

She was shaking on the inside and wanted to run. Conrad was enjoying this far too much at her expense, but what could she do? And what else was left for him to accuse her of? She had to try to stay strong.

Her ex-fiancé continued. "I forgot to mention, as did you, I presume, that you stole my Uncle Benjamin's money. You probably caused his stroke, as well. But, since there's no way to prove that, I'm willing to give you the benefit of the doubt on that point."

Now Charlotte was no longer silent. "I stole nothing! Your uncle *gave* me that money, so I could get away from *you*. Your uncle was a good man and I was sad to hear of his passing."

Conrad held out the paper in his hand and Sheriff Turner approached him. He took the paper and read it. Conrad reached out to grab her by the arm.

Sheriff Turner blocked his path. "Not so fast."

Sheriff Grant Turner stepped in and pulled Conrad off Charlotte. "I'm going to notify the circuit judge and request a hearing. He will decide whose claim to honor. I can't just let anyone ride into town with a piece of paper and carry off one of our citizens." Conrad lost some of his suave demeanor, but remained quiet for the present. "The judge can read that paper you brought and hear witnesses. You'll both have a chance to tell your story and make your case."

"Now, Sheriff, it's plain to see that I have a right to take this woman back to Philadelphia and have justice done." Conrad was showing his true colors, she thought. He was getting angry and demanding his way.

"You have a right to be heard, Mr. Walker," Sheriff Turner replied. "Until then, you can stay in town and be civil and Charlotte will go to jail."

Conrad shrugged. "This will only prolong your agony, Charlotte, *dearest.* They'll get to hear it all in court."

Niels had been quietly listening to this exchange. Charlotte reached out for him, in hopes of some support. If only she had been able to tell her side first, she thought. He turned away.

"I'm sorry Charlotte," he said softly. "I can't believe anything you say. You played me for a fool. I trusted you and told you everything in my heart. Things no one knows. I tried so hard to treat you like a lady. I believed you barely knew what marriage was." He took a deep breath and shook his head sadly. "There will be no wedding, not for you and me. You are no lady and I never wish to see you again."

Conrad was close enough to get the sense of what Niels said, if not the words. He smiled triumphantly. He stepped closer to Niels. "Mr.

Sorensen, seems we have both been led down the garden path by the same deceitful woman. Won't you join me at the local watering hole? I owe you a drink. After all, you were the one who let me know I'd find her here. Wasn't certain before." He stretched out his hand to Niels and beamed his most winning smile.

Niels pushed Conrad's arm away from him. He was not listening to Charlotte, but she took a moment of comfort in the fact that he was not accepting Conrad's show of comradeship, either. He stomped off.

Charlotte did not want to cry in front of Conrad, but it took all of her resolve to stand straight and walk to the jail with Sheriff Turner. She again cursed her bad timing. In her heart, she truly believed that if she could have explained this to Niels in her own way, he would have understood. He would likely have been mad for a time, but he would not have left her like this, nor would she have been so publicly shamed. Now, what did it matter what the judge said? She had lost the love of her life and was powerless to stop Conrad from taking everything else.

CHAPTER THIRTY

Charlotte resigned herself to her fate and followed the sheriff to the jail. There was no point in making a run for it. With all these people around she could hardly get away. Even if she had super-human speed and evaded them, there was nowhere in Soda Flats for her to hide. Though some part of her felt that she deserved punishment for her many lies, she was mystified as to the timing of her arrest. Why not wait until after the hearing? She stopped and turned to ask Sheriff Turner.

"Why are you taking me to jail now? Do you believe everything Conrad says? Why not wait until after the hearing if you are so convinced of my guilt?" She hoped this was not the case. She had counted Turner as a friend. "Surely, you don't think I would try to run?"

Sheriff Turner shook his head and explained. "I can't put my finger on it, but that Conrad fellow is too slick. After the town nearly lost its deed to that con artist, we can't be too careful. Because some fellow shows up here with a paper supposedly signed by a judge doesn't mean it's true. In my time, I've seen what can happen when someone has a mind to get their way. The safest place for you is in the jail."

She raised a brow. "You're serious."

"I've gotten to know you, Charlotte. You deserve the right to present your side. This way, he can't arrange for you to 'disappear' with him."

Charlotte was stunned. As much as she distrusted Conrad and as low as she knew he could go, the possibility of him kidnapping her back to Philadelphia had not occurred to her until now. "You really don't like Conrad, do you?"

"That's a fair statement. As I said, the man is entirely too sure of himself. He said a lot of things. Accusing you of theft and implying you contributed to his uncle's death...that didn't ring true. However, it's not up to me. It's up to the judge."

They reached the jail and Turner spoke with his deputy for a moment then faced Charlotte. "The cell is clean, but we'll see that you have a few things, if you like. Books, paper, extra blankets. Ask me or my deputy first, so that we can assure the court you aren't getting any contraband."

"As in no files in the cake, Grant?" Charlotte replied. At least her comment let them both laugh. There was little humor to be found in this day, but even a moment of relief was welcome. The men left after locking her in the cell. She sat on the bed. The day was not over yet and it had not been one of her best.

Charlotte was in jail, alone with her thoughts. She wondered who in the crowd had heard which part of Conrad's declarations. Sheriff Turner had not been present when Conrad revealed there was no Charlie, but how long would it take before he heard it from one of the others? What would he think? Would it change his treatment of her? What would any of her friends think? Others in the group had left after the initial confrontation, clearly more interested in the details of their own lives. How could *her* life have become so complicated? Conrad had found her, she was in jail and Niels wanted nothing to do with her. She had finally learned the true meaning of love, of passion, of wanting to spend the rest of her life with a truly good man and it was all over. At least, she could treasure the memory of their one night together and know that she was truly loved, in every way.

Yes, she had lied and now she was paying for it. On the other hand, Conrad was also lying. She did not deserve to be sent back East with that slime. How could she prove that she did not steal Benjamin Walker's money? What evidence could she produce for the court to support her side?

Conrad's plan for revenge seemed clear. He would have her thrown in a real jail and try to have her disbarred. How long would she be there? And what would she be able to do if and when she ever got out? Conrad's family was very influential. She would probably not be able to practice law. There would be no point in coming back to Soda Flats.

She could be old and gray by the time she got out of jail, if indeed she ever did. And what about Niels? She couldn't bear seeing him married to someone else and having a bunch of gorgeous blond children with another woman. No, the future did not look bright from any angle.

Her depressing thoughts early that evening were interrupted by the sound of someone coming into the cell room. Sheriff Turner brought her a dinner tray. "Don't have too many prisoners in our jail. Mostly drunks that need to sober up." He laughed. "Congratulations. You're the first woman we've ever had in lockup."

An hour later, the deputy came into the cell area and took her tray. "You have a visitor, Counselor."

How wonderful! A visitor? She took a deep breath. Surely, it was not Conrad. Could it be Niels? Was it too much to hope for? Soon, she realized that it was.

"Charlotte? Feel up to a visit? I couldn't bear the thought of you being in here alone." Harriet Parker breezed into the room, carrying a small bag. "Deputy?"

The deputy leaned in the door. "Yes, Doc?"

"Can you unlock the cell for me to go in and visit with your prisoner?"

He nodded and came back with the keys. After he opened the door, he waved her in. "Sorry, gotta lock you in. I'll be back in a half hour to let you out. Well, just you, Doc," he chuckled. "Rules is rules."

Harriet sat next to Charlotte and patted her hand. "How are you?" Charlotte shrugged. "Don't worry, Charlotte. You'll be safe here and we can help you figure a way out of this."

"I'm not sure there is a way." Charlotte sighed. "How did you find out I was here? I didn't see Ward anywhere near the coach today."

"Buck Larson heard the commotion and one of his ladies was on the coach. She heard it all and went to get Buck. By then, you were off to the jail, so Buck asked me to come out and check on you." She smiled. "I thought I should get a few of your things first." She indicated the small bag she brought.

"Is that okay?"

Harriet nodded. "I had it checked by the deputy before I came in."

She set it next to Charlotte and took out the items. Harriet had brought her a brush, comb, warm socks, a change of clothing, a few sheets of paper, a pencil, and the book that had been on her desk at the office. She asked if she needed anything else.

"These should do fine, Harriet. Thank you. Having a few familiar things helps." For the first time since she had seen Conrad today, she felt an emotion other than doom.

"I still can't believe that Grant put you in jail. What was he thinking? We have to get you out."

Charlotte shook her head. "Not before the trial, Harriet. I spoke with Grant. The safest place for me right now is in here. Conrad always gets what he wants, and if he thought he could get away with it, he'd drag me by the hair all the way back to Philadelphia."

"Hmmm." Doc Harriet pressed her lips together and nodded. "Perhaps this is the best place...for now. What all went on out there?"

Charlotte was too upset to say much. "I think you got most of it from Buck. What about Niels? Have you seen him? Where is he?"

"I really don't know. I haven't seen him, nor heard anything about him, but I'll ask Ward if he fared any better. He went out after him. Try to get some rest and we can talk later about what to do to settle this."

"Thank you, Harriet. Yes, I'll do my best. It's been a very trying day."

Niels was still fuming after the scene at the stagecoach. How could Charlotte have lied to him? She was no widow. She hadn't even been married, but if Conrad were to be believed, she was also no innocent maiden. By the look on Charlotte's face, this charge was also true. How could she act as if none of those things had ever happened? He had believed her. He had fallen for her and some small part of him wanted to believe that the awful scene today was only a bad dream. But it wasn't and there was no forgetting the guilt betrayed by her eyes.

He had gone back to his room and was pacing the floor. There was a knock at the door. He did not care who it was. "Go away!"

"Niels, it's Ward. I want to talk to you."

"I have nothing to say."

"Well, I do. Let me in."

Niels growled but did as he was asked. He opened the door and let Ward enter the room. "You're in now. What have you to say? That I am a fool for trusting her? When that fellow Conrad started talking, I thought he was crazy, until I saw Charlotte's face. She's been lying to me, lying to all of us."

Ward stood his ground and looked directly at Niels. "I know what he said. Harriet told me. But I also believe there's more to the story."

"I do not wish to hear it." He turned away and resumed pacing. The faster he paced, the faster he talked and the angrier he felt. "The truth is probably even worse than we've heard so far. If she can lie about so many things, like being married, why should we not believe that she ran off with an old man's money? Hell, maybe she did cause his stroke."

"Niels! Calm down! What are you saying? You know her. We all do. Do you really think she could do something like that?"

Niels had an ugly feeling in his heart and it had to have shown through to his face. "Did we think she would lie about being married? About being a widow?" He paused briefly in his furious pacing. "No, of course we did not. So why should we believe she is not a thief?" He resumed his frantic walking back and forth in the room, gesturing as he went. "And I trusted her."

"And we owe her a chance to tell her side," Ward countered.

"Side? What side? Did she deny the charges? She does not even have a damned brother! She made him up. It was her all the time. Did anybody know?"

"Charlie was...Charlotte?" Ward stopped for a minute. "That *is* interesting." He rubbed his jaw. "I still say we need to hear her side. She must have had a reason. Coming out here alone as a woman is risky. Ask Doc."

Niels shook his head and kept walking. "I was not here when she came to Soda Flats." He stopped and looked at Ward. "She never made up a fake twin brother."

Ward took Niels by the shoulders and shook him. "She came here with a husband! Me." He let go and paused. Niels seemed done with his ranting. "So, what are you going to do?"

"Do? The only thing that makes sense. I take the next stagecoach to the train and go back to work. My gear is still packed."

"Suit yourself. I'll send you a telegram when the hearing is set."

"So I can hear her 'side'?" He stopped. "If that is what you want." He shrugged. "Now, leave me alone."

Ward threw up his hands and left.

In the morning, Sheriff Turner brought breakfast for Charlotte. She was not very hungry, but knew she had to keep up her strength for her mind to stay sharp. When he returned and took the tray, he told her she had another visitor. "I must say that you are the most popular prisoner we have had in some time." He left, and returned with a chair that he set up across from the cell door. "Might as well be prepared. I suspect we have not seen the height of your popularity."

Pearl came in behind him, carrying a sheaf of papers. She thanked the sheriff and sat in the chair. "How are you, Charlotte? You're one up on me. I've never been in jail."

Charlotte smiled. "Being in jail hasn't been so bad. It's what happened before I got here that I wish I could forget."

"I heard." Pearl waited a moment. "I went over to see Buck when you didn't come to the office this morning. He told me all about it and pointed out Conrad to me."

"Oh? Where was he?"

"He came into the saloon for a drink and was spewing his filth about you. Buck threw him out not long after I got there." She shuddered. "Your ex is a good-looking fellow but no gentleman."

Charlotte nodded sadly. "I wish I had seen that sooner."

"Advantage of my former profession. Have to size 'em up fast. Anyway, I'm not here to tell you that I agree that Conrad is a rat. There's work at the office and Grant says I can bring you papers every day to keep things going. So, what do you say we get to work, and if there's anything I can do to help you with your case, name it."

Charlotte agreed. "Thanks." She took the stack of papers and they reviewed them. Before Pearl left, she said, "Keep your eyes and ears open to what Conrad is doing and saying. Maybe you can ask Buck to let him back into the saloon, so we'll know what he's up to."

"I'll ask him, but I'm starting to think Buck has even lower opinion of him than you do."

Really? Charlotte blinked. *At this point, that would be next to impossible.*

Chapter Thirty-One

Two days later, an hour or so after Pearl's daily morning visit, Grant informed her that she had yet another visitor. This time it was Buck Larson.

"Sheriff tells me you have to take a number to visit you." Buck pulled the chair up and flipped it around before he sat. He leaned his arms on the back of the chair, his legs straddling the seat. "Your...well, I don't know what to call him. He's not your husband, for which you can be right grateful, and he's surely not your friend." He scratched his chin. "I'll just refer to him as your...former classmate. Anyway, Conrad Walker is a real piece of work. Believe me, I can spot 'em. He dresses sharp, but he's lower than the dirtiest card sharks I've tossed out of my establishment."

"I see that his popularity continues to increase." She made a face. "That worm."

"You're bein' charitable." Buck laughed and pulled a short cigar out of his vest pocket. He didn't bother to light it, merely twirled it in his fingers. "Not that he hasn't found a few men who nod and agree with him. Most of them have no idea who you are. They hate women in general, unless they're underneath them and don't have any opinions."

Charlotte could not hide her surprise. She was getting support from unexpected sources. "What's he saying, specifically?"

"That his uncle had a soft spot for you. That he can prove that you took advantage of that and stole money from him." He recited these charges in bored tones, clearly unimpressed. "The stress of the betrayal caused his stroke, and so on."

"And what do you think?"

"Besides the fact that the man is a horse's ass?" Buck laughed and gestured with the cigar. "I think he's a greedy son of a bitch who thinks he's being done out of an inheritance." He cleared his throat. "He wouldn't know the truth if it hit him in the face."

"Do you think he'll be able to convince the judge of his claim?" This is what kept Charlotte awake at night.

Buck crossed his arms and did not answer immediately. "Unfortunately, Charlotte, men like him tend to get their way, in and out of court." He gestured again, waving the unlit cigar. "He's a pompous bastard, but he's not stupid. And he's rich. He's also acting awfully confident, swaggering around town saying he's got an 'ironclad case' against you." He stopped and inspected the cigar. "But I do have a funny thought."

"Oh? It's hard to laugh about this." Charlotte hung her head. "So what am I to do?"

"You can always come work for me." He grinned. "Okay, I'm joking. Here's what I really think: If I was a violent man, I'd make Walker disappear." Charlotte gasped and he waved her off. "No, I won't go that far. But, we've got eyes and ears on him all the time. He's bound to make a mistake. Not only that, you have friends in this town. If the court finds against you, we can break you out of jail." He stuck the cigar in the corner of his mouth and grinned.

A life on the run? And without Niels? Not exactly her idea of a great future. "I hope it doesn't come to that." She stopped and thought. "I have no idea what kind of 'proof' Conrad could have. How can there be proof of something that didn't happen?"

Buck waved his cigar. "If you have no conscience, there are ways, Charlotte. He's been throwing money around looking for people to testify against you. So far, no takers, not from anyone who actually knows you. Some dude from out of town nicked him for ten bucks, then left on the next train." He paused and seemed to contemplate his cigar. "Tell you what I think. You got more balls than your ex or whatever can hope for. Even though I figured out the twins thing, it doesn't matter. I like you both."

"Thank you, Buck."

He chuckled again. "I also don't care if you have the old dude's money or not. Walker sure as hell doesn't deserve to have it." Buck wagged his head. "Stay out of trouble, Charlotte." He got up out of the chair and put it back. "See you in court. I'm going to close up the day of the hearing. The ladies and I will be there." He bowed slightly at the waist and departed.

Charlotte marked the days by completing her morning paperwork with Pearl, dictating letters and delivering pieces she had written during the previous afternoons. Pearl brought books and took back the ones her boss no longer needed. Charlotte wondered when the hearing would be and tried not to think about Niels. Would she ever see him again? The hardest time was the nights. She dreamed about him, sometimes even to the point that she could almost imagine they were back in her cabin and could feel him next to her in the bed. Their one night together had been magical and, for a short time, she had dared to think it was a preview of the rest of her life. How she longed to be able to accept his proposal! And now, the dream was gone. Niels had withdrawn his offer of marriage and left.

After she had been in jail for four days, Harriet came to see her again. The deputy let her into the cell with Charlotte and left. She brought a basket with cornbread, cider and a novel. "Harriet! Thank you. You know how much I love cornbread."

"And this is a copy of a novel I just read. She pulled out a book. "It's called 'The Picture of Dorian Gray'. It's pure fantasy, which is what you need right now."

Charlotte couldn't agree more. Reality was not so pleasant these days. "Well, I can't use the excuse that I don't have the time." She picked up the book and paged through it. It was going to be good. But as distracting as the book promised to be, she had to ask Harriet about what was uppermost on her mind. "Have you heard from Niels? What did he do after we...argued?"

"He went back to Denver on the next train." Harriet sighed. "Ward tried to stop him but he was having no part of it. Told Ward he was better off staying at the site until the stonework was complete."

"Oh."

"For what it's worth, I don't believe anything I've heard about what Conrad has said."

Charlotte was pulled back to the sad reality that faced her. Her future seemed bleak and there was nothing she could do. She could feel herself breaking down. She didn't want to, but all of the disappointment and sadness she had been holding back finally burst through. She covered her face with her hands and started to sob quietly.

Harriet offered her some cider and it eased her sobs.

"Would it help to talk?"

Maybe, maybe not, but could it hurt? At this point, there were no more secrets to expose. It was only a matter of how much Harriet knew. After a moment, Charlotte pulled herself together and started to tell Harriet her story. She started with her family. "I so admired my father. The more I learn about what he was doing and what he was trying to do, the more impressed I am. He was so brave."

"Yes, to be a Northerner trying to heal the wounds after the war was dangerous. Many still do not wish to forget." Harriet nodded sympathetically and waited for Charlotte to continue.

She went on to explain about how she went to college, managed to get a spot in the law school but then ran out of money. The more she told, the more she got deeper into the details. She talked of her desperation at the prospect of leaving law school, the opportune scholarship, of meeting Conrad and being swept off her feet by his fine treatment of her, at least at first. Charlotte also told her of how Conrad had not been the best student, and begged her for help, promising her a position alongside him in his father's prestigious law firm.

"Actually, Harriet, had he not been his father's son, he would not even have been admitted. He struggled with every class, and his briefs were positively awful. Unfortunately, I was so blinded by love that I took it as a personal mission to tutor him and help him get through his exams. It's not that he's dull, but he lacks the discipline to study without direction and without the threat of dire consequences should he fail."

"Dire consequences?" Harriet asked.

"His father's wrath. He would have cut Conrad off financially and denied him a position had he not made the law review and passed the bar." Charlotte grimaced. "I spent countless evenings reviewing the points of law with him. We did so before each exam and double for the bar. I had to re-write those frightful briefs, but still have them sound like he had penned them himself. Not an easy task, mind you." She stopped to think about what to tell next. She decided on the engagement, the party, meeting Conrad's uncle, and ending with the fateful night when he seduced her and then rejected her.

"My God, Charlotte!" Harriet put her hand on Charlotte's arm. "How monstrous!"

"It was worse than that. He told me that the scholarship was only a ploy to gain him a tutor, and that he never intended to place me in the firm. Lastly, he said his family would prevent me from joining *any* firm in Philadelphia." She took another swig of the cider to steady her voice. "I was on my way out of town when I got a letter from his uncle to come by. He was always so kind to me that I had to go. Uncle Benjamin gave me money and wished me well. He said his nephew was a fool and I best stay far away from him."

"Where did you go then?"

"I took the train out to Pittsburg, got a room and looked for work. When I read in the paper about Uncle Benjamin's passing and that the family was looking for me, I had my trunks sent to the train station and faked my death."

Much to Charlotte's surprise, Harriet smiled. "How clever of you. Tell me how you managed it."

She explained how she had staged a breakdown in her apartment, yelling and screaming about "Conrad." She cried that she would sooner rid the earth of any trace of herself and her possessions rather than face him. "I hinted that I would throw myself off a bridge. I knew that my pleasant, but terribly busy-body landlady would tell everyone, which was the point." She also told Harriet about writing the note and tossing the dummy in the river. She chose a time that would assure witnesses to the act, but dark enough that they could not see clearly. "I dressed in black, put on a hat with a heavy veil and took the next train to Chicago. I spoke to no one. After that, I knew that the only person I could trust was Charlie." She couldn't stop a fresh round of tears.

"Charlie?" Harriet asked. "But Ward said that Niels was going on and on about there wasn't any Charlie. What was all that?"

Charlotte wiped her eyes and said, "It's all me- I'm Charlie. I have no brother, but since my parents have been gone, he has been as real to me as if I did."

Harriet nodded. "Children left alone often have imaginary friends, though I've never known one to carry it that far."

"Traveling West as Charlie seemed the only safe way to get here. That way, he could make all the advance preparations for me and then conveniently move away before I arrived."

"What about the letters?" Harriet wondered aloud.

"I wrote all the letters and arranged for them to be sent to Charlie." Charlotte paused. "When Charlie went to Denver to check on my crates, I became Charlotte again." Charlotte was spent. She had no more to tell. "It no longer matters. Even Charlie can't help me now."

Harriet gave her a hug. "Your friends will stand by you." The deputy came in to tell her that the visit was over and Harriet left.

Two days later, Charlotte learned that the hearing had been set for two weeks hence. She passed the time as she had during her first days in jail, but now also had daily outings accompanied by the sheriff or his deputy. They would take a short walk away from town and back, to avoid being seen by most of the townspeople. The only difference between them and any other couple out for a stroll was that Charlotte was handcuffed to the person accompanying her. This was for general security and to prevent any attempted abduction. Sheriff Turner was not convinced that Conrad was above a kidnapping disguised as a jailbreak.

She had no new ideas about how to counter the charges. She was mystified about what type of proof he planned to offer the judge. Harriet and Pearl brought her clothes and Sheriff Turner agreed that Harriet could supervise Charlotte so that she could clean up and dress for the hearing.

Reverend Bob Miller came to see her to offer a prayer on her behalf. He did not ask Charlotte to explain anything. "How do you fare, Charlotte?"

"I would be better if I were not in jail facing a possible trial, but I appreciate your concern."

"Trust that God's will shall be done and if Conrad's claims are false, they shall be proven so."

Charlotte silently begged God for forgiveness and asked that justice be done. She placed her fate in His hands and asked that He grant comfort to Niels, whatever he decided to do. With a last selfish wish, she prayed for a miracle: that Niels might forgive her.

Chapter Thirty-Two

Despite being in jail, Charlotte remained remarkably busy with her law practice. Pearl brought her papers and messages every day. Since she had been working for Charlotte, the former saloon employee's look and her wardrobe had changed drastically, but there was no hiding the fact that Pearl was a beautiful woman. She wore her hair pulled back into a conservative updo and her dresses were similar in style to those Charlotte favored, though her choices were more colorful.

"One would almost think that being in jail was a way to attract business, Charlotte," Pearl told her as she passed her another bundle of papers. "You are getting work from some of the people in town that I never would have thought would come to you. Before this, they would go all the way to Denver rather than consult a woman. Hard to figure."

"Think it might have to do with the idea that if I'm mixed up in something worth going to jail for, that I might know my way around the system?" Charlotte laughed. It was a weird idea, but the only one that currently came to mind.

"I have spent much of my life dealing with the strange ways men's minds work. You may be more right than you think," Pearl countered.

"I can only hope that I am still in demand should I win my case and get out," Charlotte muttered.

Pearl smiled. "I have no doubt that you will win and that Conrad will have to leave town with no more than he came with." She shuddered. "He's good-looking, but he makes my skin crawl."

"I'm ashamed to say that I really thought I loved him." She grimaced. "Now, I can barely stand the sight of him."

"Are you mad at him or disgusted?"

Charlotte sighed. "I suppose some of both. I'm not mad enough to want to do away with him, but the fact that he has the nerve to lie so audaciously...that makes me just plain furious." She paused a moment. "Let's not waste the day talking about Conrad. What did you bring me?"

"First, we have a deed transfer. When old man Rankin died, his only heirs were back East and they wanted to sell the ranch rather than move here. Bradwell bought it, though I doubt he's interested in running the ranch himself."

Charlotte laughed. "Can you see him on a horse rounding up cattle? Or wearing chaps?" The thought was ridiculous. "I suspect he will either hire someone to run it for him or divide up the land into smaller plots and sell them to the newcomers for houses and farms."

"No doubt."

Charlotte looked over the papers and signed off on the sale. "What else do you have for me?"

On the day of the hearing, Harriet and Pearl helped Charlotte get properly cleaned up and ready. She arranged her hair in a braid and wore a simple, dark blue dress. She took paper and pen to make notes, but had no documents to present to the judge. How could she counter a charge that had no proof to begin with? The two women accompanied Charlotte and the sheriff to the hearing. This time, instead of the saloon, the sheriff had prevailed upon Reverend Miller to use the church hall. He anticipated a large crowd and his instincts were correct. Volunteers had set up chairs and benches in the main section of the hall. There wasn't an empty seat in sight.

Charlotte had a table on one side towards the front, and Conrad was seated at a table on the other side. He had another gentleman beside him. She had never seen the other man before. There was a third table set up beyond near the back wall for the judge, his assistant and the person scribing the proceedings on long sheets of paper. Harriet went to sit with Ward, and Pearl joined Charlotte at the front table. She brought a stack of papers and books and placed them on the table.

"What's all that, Pearl?" Charlotte whispered.

"With someone like Conrad making trouble for you," Her assistant whispered back, "you need to make a good impression on the judge. I know we don't have much, but it needs to look like a lot. Besides, I hear he has a surprise witness."

"Yes, I heard a rumor about that." There had been all kinds of rumors about the hearing and her visitors had passed on everything they had heard. As to the veracity of any of them, she would find out all too soon. "Maybe that's the fellow sitting with him." Further conversation was halted by the sound of the judge banging his gavel on the table in front of him.

"Order! I will have order!" the judge barked.

The judge's assistant rose and addressed those assembled. He was a tall, slender man in his mid-thirties, well dressed, with a head of dark hair that was beginning to recede. "We are here today to hear the case of Conrad James Walker the third against Charlotte Baker, also known as Charlotte Walker. District Judge Frederick Samuelson will preside, hear the evidence and render his judgment. Do both parties swear to tell the truth?"

Conrad and Charlotte both swore that they would.

Judge Samuelson stared out at the assemblage. He was a man of about sixty, with a full head of grey hair and an expression that indicated that he was in no mood for any foolishness in his court. "The purpose of this hearing is to settle the matter of whether Conrad James Walker the third has justifiable cause to extradite one Charlotte Baker, also known as Charlotte Walker, to Philadelphia to stand trial for theft and fraud. Each side will have the opportunity to present evidence and witnesses to support their claim." He shifted his weight in his chair and nodded to the scribe. "Mr. Walker, who is representing you?"

Conrad rose and nodded to the judge. "As a duly accredited member of the bar, I shall be representing myself."

This seemed to have no effect one way or the other on Judge Samuelson. "Very well. Proceed, Counselor. Present your arguments and any evidence that you have."

"First of all your Honor, I wish to present you with this writ from Judge Edward Lothrop of Philadelphia. It states that Charlotte Baker, former resident of the city of Philadelphia, is ordered to return to Philadelphia to face the charge of theft from Benjamin Walker." He paused. "Please note that the woman appearing here, who has been calling herself Charlotte Walker, freely admits that she is indeed Charlotte Baker."

"And who is Benjamin Walker, sir?" the judge asked.

"My beloved uncle, now sadly deceased." Conrad put his hand over his heart, and made a point of not only looking at the judge, but also turning to glance at Charlotte and the assemblage.

It took all of Charlotte's self-control to keep her reaction to a stifled cough. Conrad was always the showman. She would have to stay calm and present her side rationally when she had her turn.

"How do you know Miss Baker? What was your relationship?"

"She was my classmate at the University of Pennsylvania and we saw each other socially."

"And what were the circumstances of the alleged theft? What was taken and when?" Judge Samuelson gestured as he tried to move things along.

"My uncle met Miss Baker at a party at my father's home. He liked Miss Baker and trusted her. Later, Miss Baker went to his home and stole a large amount of cash and valuables from him. The following day she left town, and several days after that, my uncle suffered a stroke. He lingered for a time, but sadly, he took a turn and died. It only seemed reasonable for me to assume that the stress of being deceived and robbed by someone he trusted brought on his attack. Miss Baker knew that he was in poor health, but that did not stop her from using her feminine wiles to take advantage of a sick old man." He paused dramatically. "It was because of these facts that the judge issued the writ."

Judge Samuelson nodded. "Is there anything else you wish to add at this time?"

"Only that the sooner we conclude this, the sooner I can take Miss Baker back to Philadelphia and seek justice for my uncle."

Charlotte forced herself to keep her face neutral. Conrad was using every bit of his considerable charm to paint her as a conniving, heartless witch who would steal from a sick, old man. *How dare he?*

"Miss Baker?"

"Yes, Your Honor?"

"Have you representation?"

She rose to address the judge. "As Counselor Walker stated, we were classmates. Classmates at the University of Pennsylvania School of Law. I am a member of the bar in this state and shall represent myself. As for how to address me, while the people of Soda Flats call me Counselor Walker, for the sake of clarity in this hearing, Counselor Baker will be appropriate. My diploma so reads, after all."

"Well now," the judge said. "I thought this would be a routine matter. Now I see my mistake." A trace of a smile appeared momentarily. "A most interesting development. Proceed, Counselor."

Charlotte rose and spoke to the judge. "Counselor Walker and I were more than classmates. We were engaged to be married."

The judge raised his eyebrows. "I presume you will explain the relevance?"

"Yes, Your Honor. This is relevant because of how it came about and how I met Mr. Benjamin Walker. When I got to the law school, I had only enough money to pay for the first semester. I met Conrad in the Dean's office after one of my appointments to apply for financial aid. He asked me to dinner. Later, I was called to the Dean's office and informed that I had been awarded a full scholarship and a stipend for living expenses. I was overjoyed. Conrad and I often went out socially and also studied together. When he asked me for help, I thought nothing of it. He was my friend, and later, also my fiancé."

Charlotte paused. "I did indeed meet Benjamin Walker at a party at the Walker mansion. He was a charming, intelligent man and I enjoyed his company. Conrad did not care for him much, but I gathered that he did not spend much time with his uncle.

"As we progressed in our studies, I did more and more of Conrad's work, but at the time I did not mind. Conrad told me that his father expected him to join the firm, but said if he did not do well at Penn, he could forget that. Conrad promised that if I helped him, he would see that his father would also hire me after we graduated."

The judge raised his hand to interrupt. "I presume there is a point here?"

"Yes, your Honor. Pardon the lengthy explanation. After graduation, we passed the bar, Conrad just barely, but this was good enough for his father. We celebrated our future and Conrad made a lot of promises to me...and then compromised me. The next day, he informed me that, now that he had been admitted to the bar, he had no further need of me. I would not be joining the firm, nor did he have any interest in marrying me. The 'scholarship' was a fraud. It had been his way of buying a tutor. He said that if I tried to join any firm in Philadelphia, his family would ruin me." She looked directly at Conrad for effect, then turned back to face the judge.

"I decided to leave and packed up my things. Benjamin Walker sent me a message to come to his home. I went. He told me that he thought his nephew was a fool and had treated me shamefully. He wished me well and gave me money, advising me to go far away from Conrad. I did." Charlotte stopped there. She had no desire to include more detail than was necessary. This much was humiliating enough. She returned to her seat.

Judge Samuelson looked over at Conrad. "Have you anything else to say?"

"Yes, indeed, Your Honor." He rose and smiled at the crowd and the judge. "Miss Baker paints me a cad. I submit that while I do not deny the general outline of what she said, she did it all willingly and without any threat to herself. The scholarship was genuine, a gift from a wealthy alum. As to our engagement...with great regret, I realized that we were not a good match." He put his hand over his heart again and gave a quick glance at Charlotte. "I tried to break our engagement gently, but she begged me for another chance and threw herself at me. I suppose she hoped that a night of passion would change my mind."

Charlotte nearly gagged. What in the world was he thinking? Telling all these lies?

With a face full of such sincerity that Charlotte could almost believe him, Conrad went on. "Your Honor, I'm only human, so I accepted what she offered, but it didn't change anything. When I told her it was over, she became hysterical. She took her revenge on me by stealing money from my uncle and doing God knows what to cause his stroke. The old man liked her and she turned on him. And to make it all the worse, when I found out about what she had done to poor Uncle Benjamin, I had a detective track her to Pittsburg. There, I learned that she was reported dead of a probable suicide." He went to his table and then handed the judge a paper. "This is the newspaper report."

The judge turned to Charlotte. "Counselor Baker, would you please explain this? You clearly did not die in Pittsburg."

She rose. "After Conrad used me and told me that the offers of marriage and a position in his father's firm were lies, Conrad's uncle *gave* me the money to get away. I took the train to Pittsburg. Later, I read about Benjamin Walker's death and that Conrad was intent on following me to the ends of the earth for stealing from him. I knew that only my death would stop him from continuing to ruin my life. Hence, I made it appear that I *was* dead. I hurt no one. It was only a dummy that I threw off the bridge." Charlotte could sense the mood in the room. There was strong sympathy for her situation.

Conrad fairly jumped to his feet. "She lies! She's been spinning a web of lies and I can prove it."

Chapter Thirty-Three

Conrad was on his feet, his hands pressed to the table in front of him. His face was filled with rage.

Judge Samuelson banged his gavel. "Counselor! Please control yourself. You say you have proof. Please, present it."

He quickly composed himself. Charlotte could barely believe how rapidly her former fiancé resumed his calm, suave demeanor. "Your Honor, pardon my outburst. It is hard to remain silent under these circumstances." He paused. "I have brought a witness. I ask that he be heard now."

"Very well. Present your witness."

Conrad nodded to the man seated at the front table with him.

"Come forward, sir," the judge said. The man rose and walked towards the chair next to the judge's table. The judge's assistant spoke. "State your name, please."

"Edward Smythe."

"Raise your hand, sir." Mr. Smythe did so. "Do you swear to tell the truth?"

"Yes, sir."

"Please be seated." The witness took his seat. Judge Samuelson motioned to Conrad to begin.

Conrad approached his witness. "Mr. Smythe, please tell us what your position is."

"I am the vice president of the First National Bank of Philadelphia."

"How did you know Benjamin Walker?"

Mr. Smythe smiled slightly as he answered. "He was a valued client of our bank."

"When did you last see him and for what reason?"

"On May tenth of last year he sent me a message to come to his home. He wished me to witness some papers and take copies to the bank for safekeeping."

"And what transpired during that meeting, sir?"

Smythe seemed to be more comfortable as he discussed bank business. "Well, I explained all the documents to him and he made a few minor changes. We discussed his current holdings in the bank and his plans to consolidate some of his investments."

"Did you have occasion to inspect the contents of the safe at the house?"

"Yes. He opened the safe and asked me to get out a specific document that we needed to complete the business I went over to discuss."

Conrad moved closer to the witness and looked out at the gathering, then glanced at Charlotte before turning back to the witness. "And what did you notice about the contents?"

"Benjamin Walker always kept cash and jewelry in his safe, along with various papers. On that day, there was no cash and I saw no jewelry pouch."

"Did you mention this observation to Mr. Walker?"

"Yes sir, I did. I asked him if he had made any large purchases that week."

"And what was Mr. Walker's response?"

"He was...surprised. He said he had not made any such purchases. That surprised me. You see, I had personally delivered a large sum of cash to the house the previous week. I asked him who had been to his home recently."

"What was his reply?"

"Charlotte Baker." Smythe paused and cleared his throat. "It was then that he suddenly took ill and fell to the floor. I sent for his doctor and he was taken to the hospital, but he died several days later. They tell me he never woke up."

"Thank you, Mr. Smythe. I think that says it all."

"Have you any questions of this witness, Counselor?" Judge Samuelson asked Charlotte.

"Yes, Your Honor, I do." She came forward to face Mr. Smythe.

Charlotte smiled at Smythe and spoke pleasantly. "Did Benjamin Walker specifically state that he knew where the money had gone?"

"Well, no. But he named no one else as a visitor."

"Did he specifically state that he was robbed?"

"No, but the money was gone and he denied making any purchases."

"So, he never said that he was robbed, correct?"

"He did not. However, the money was gone and when I asked him about who had been there, yours was the only name he mentioned. The stress of that memory must have caused his stroke. It's an obvious conclusion."

"But not one he uttered." She nodded to the judge. "I have no other questions of this man."

Judge Samuelson excused the witness and asked Conrad if he had any other witnesses.

"Yes, Your Honor. I wish to call Mr. Winston Bradwell."

Bradwell came forward and was sworn. Charlotte noted that he did not seem particularly pleased to be there.

Conrad smiled at the local banker, as if they were long-lost friends. Bradwell did not smile back. "Mr. Bradwell, you are the president of the bank here in Soda Flats?"

"Yes, sir."

"And Charlotte Baker is a depositor in your bank?"

"Charlotte Walker has an account at my bank, yes sir."

"I stand corrected." Conrad tried another smile. This expression got no better response from the local banker. "I'll get to the point. Miss Walker deposited a substantial sum in your bank?"

"As I said, she made a deposit."

Conrad looked at the judge. The judge shook his head slightly. "I believe this witness has answered you, Counselor."

Conrad shrugged and asked another question of the banker. "Did she ever approach you for a loan?"

"No, sir."

"And yet, she was able to pay for materials to build a cabin, rent an office and purchase supplies for it?"

"You would have to ask the merchants about that."

"Very well, then. I will call..."

Judge Samuelson interrupted. "First of all, do you have any questions for this witness, Counselor Baker?"

"Not at this time, Your Honor."

"Very well. I doubt that any testimony from the local merchants can prove the source of the funds spent." The judge addressed Conrad. "Do you have anything else to present?"

"I do, Your Honor. Much of your decision has to be based on the veracity of the principals. After Charlotte faked her death in Pittsburg, she came West, but not as Charlotte Baker. She posed as her twin brother, Charlie Fletcher and deceived the good people of this town for months. There is not and never was, a Charlie Fletcher. There is only Charlotte Baker, now passing herself off as Charlotte Walker. These are two more examples of her lies. She lied about who she was, about being a widow, and admittedly faked her own death to escape prosecution for her thievery when she knew we were after her. I ask you, Your Honor, if she lied about these most important things, why should we believe her now?" Conrad made a sweeping gesture, making brief eye contact around the room, lastly settling on Charlotte.

Charlotte was appalled at Conrad's misrepresentation and distortion of events. He was twisting every point he could to paint her in the worst possible light and resorting to outright lies if he did not have enough to bridge one point to the next. She looked up as the judge addressed her.

"What have you to say about these accusations?"

"Benjamin Walker called me to his house of his own free will. He had no great love for his nephew Conrad. He heard Conrad's father making sport of what Conrad had done, saying it showed that his son was a clever boy, after all." She wagged her head to demonstrate her disgust. "After realizing there was nothing left for me in Philadelphia, all I wanted to do was start over without causing a fuss. That is why, when I came to Soda Flats, that I said I was a widow. I didn't want to have to tell my story about being seduced and jilted. A single woman is a hard thing to be out here. Being a widow is respectable." She took a deep breath and risked adding a bit more of the truth. "I never dreamed that Conrad would go to such lengths to find me."

"Have you any witnesses you wish to call, Counselor Baker?" the judge asked.

"Yes, Your Honor, I do. I would first like to call Dr. Harriet Parker."

The judge's assistant spoke. "Dr. Parker, please come forward and be sworn."

Harriet rose and took her place in the chair next to the judge's table. Charlotte faced her. "Dr. Parker, what is your position in Soda Flats?"

"I am the town physician and surgeon."

"Have you anything to say about this case?"

"I believe I do. I met Charlie Fletcher last year when he came to Soda Flats. You came to town in May. I got to know you much better than I did Charlie. I cannot for a minute believe that you took money from Benjamin Walker or caused any harm to him. You spoke well of Benjamin Walker and in truth, you talked more of him than of your supposedly late husband. It made sense when you later told me that you had never married, that your fiancé had left you under rather unpleasant circumstances."

"So, you knew about all of this before Conrad came to Soda Flats."

"Yes, you told me about him in confidence."

"Did you think less of me because of this deception?"

"Hardly. It is a brave thing for a woman to come out here alone under any circumstances." She looked directly at the judge. "I have found Charlotte, whether she was herself or in the persona of her brother Charlie, to be bright, honest and hard-working. She has been treated dreadfully, and sending her back with this man," she pointed at Conrad, "would be a travesty."

"Thank you. That will be all," Charlotte said.

The judge asked if Conrad had any questions and he merely waved him off.

Charlotte continued. "I would next like to call Ward Parker."

The judge called him and he was duly sworn.

"Mr. Parker, what is your profession here in Soda Flats?"

"I am a builder and carpenter."

"And did you have occasion to know Charlie Fletcher?"

"Yes." Ward looked over at the judge, then back to Charlotte. "He wanted to build a cabin for his sister and needed my help."

"And the two of you built this cabin?"

"Yes, we did, except for the stonework by Niels Sorensen, the stonemason. Charlie impressed me by his hard work, honesty and dedication to the project."

"And how did you feel when you learned that Charlie and I were the same person?"

"A trifle surprised, but I had to admire the determination it took to do that."

"Have you any other comments on this case?"

"Only that I am proud to know both Charlie and Charlotte and find the charges impossible to believe. You have dealt fairly with everyone, including those who have not been fair with you."

"That is all. Thank you."

This time Conrad did not pass on his opportunity to ask a question. "Mr. Parker, didn't you find it odd and somewhat distasteful that a woman would pass herself off as a man to gain the trust of this town?"

Ward smiled and shook his head. "Mr. Walker, you may live your life with your head in the ground, but I don't. Doc Harriet and I have been married a long time, and I've seen how men like you treat women who are 'different.' We should celebrate people's talents and not assign them to only men or only women."

Conrad opened his mouth to speak and then closed it, apparently thinking the better of whatever he was going to say next. "That is all, Mr. Parker." Charlotte returned to her seat and spoke with Pearl, to confirm the presence of her next witness, Buck Larson.

Conrad rose to speak first. "Your Honor, I object to this parade of character witnesses. While they are all fine people, I am sure, they have no specific knowledge that pertains to this case."

Judge Samuelson nodded and considered. "Counselor Baker, have you any witnesses that can speak to the facts of this case? That is, any person who has information regarding the charge of theft?"

This was one of the things that Charlotte feared. She had no such witness, nor did she possess any documents that would support her position. She rose to face the judge. "No, Your Honor, I do not. However, I would point out that the outcome of this hearing hinges upon your judgment of my character. Therefore, I do feel that character witnesses have a bearing on the case."

"The point is well taken," Judge Samuelson replied. "Are there others present in this court who would attest to Counselor Baker's character? You may raise your hands." Charlotte turned to see. Perhaps two dozen hands went up, including Buck's and those of his ladies. "I see. I believe with that, I have heard enough."

Conrad jumped to his feet. "I demand that Charlotte Baker be released immediately to the custody of the Marshall that came with me. We can leave tomorrow."

"Counselor, I did not finish my statement." The judge glared at Conrad. He sat. His expression was sullen. "I have a great deal to consider. This case has taken more time than I anticipated and this young woman's future depends on my ruling. The accused will return to the custody of the sheriff. I have another case to hear in a neighboring town. I shall give my ruling after that case is concluded. Court is dismissed." He banged his gavel.

Pearl picked up the books and papers and walked with Charlotte and Sheriff Turner back to the jail. She told Charlotte she would see her the next day and they could discuss the case then.

Back in her cell, Charlotte thought about the witness Conrad had brought, Mr. Smythe. What inducement had Conrad offered to get him to come all the way out to Soda Flats? At the very least, he had paid the man's expenses and lost wages. Why would Smythe accept? She analyzed what the bank officer had said, going over her notes. He had not actually *seen* her take anything or do anything, but the circumstances were damning and presented more specific evidence than she could in her defense.

Her first instinct had been to assume that any witness Conrad would bring had to have been paid off to lie. But Smythe was a well-respected banker and on close inspection, could have been telling the truth, at least as he saw it. Benjamin Walker *might* have been about to tell the banker that he had given the money to Charlotte, but had not been able to get the words out. The stroke simply came at an inopportune time, at least for Charlotte. And was Conrad blameless in his uncle's distress? What might *he* have said to his uncle after she left Philadelphia? He was not above spewing his version of his relationship with Charlotte to any who would listen and might well have said something to his uncle to explain why she left. Maybe he wanted to prove to his uncle that he was right about Charlotte and his uncle was not.

That night she dreamt about many things, including Benjamin Walker's words about the box. "This will give you everything you need to fight Conrad." In the morning, she asked the sheriff to send a note to Harriet.

Chapter Thirty-Four

Charlotte was back in jail and wondered how many more nights she would spend there. While she tossed and turned early in the morning, she reviewed the pieces of evidence for and against her, as they might be interpreted by the judge. *She* knew she was not guilty of theft, but the whole point was being able to prove it. Would she be able to? She had produced character witnesses, but the circumstantial evidence was formidable.

Conrad had shown that Benjamin Walker kept large sums of cash at his home. His uncle had made a substantial withdrawal only days before she went to his house. She herself had testified that she went there to meet with Benjamin Walker. Mr. Walker asked her to come. Unfortunately, she no longer had Mr. Walker's note for evidence. With her many moves, it had been left behind. Conrad argued that she went over on her own volition to badger the older man and steal his money.

The banker Conrad brought out from Philadelphia had made matters worse. When asked what happened to the money in his safe, Mr. Walker said her name, then had his stroke. Conrad wanted the judge to believe that this was a declaration that she had stolen the money. She truly believed that his uncle was trying to explain that he had *given* the money to Charlotte, and the stress of thinking about Conrad's perfidy had brought on the stroke.

Even though Bradwell had essentially avoided most of Conrad's questions, she could hardly deny that she had money. Bradwell might not be able to say how much, but his discomfort spoke volumes. She had paid cash for her materials to build the cabin and furnish her office. She had money for food and to pay Pearl. When she first came to town, both as Charlie and then as Charlotte, she was not working.

Her cover story had been for people to assume that Charlie had saved his money to come out ahead and that Charlotte had inherited from her late husband and given her brother enough money to build her home. Now that she was revealed as never having been married in the first place, would the judge wonder where she got the money?

Speaking of the non-marriage, would the judge understand why she had resorted to lying about it? She had admitted a number of deeds that he might not feel he could ignore. In her defense, she had not physically harmed anyone when she faked her death, nor had she benefited financially by it, at least not directly. Conrad would argue that she did this to try to cover up her theft and keep him from finding her. Well, she granted, he was partly right. The goal *had* been to evade Conrad. It had worked until her article was published in the law review for the University. But days after she reached her greatest accomplishment, her life began to unravel.

And what did the judge think about her posing as Charlie? Conrad made quite a point out of saying that if she lied about that, how could anything she said be taken as truth? She had no choice but to admit there was no Charlie, but she had her reasons. She had done her best to explain this to the judge, but it was not exactly the kind of behavior expected of a respectable young lady. She sighed and turned over on the cot. Was being a lawyer, being a member of a "man's" profession, considered any more respectable for her?

She still felt that the whole point *was* her character and that her witnesses should count for something. Wasn't part of Conrad's most telling argument that he had not seduced her, but that *she* had thrown herself at him? This would not be the action of a woman of good character, so proving that she was should bolster her version, the true version. She tossed to lie on her other side. How could anyone believe Conrad's story? She shivered. He was a much lower form of life than she had thought. She punched the thin pillow. Should she be punching herself instead? How could she have fallen for this man whose moral compass never seemed to point to the truth?

The sound of the door opening to the cell room roused her to full wakefulness. She shook herself.

Sheriff Turner came in with a tray of food. "Time to be up, Charlotte." He unlocked the cell door and put the tray on the small table. He closed the cell and sat down in the chair outside it. "I know this is not exactly like staying in a hotel, but I want you to know that I'm doing my best."

"I know, and it's not your fault that I'm here. I only hope that the judge will find in my favor." She sighed. "Though there isn't much hope for that."

Sheriff Turner wagged his head. "I'm not happy to have to keep you there. I think that this Conrad fellow you were mixed up with is a low-life."

Charlotte picked at her breakfast. "I wish I had known what a toad he was before I let him use me to get through law school. In fairness to him, he's bright enough, but he isn't very logical. He couldn't write a proper legal brief if his life depended on it. Fortunately for him, he's very charming and he has no trouble getting other people to do his work for him."

"Hard to respect an able-bodied man who doesn't put in an honest day's work. He hasn't made many friends here in town." Sheriff Turner stretched and shook his head.

"I suppose not." Charlotte picked at her tray. "Even Bradwell didn't look particularly pleased to be called as a witness. That says a lot. He only puts up with me because I'm a customer."

"I wouldn't know about that, but he sure doesn't care for Conrad Walker."

"Oh? How so?"

"The man waltzed into the bank here and acted like he was some kind of big shot and made some crack about the Soda Flats Savings and Loan being...let me get this right." Turner stopped to think. "I believe he called it a 'giant piggy bank.'"

Charlotte's eye went wide. Bradwell might be a trifle full of himself, but he had established a strong bank, albeit with some help from his father. "I would hardly call a bank with a partner in Denver a 'piggy bank.' It's Bradwell's life. No wonder he hates Conrad." What a choice for the banker, she thought! He could spite her to help Conrad, or spite

Conrad to support her. Clearly, he disliked Conrad more. "Too bad this isn't a trial by jury. Conrad is his own worst enemy."

"We're with you, Charlotte, but the law is the law. I hope something turns up to show the truth."

She sighed. "No more than I do, Grant."

She got her usual visit later that day from Pearl. Today, Buck came with her. He pulled up a chair outside the cell. "Sorry I didn't get a chance to tell the judge what I thought."

Charlotte needed some amusement. "And what would that have been?"

"That I've run across a lot of pompous jerks in my line of work, but Conrad Walker is the biggest horse's ass I've ever met. He's spent a lot of time over at the saloon. I don't mind taking his money, but he acts like he's better than all of us. Just because he wears a fancy suit!" He turned his head and spat.

For the first time since Conrad had arrived in town, Charlotte laughed. Pearl joined in. Nothing had changed, but the weight of worry about her future had lifted just a bit. "Buck, where have you been all my life?"

Buck merely grinned. "Okay, ladies. I see my work here is done." He got up and nodded to them. "Charlotte, Pearl. I'll see you in court."

Pearl handed her a stack of papers. "Court or no court, these still need your signature. You are very popular."

An hour after Pearl left, Sheriff Turner told her that she had another visitor. Charlotte assumed it was Harriet with her box. Surely, she hadn't forgotten about it. Charlotte had to see if she was missing what Benjamin Walker had said to her. She was excited to get the box in her possession and fairly leaped up from her cot. She heard the sound of the door as the sheriff opened it, but as she turned to greet her, she saw that it wasn't Harriet who had come to see her,

Charlotte could not believe what she was seeing. It couldn't be true, could it? She had hoped and prayed, but with the last she had heard, the chance of this happening was so remote. Could it be?

"Charlotte?"

She did not realize she was staring until she heard her name called the second time.

"Charlotte? Please, speak to me."

Shaking herself, she focused. Standing in front of her was...Niels! She nearly fainted. He no longer looked angry, he looked...sad?

"Niels?" Charlotte kept staring. She spoke so softly, it was nearly a whisper. "I can't believe you are here."

Niels returned an uncertain look. "Harriet sent Ward to get me. He made me go to the hearing." He moved his hands from behind him, and she saw that he had her box. "I must go back to the job later today, but Harriet said you needed this." He passed the box through the bars to her.

Her mouth was dry. Words would not come to her. She set the box on her cot. "Yes, yes, I do."

"I did not wish to go to the hearing. Ward threatened to drag me there if he had to."

Charlotte had scanned the crowd several times. "I didn't see you with them."

"Because I stayed at the back of the hall. I was not ready to have you see me. It was too...hard."

"But you came. That is enough."

"I listened to Conrad, at the hearing. He reminds me of the traveling man with the patent medicines. He says whatever you wish to hear to make you buy what he has to sell." He breathed deeply. "I should have let you talk to me when he first came here."

Charlotte blinked. This could not be real. She had to be dreaming, didn't she? What was she to say? For a moment, she was speechless, then she found her voice.

"I wanted to say that I let you believe I was someone I was not, that I had a brother who did not exist. Now, it looks like the man who I claimed was dead, who is not dead, will be taking me back to Philadelphia in chains for theft and causing his uncle's death."

"No!" Niels grabbed the bars of the cell, then dropped his hands as if the bars were on fire. He turned away from her and Charlotte was in turmoil. She had thought he was going to forgive her, but now...

Niels shifted his gaze to look directly at her. "It is true that you have...told lies. But you would not steal from an old man or cause his death." He paused. "What about the box? Harriet said it was important."

"Oh! Yes, the box!" She picked it up and looked inside. She had not left much in it. The remaining money and jewels were secreted in her cabin. She looked it over and showed it to Niels. He shrugged. She shook it out, and only got lint and two pencils. Nothing that looked remotely like it could save her.

Niels frowned. "I thought I had the key to your freedom."

She sighed. "So did I." This setback tempered her joy at seeing Niels. "Thank you for bringing it." She paused. She had to know. "If I can prove my case, is there hope for us?" She looked into his eyes, searching for the answer.

He looked away. "I...I will be at the court." He opened his mouth as if to say more, but closed it without speaking. He turned and left the jail.

When he was gone, she cried.

Later, she finally felt calmer, and thought again about what Benjamin Walker said. She replayed every moment of that last, tense meeting. That night, as she slept, she did so one last time. After Conrad dumped her, she was frantic to leave Philadelphia, but could not ignore Benjamin Walker's request to see her. After all, she liked him and did want to say good-bye. He was the only one in that family who was worth the risk of delaying her departure. So, she went to his house. He wished her well and gave her the box. The box! Yes, the box. It had to be the box. Something special was in it. But she and Niels had looked through it again, to no avail. Why couldn't she find what she needed to stop Conrad? Benjamin Walker seemed so sincere in his disapproval of Conrad. He assured her that the box he gave her held everything she would need to protect herself. What could she possibly have missed?

CHAPTER THIRTY-FIVE

In the morning, Sheriff Turner informed Charlotte that the new hearing date was set for the following day. "Got the telegram this morning. Judge Samuelson finished his other cases and will be back for any final words and to render his decision. Anyone you need me to send for?"

Charlotte wanted to be out and have another chance with Niels. "No, thank you. I'll talk with Pearl when she comes and see what we need to do."

Pearl arrived mid-morning and Charlotte gave her the news. "I don't know whether I should be happy or sad, Pearl. On the one hand, the suspense will be over, but on the other..." She shrugged.

"Charlotte, I refuse to believe that Conrad will be able to take you away." She touched Charlotte's arm. "It's not right."

"Unfortunately, what is right and what is the law is not always the same thing." Charlotte mostly dealt with contracts, deeds and wills. What she had seen of criminal court had convinced her that verdicts often depended on the skill of the lawyer in interpreting the law and not what she felt was morally right. She hoped that between her legal skills, her story and perhaps some luck, she would ultimately prevail.

The day of the second hearing began much as the prior one had. Pearl and Harriet came to the jail to help her prepare. Harriet supervised her appearance and Pearl brought her papers. Charlotte debated for a moment. Should she take the box? While she had not found anything in it, she felt that it might bring her that elusive bit of luck she needed.

When the principals reassembled in the church hall, Charlotte looked over at Conrad. He looked confident and pleased with himself. She did not wish to go back to Philadelphia with him. Could she escape if the court found against her? Would Niels come with her? Even if he would, she would not let him do that. It would only ruin his life.

Judge Samuelson entered the court and sat at the front table. He scanned the room. "I see that both parties are present. I have spent a good deal of time considering this case, but I wish to ask each of you if there are any final words or additional evidence." He looked over at Conrad. "Mr. Walker?"

"Yes, Your Honor. I have one additional witness to call. Mr. Richardson, please come forward."

Herman Richardson, the proprietor of the local mercantile, came forward and was sworn. Charlotte doubted he had much to add, but was curious as to what Conrad wanted to ask.

"Sir, did Charlotte Baker come to your store?" Conrad pointed to her.

"I knew her as Charlotte Walker, but yes."

"Did she place any large orders though your store?"

"Yes, sir, she did. She ordered shelving and furniture for her office. Nice quality, too."

"And how did she pay for these?" Conrad began to pace. Charlotte recognized his signature moves. He was trying to create some drama.

The proprietor showed no particular reaction to Conrad's movements. "Cash in advance."

Conrad stopped his pacing. "Indeed. Did she try to negotiate a lower price or seem to have any difficulty paying?"

"No sir. She knew what she wanted. She didn't pick out the most expensive items, but she knew quality. Knew how to get the most for her money." He nodded at Charlotte.

"Well, that's all very nice, but we are only concerned with her ability to pay, not her shopping acumen." Conrad gave a slight smile, oozing charm and reasonableness. Charlotte tried to keep her face neutral. "Are you aware of her having any clients, or other gainful employment, when she first came to Soda Flats?"

"Not to my knowledge. Of course, I can't say that I know *everything* that is going on in town."

"Fair enough. However, she had the money to pay for whatever she bought, correct?"

"I believe I have already said so, sir."

Judge Samuelson shifted his weight in his chair. "Counselor, you have made your point. Is there anything else you wish to ask of this witness? It would seem we covered this before." Conrad shook his head. "Very well. Counselor Baker, have you any questions?"

"No, Your Honor. I am willing to concede that I have never tried to buy anything in his store that I could not pay for." She offered Conrad a challenging look, as if to say, "so what?"

The judge heaved a sigh. Charlotte saw that he was not impressed by the "new" witness. However, the previous evidence was made no less by it. He spoke. "The witness is excused. Counselor Baker, have you anything to present?"

Charlotte rose and collected her thoughts. "Your Honor, I stand by my statements at our first session. Conrad Walker is a shameless user of anyone who can help him get what he wants. He will tell any lie, use any manner of deception to further his own interests. The worst of it is that he sees nothing wrong in this. He believes that he is entitled. I was merely his means to an end."

The judge sat quietly and considered. "Even if that is all true, how does it speak to the charge of theft? One could argue that Mr. Walker's behavior was your motivation to get even."

Conrad rose. "While I deny all of the heinous charges hurled at me by opposing counsel, the fact that she believes them to be true provides more than enough incentive for her to exact revenge by stealing from my uncle and driving him into apoplexy." He glared at Charlotte and sat down.

Charlotte took a moment to choose her words. "I grant that I have no love for Conrad Walker, but his family did make it possible for me to finish law school by tutoring him, and his Uncle Benjamin was always kind to me. I would never wish any harm to come to him. Reading about his death in the newspaper was a shock. Had it not been for Conrad's threats as to what would happen if I ever set foot again in Philadelphia, I would have returned for the man's funeral."

She took a deep breath and turned to her table. She picked up the box and held it out. "Benjamin Walker told me that by giving me this box and its contents, Conrad could never have control over me again. He said that it held everything I needed to be free of him forever."

Jumping to his feet, Conrad began to sputter. "That's uncle's favorite cigar box! And she admits, *admits* that she has it! She even has the audacity to bring it before Your Honor!" He strode over to confront Charlotte. "Give that to me! You have no right to that!" He grabbed for the box but Charlotte held it tight in her grip. He shoved Charlotte into her table. They fought for the box once again and as Conrad wrested it from her hands, it fell to the floor and appeared to break. Charlotte dove on top of it.

Judge Samuelson banged his gravel. "Order! Sheriff, please restrain Mr. Walker! Miss Baker, are you all right?"

As Sheriff Turner pulled Conrad back to his chair and forcibly sat him down, Charlotte got up and momentarily took stock as she smoothed her dress. "Yes, Judge, I'm fine." She placed the box on the table. It looked sad. Then, she took a second look. In the scuffle, something had triggered the release of a hidden compartment, a false bottom in the elaborate box. She saw the edge of a paper. What could this be? It hardly mattered at this point. It was all over, save for Conrad's bad behavior. Her hands shook as she thought about having to leave Soda Flats, and not being able to be with Niels. She pulled out the paper. It was a letter! She looked it over and held it up before the judge. "Your Honor, I believe I have something I should read to the court."

"Please do," Judge Samuelson said. "Anything but further combat, please." Conrad opened his mouth. The judge put up his hand and Conrad remained silent. "What have you?"

"I have a letter which was hidden in the false bottom of this box. I have to thank my fellow counsel for assisting in its discovery." She bowed slightly to Conrad and he scowled in return. Holding the letter in full view of those gathered, she stated: "This letter is dated May of last year." She took a deep breath and read.

"Dear Miss Baker, in addition to the contents of this box, I fear you will find need for this letter. My nephew, Conrad, is as persistent as he is ambitious. Should he find you, he will likely hunt you down and demand you return my gifts. Under no circumstances should you comply.

"You have worked very hard to achieve your goal of entering the law. It was not easy to work at your family's store and attend school, even harder to disguise yourself as a man so that you could continue to earn money by delivering furniture and doing upholstery."

Charlotte paused. She was completely shocked. She had no idea that Benjamin Walker knew so much about her. Yes, she had told him about working in the shop, but he knew about Charlie, too? As she continued to read, the judge's expression darkened as he glared at Conrad. Conrad was about ready to spit.

"You are the best thing that has ever happened to Conrad and he never would be where he is now without your help. He has proven his poor judgment by discarding you in a most shameful way. I know his reputation with the ladies and I can only surmise that his behavior would not be considered as gentlemanly. Conrad Walker the third is a shallow, selfish and somewhat dim-witted excuse for a man, and I am embarrassed to be his relation.

"To be absolutely clear, I give the cash and jewelry contained in this box to you freely and I expect nothing in return. Use them to build your future away from Conrad. You have much to offer the world and I feel fortunate to have known you, Charlotte. (If I may be so familiar. I do feel closer to you than to many of my family.) Goodbye and God bless, signed Benjamin Walker."

Charlotte lowered the letter and looked at Conrad. He was already on his feet, his face deep red. He screamed, "It's a fake! It's all a lie! How convenient that she has 'found' this letter now. I demand my right to examine it!"

Judge Samuelson waved him away. "Please, I wish to see this letter." Charlotte passed it to him and he looked it over. The judge motioned Conrad to approach him. "Look at this letter." Conrad moved to take it. The judge pulled it away. "No, just look."

Conrad had never been good at bluffing. When the judge showed it to him, his ashen face gave away the truth. Still, the judge had a request.

"Will Mr. Smythe please come forward?" The Philadelphia banker approached the judge. "You are familiar with Benjamin Walker's handwriting?"

"Yes, Your Honor."

"Please, examine this letter. Could this have been penned by him?"

Mr. Smythe adjusted his spectacles and studied the letter. He nodded slightly. "This is most definitely written by Benjamin Walker. It is his handwriting and his style." He passed it back to the judge. "Your Honor, I had no knowledge of this arrangement. I only knew that he had withdrawn a large amount of cash and that it was not in his home. His nephew," he pointed at Conrad, "persuaded me that he had been robbed and paid my way to come out here to testify." He shook his head. "That was low, Conrad. Miss Baker is nothing like you portrayed her."

Charlotte looked over at Conrad. He knew the letter was real *and* in his uncle's hand. When he started to sputter, the judge spoke.

"Mr. Walker, if this court were in the State of Pennsylvania, I would likely move to revoke your right to appear at the bar. You are most fortunate that we are in Colorado." He turned to Charlotte. "All charges are dismissed." He wagged his head in disgust. "Conrad Walker, I order you to be out of town tonight and to take the next train East out of Denver. It would be in your best interest to stay there." He banged his gavel. "This proceeding is over."

The crowd began to disperse and Charlotte let out a deep breath in relief. Niels approached her and stood in front of her, looking awkward.

"Niels?"

He took her hand and went down on one knee. "Charlotte, please forgive me. Letting you go to jail was a terrible thing. I should have let you explain when you wanted to."

Even in her dreams, she did not envision seeing him in such a position. In her dreams and hopes, *she* was the one begging for forgiveness. "Will I forgive you? There is nothing for me to forgive." Her eyes filled with happy tears. "I am the one who lied and ruined everything."

"How can you say that?" Niels responded. "Your lies hurt no one.

They were meant only to keep Conrad far away from you, where he belongs." He then spoke softly. "You belong with me." He rose and held both of her hands.

Charlotte choked back tears. He believed her. She looked at him and for a long moment, she basked in the joy of looking at Niels. He smiled at her. She was lost in the depth of his blue eyes.

Finally, Niels spoke. "You will still marry me?"

For a moment she could not find her voice. It finally came to her as she cried, "Yes, oh yes!"

Niels pulled her into his arms and kissed her without reservation. The judge came over to them.

"I would gladly sign a marriage license today. It would be much better than an extradition decree or an arrest warrant."

They both smiled sheepishly. Niels whispered to her. "Shall we accept?"

CHAPTER THIRTY-SIX

While having Judge Samuelson marry them that very day was tempting and had a certain romantic air to it, Charlotte wanted more of a wedding. She had to know what Niels thought. "Would you mind very much postponing our wedding long enough to organize a proper ceremony?"

Niels smiled. "After all you've been put through, you deserve to have a grand wedding with all of our friends there to celebrate with us."

"I like how you think." She hugged Niels, then turned to the judge. "I'm afraid we must decline your thoughtful offer, Your Honor. However, if you are back here in say, a month's time," she looked at Niels and he nodded assent, "we'd love to have you attend."

A disgraced Conrad did leave that very night. He hired a wagon and driver to take him to Denver, rather than wait for the next stagecoach. Mr. Smythe decided to stay in town for a few days, instead of traveling back with Conrad Walker. He and Winston Bradwell had met at the hearing and Bradwell was in his glory showing the eastern banker around town. He had even arranged a foursome for dinner at the hotel with two eligible young ladies from Cedar Springs.

Niels and Charlotte joined the Parkers for dinner in their home to celebrate her vindication. Harriet took her aside as they cleared off the table after the meal.

"I hear you're planning a big wedding in a month," Harriet said. "You think that's enough time? What about getting a dress made?"

Charlotte paused. "One of the trunks I had shipped out to me has about everything we need. Much of it was sent to my room in

Philadelphia after Conrad... called everything off, but no one asked me to give it back, so I kept it all."

"What do you have?"

"There's a lot, actually. How about you come over later and I can show you. Then you can tell me what other things I might need. Besides, I'm not sure the men are all that interested in the details."

"They do say that a picture is worth a lot of words. Tomorrow afternoon? I can stop by your office when I finish with patients."

Charlotte nodded. "Sounds perfect."

The next afternoon, Harriet followed Charlotte out to her cabin. They went in and Charlotte lit a lamp. "I have the trunk over here." She had been using the large trunk as a side table in the dining area. She cleared things off the top and opened it. "I packed everything the store sent. I wasn't about to let Conrad have these, but he never seemed to care."

She started to pull the contents out of the trunk. "His family paid for this. One-of-a kind and specially fitted for me." She produced a long, formal wedding dress with genuine French lace, a matching veil, shoes and a small handbag.

Harriet gasped and put her hand to her chest. "Charlotte, this is gorgeous! I've never seen anything like this. The workmanship is exquisite!"

"You don't think it would be peculiar for me to wear this, since Conrad's family paid for it?"

"I think it would be much more peculiar if you didn't. Conrad never saw this, did he?" Charlotte shook her head. "His family never asked for it back, you say?"

"No. I think they believed that any price was cheap to be rid of me. The store went ahead and delivered it and told me it was paid for. They also sent along a formal wedding suit. Conrad may have ordered it but he never asked about it. He certainly never intended to wear it. I think it was sent along with the dress by accident, but it was also paid for. I presume the store wanted to deliver it somewhere. By then, I was so angry at Conrad, that I was going to keep what I could."

Harriet nodded. "He certainly didn't deserve anything. By the way he practically ran out of town yesterday, he knows it." She smoothed the fabric of the dress, clearly admiring it. "I saw the wedding rings you hung over the picture on your mantel. Are they family heirlooms?"

"No, Harriet," she laughed. "When Conrad bought my engagement ring, the jeweler also sold him a set of wedding rings. When they sized my ring, the jeweler delivered the entire set. I told Conrad, but he simply waved me off. Never even asked about having them engraved, so they aren't. Money means nothing to him, as long as he is the one in control. It was only a detail and he didn't care enough about it to remember."

"Looks like all you need to do is speak to Reverend Miller and pick a date. Then we can air out these clothes and check the fit. The suit should fit Niels with some alterations. They are about the same height, but Niels is leaner."

"I really have to wear this?" Niels asked. He had brought Ward Parker with him to the tailor shop to have the wedding suit fitted.

"It's only for a day and Charlotte will appreciate it. Besides, as best man, I have to wear a suit, so it's only fair." Ward looked him over. "You clean up well."

The tailor came in and fussed and measured. "This should work. Have to take the waist in a bit and let out the back seam for the shoulders. It's exceptionally fine quality and the seam allowances are generous." He pinned and drew lines with tailoring chalk, "There! That should do it."

Niels looked in the mirror. "I suppose." He turned to Ward. "The idea of dressing up for a special day is not so bad."

The tailor told Niels to change back into his other clothes. "The suit will be ready in a week, sir. I trust that will be satisfactory?"

The wedding took place only a month after Conrad's ignominious departure. The crowd filled the church and spilled out onto the grounds. Those who did not have seats waited outside to watch the members of the wedding party file in and to offer their congratulations afterwards.

Niels stood inside while Ward walked in with Harriet, who served as Matron of Honor. Next was Pearl, her bridesmaid, escorted by Buck, who had ushered in many of the female guests. Sheriff Turner walked with Charlotte. Obviously, her father could not be there. She joked that she would have asked Charlie, but...that would not work, either. A somewhat surprised Sheriff Turner accepted the duties with pleasure.

Rev. Bob Miller officiated and the couple exchanged vows. As they walked down the aisle to leave the church, those present offered their congratulations. She noticed that even Bradwell was there to ingratiate himself. Did he hope she would deposit more of her fortune in his bank? When they appeared outside the church, the crowd burst into cheers. Niels pulled her close and kissed her. The cheering began anew. Charlotte hugged her husband. This was not how she thought her life would be. It was better, much better.